TH[...]
LOV[...]

This story is set i[...]
little is known. Denis[...]
parts a good deal of [...]
island.

Lucie Gresham, a secretary at the British Embassy
in Cairo, was desperately anxious to visit Cyprus, and
she did so with the help of Adrian Ollivent, a rich
shipping magnate, to whose mother she becomes
companion. The moody, sombre, embittered Ollivent
is one of the best studies Denise Robins has given
us. The secondary characters—particularly Aphra,
the Greek girl—are beautifully drawn in a novel
especially rich in portraiture. The plot has that
compelling interest which readers have learned to
expect from this author.

THE CYPRUS
LOVE AFFAIR

DENISE ROBINS

Originally published by Hutchinson and Co., Ltd.
Hodder Paperback edition 1970

*Printed and bound
for Hodder Paperbacks Ltd.,
St. Paul's House, Warwick Lane, London, E.C.4,
by Richard Clay (The Chaucer Press), Ltd.,
Bungay, Suffolk*

SBN 340 10522 4

'Love hath an island,
 And I would be there;
Love hath an island,
And nurtureth there
For men the Delights
The beguilers of care . . .
Cyprus, Love's Island;
And I would be there. . . .'

EURIPIDES (Bacchæ)
J. F. R.

ONE

LUCIE GRESHAM walked down Kasr El-Nil Street in Cairo on that hot dusty morning in May, looked through her dark glasses at the familiar sight of the cosmopolitan crowds thronging the streets; at the white turbans and *gallabiehs* of native *suffragis*; at the sleek high-powered cars carrying wealthy Egyptians wearing the scarlet tarboosh; at everything which spelt *Cairo* . . . and felt profoundly depressed.

She was having to say good-bye to it all. Good-bye to Egypt and the Middle East ... to all the fascination which had got under her skin . . . and the work she had done at the Embassy as a stenographer for the last eighteen months.

It was all over. That last visit to the oculist had settled the question. The blinding glare of last summer and too much concentrated typing had resulted in severe eyestrain. She simply must relinquish her post.

Yesterday she had gone to the Embassy for the last time. And now she was supposed to be waiting for a boat to take her back to England.

Dejectedly, Lucie strolled along the fine boulevard. She did not mind the heat of the sun. She was drenched with it, bare legs and arms tanned to a deep gold, fair hair bleached almost to silver. She loved the sun, just as she loved Egypt. She had never been homesick out there, like so many of the other girls. Perhaps that was because she had no family ties, no home to pull at her heartstrings.

Her father, a doctor with a one-time practice in the Lake District, had died in harness two years ago. Her mother had died when Lucie was born. She had been trained both in shorthand typing and languages and been only too glad to go out to the Foreign Office clerical job in Cairo, when it was offered her.

There were a number of secretaries living in one of the many quiet English *pensions* which abound in Cairo. For Lucie it had been a year and a half of interest and happiness—in her own quiet way. She was a shy girl who found it difficult to make friends, and little of the capacity of her associates to rush around with any young man who wanted to take them out. Lucie suffered perhaps by being too fastidious, and the only boy who had begun to interest her in the Embassy had been transferred to Ankara. So Lucie's little romance had been nipped in the bud.

She had not minded. It was not serious. What she really enjoyed was all the colour and glamour of life abroad; the exciting change after 'austerity England'. She adored the desert, the trips they made down the Nile, the beauties of sunrise and sunset, the imperishable mysteries, the historical tradition of ancient Egypt.

This summer she had planned to go to Cyprus. Cyprus, which they called '*Love's Island*'. Some of her girl-friends had been on holiday there and came back telling rapturous stories of its beauty and fascination. Lucie had heard so much about it that she was filled with a tremendous desire to go to Cyprus. She had saved for that purpose. She read books about it; studied photographs, steeped herself in all the charm of its atmosphere.

And now it seemed that her great ambition would never be realized. She had to save every penny in order to keep herself once she got back to London, until her eyes recovered sufficiently for her to resume work.

This morning her irresistible longing to see Kyrenia returned in full force, and drew her to a certain Travel Agency which was in this very boulevard and wherein bookings could be made for Cyprus, by sea or air. They had already supplied her with pamphlets about the Island.

Of course it was just a waste of her time ... and yet ... supposing there were some way of getting back to England *through Cyprus*, without spending too much money, Lucie asked herself. She looked at a big coloured poster of the famous Castle in Kyrenia ... at the radiant sea which was like lapis lazuli ... the olive trees on the green slopes leading down to the small white harbour.

She would always feel that she had missed something in life now that she would never set foot upon its enchanted shores!

It was quiet, dark and cool in the little office after the blinding heat outside. The clerk was busy. Lucie sat down, took off her sun-glasses, blinked and began to dab her damp young face with a handkerchief. How sore her eyes were, she thought, looking in a mirror. And how plain she looked. Those light coloured golden hazel eyes with their long lashes, were the only good feature in her face. Today they were red-rimmed and tired. She had grown very thin out here ... her face was too drawn. The fine-cut delicate lips had a weary droop to them. With her bleached hair drawn into a knot at the nape of her neck she looked drained of vitality, even austere. Yet, she felt full of enthusiasm, courage—the spirit of adventure.... It was all there still behind that colourless exterior.

She sighed, returned her mirror to her bag and looked up at a tall, broad-shouldered man who was having a serious discussion with the booking clerk. His back was arresting ... like his rather massive head, with thick dark brown hair. He wore a light-coloured garbardine suit. He was saying:

'I don't care what the bookings are, my dear Wilson, you've got to get me on to that 'plane. I want to be in Kyrenia the day after tomorrow.'

'I'll do my best for you, Mr. Ollivent,' said the clerk.

'It's an infernal nuisance,' the tall man with his back to Lucie spoke again. 'I really meant to get up to Khartoum this weekend—I've got so much to do. But my mother isn't fit to be left alone. Her health these days is such that she's tied hand and foot to the Villa. She *must* have someone with her.'

The clerk sympathized.

'Very trying for you, Mr. Ollivent, and I can remember you telling me you were so pleased with that Miss Little, who lived with Mrs. Ollivent.'

The man called 'Ollivent' shrugged his shoulders.

'Miss Little was an excellent companion, but my mother's letter says they had to fly her home at a moment's notice for this wretched operation, and that she is never likely to return.'

'And how are you going to replace her, Mr. Ollivent?'

'That's the devil of it. I've got about twenty-four hours in which to find somebody suitable. I won't manage it of course. She has to get just the *right* person. Not easy. So I'll have to advertise, and arrange for my mother to be looked after meanwhile. Fortunately, she has a good staff.'

Lucie sat still. She found herself an unwitting eavesdropper. It was interesting, to say the least of it. *Kyrenia!* ... that

9

haunting name!

What a wonderful chance for somebody ... somebody who would fill the shoes of the departed Miss Little, as companion to the old lady in her Kyrenian villa!

'Mr. Ollivent' turned and walked out of the office. He cast a brief disinterested glance at Lucie. Her small figure was inconspicuous, and her face in shadow, but the light from the door fell upon Mr. Ollivent's face and showed it up clearly to the girl. Like his back, it was remarkable. What a strong, proud, bitter sort of face, she thought, with a granite strength of mouth and jaw, and curiously light-coloured blue eyes.

There was something unusual about him. Lucie walked to the desk.

'Who *was* that?'

'Mr. Adrian Ollivent,' the clerk answered, and being an affable and garrulous young man who liked to air his knowledge, added: 'Everybody knows him. Big shipping interests in the Middle East, and has a villa in Cyprus.'

'Yes,' said Lucie slowly, 'I ... couldn't help hearing.'

The clerk tapped his pencil on the desk.

'If anyone can get on a 'plane to Cyprus at a moment's notice, *he* can. It's wonderful what money and position can do. But I'm not quite sure how he's going to find a companion to suit his mother, in a hurry.'

It was then that Lucie Gresham had what she afterwards described to herself as 'a rush of blood to the head'.

Breathlessly she said:

'Oh, I wish *I* could apply for the job!'

Mr. Wilson gazed a trifle coldly at the slim English girl, with her bare brown legs and sandals. ...

'You!' he exclaimed.

Lucie felt herself growing hot. That heart of hers was pounding now. She said:

'Well, why not? I want to go to Cyprus. I'm *dying* to see it and I need a new job. I've got excellent references. I worked at the Foreign Office in London for a year, and I've been at the Embassy here for a year and a half.'

The clerk pricked up his ears. Of course, if the young lady was from the Embassy ... he looked at her with new respect. She was a very ladylike girl, and had a sympathetic voice. She might turn out to be a godsend to Mr. Ollivent. She was a bit young ... Mr. Ollivent wanted an elderly companion for his mother ... but there would be no harm in him seeing this young lady. She could call at Mr. Ollivent's apartment in Gezira.

Lucie left that office with a slip of paper bearing Adrian Ollivent's address in her bag, conscious of a wild hope that she might yet see Cyprus—and settle her future into the bargain.

TWO

THE first few moments of Lucie's interview with Adrian Ollivent were disappointing.

When he found her in his flat and heard how and why she had come, he seemed annoyed.

'Ridiculous of Wilson to have sent you all this way, Miss —er——'

'Gresham.' Forlornly, Lucie supplied the name. 'Lucie Gresham.'

'Well, I'm sorry, Miss Gresham, you're much too young. My mother's recent companion was a woman of fifty, and I'm looking for somebody about the same age. My mother is over seventy. She doesn't want a teenager in the house.'

Lucie gave an indignant gasp.

'I'm twenty-four and I've been earning my own living for the last four years. I assure you, the Embassy will give me the highest references.'

Adrian Ollivent stared down at her. He had not thought her as old as twenty-four. Now she had taken off her sun-glasses and was looking up at him. He could see that she had beautiful, weak-looking eyes, and slender expressive hands, but otherwise was unimpressive. She was telling him about her job in Cairo, her eyestrain, and the necessity for her to return to England.

'I don't want to go!' she ended. 'I've nothing to go back for. Nobody ... and I'm *terribly* anxious to see Cyprus. Believe me, I'm ready to devote all my time to your mother. I don't care much for parties or anything. I love books and music. I play the

11

piano—by ear. People say that it's quite pleasant to listen to. Your mother might like me to play to *her*.'

That was the point at which Adrian Ollivent hesitated. He was tired and disgruntled by excess of work in these troubled times, and by the necessity to go to Cyprus just now, which he deplored—much as he loved his mother. His first instinct was to get rid of this girl as soon as possible. She wasn't what he wanted; but he loved music. His mother loved it too. There was a grand piano in the villa in Kyrenia: rarely played upon now. He had often heard his mother say she had wished Gertrude Little could play. She disliked gramophones or radio.

This little girl said she was a pianist....

Yes, but was she a *good one*, or just a 'thumper' whose second-rate improvising would drive his mother mad?

Lucie's voice pleased him:

'Mr. Ollivent, I know you think this is very unorthodox and that perhaps I had no right to listen to your conversation, but I couldn't help it. I'd gone into that office to see if I couldn't possibly get to Cyprus *somehow*. You don't know what it means to me to have to go back to England. I've nothing ... no ties. I could devote my whole time to your mother. Please do consider me, if only as a temporary measure until you find somebody else. Please give me a chance. You can ring my chief at the Embassy.... Look, he gave me this....'

She thrust a note into his hand. A persistent young woman, Adrian Ollivent reflected, and half amused, half nettled, read what had been written about her.

Certainly it was all to the good. *First rate secretary ... intelligent and reliable ... tactful ... very sorry to lose her ...* etc....

Tactful! That was a word that caught Adrian Ollivent's Fancy. Gertrude Little had often annoyed his mother because she lacked tact. He walked to the window and stared out. The sun had gone down. The first evening star hung glittering in the hot blue sky. His thoughts winged from Cairo to Cyprus ... to Villa Venetia, his mother's home. How would his mother like a companion as young as this girl? Maybe it would be a change for her to have something fresh and youthful in the house. There was something curiously old-fashioned about this little creature. She had a gentle voice.

'I may regret this decision, and I still think you're too young. But I'm a busy man, and I'm anxious to get my mother settled as soon as possible. I'll ring up the Embassy, and if what they tell me is as satisfactory as this written reference, I'll suggest to my mother that she gives you a month's trial.'

Lucie caught her breath. The colour rushed to her thin young face which held that look of anxious strain which had first roused his pity.

'Oh, thank you, *thank you* very much!' she breathed.

Her rapture seemed to annoy him. He had no charm, she afterwards told herself. He was curt to the point of rudeness.

'Your way of thanking me will be by doing your absolute best for my mother, whose happiness is of extreme importance to me. I hope you meant what you said about not wanting to rush round to parties. My mother won't want you to make a lot of friends and fill the Villa with noise. Naturally, you'll have your time off, but my mother needs concentrated attention. She is almost helpless with arthritis, and walks slowly on two sticks. You will need to be with her everywhere. If you think it's going to be too dull and exacting, you had better say so now.'

Lucie's hazel eyes met his gaze squarely.

'I shan't find it dull, or exacting. When do you want me to start?'

'Are you free now?'

'Absolutely.'

'Then we'll fly the day after tomorrow. Ring my office in the morning and I'll tell you the time. My chauffeur will pick you up and take you to the airport.'

A little gasp from Lucie. This was getting what she had set out for, in no uncertain manner. Adrian Ollivent was certainly a man who acted quickly once he made up his mind. *The day after tomorrow* she would be flying to Cyprus. What stupendous luck!

Adrian Ollivent's curt voice broke in on her ecstatic reflections.

'Not too much luggage, please. A couple of suitcases only in the 'plane. I'll have your heavy stuff shipped to the Island later.'

'Very well,' said Lucie meekly.

Then suddenly a thought struck her ... a shrewd and practical thought. It did not do for any girl to be too impulsive. And if she was going to be flown out of Egypt so suddenly, away from all her friends ... she ought, surely, to make a few enquiries from *her* angle.

Stammering a little, she said:

'You won't mind if I ask a few things about ... about *you* and ... and ...' she broke off, scarlet with confusion, half afraid that she might so annoy him that he would cancel the wonderful offer then and there.

He stared down at the young flushed face, noting the nervous way she clasped and unclasped her hands. Suddenly he understood and a look of ironic amusement shot into his light blue eyes. He gave a short laugh.

'I see. You want to make quite sure that I'm not a wolf in sheep's clothing about to lure you into a trap. How comic. But of course you're quite justified. You took rather a chance offering your services to an unknown gentleman in Cairo. But by all means make full enquiries. My name and the name of my firm are well known throughout the Middle East. I have offices here, in Alex, in the Sudan, in Greece. And I think my personal character can be vouched for by the gentleman for whom you have recently been typing. I worked with him when I was a *liaison* officer in the war. You really need not bother about *my* character.'

This speech did little to ease Lucie's embarrassment. She felt slightly resentful. He really was a most difficult, unfriendly person! Before she could reply, his mood changed and, less harshly, he added:

'However you were justified. All being well, we'll meet at the airport the day after tomorrow. Thank you for offering your services.'

Now he gave her the faintest possible smile, and it seemed to Lucie to transform him into a human being. In a rugged, massive way he really was very good-looking. And quite young —surely in his early thirties.

Had he a wife? Presumably not ... he spoke only of his mother. Had he had an unhappy love-affair?

Lucie, with her incurable sense of romance, found herself speculating about him. But the most important thing in her mind at the moment was the wonderful knowledge that, after all, she was going to Cyprus.

Her friends listened to her amazing news and were in turn envious, full of congratulations, astonished, and some of them dubious.

When her recent employer heard the name Adrian Ollivent, he said at once:

'Oh, Ollivent! Fine type. Did a damned good job in the war.

14

Full of money. Inherited that shipping business from his father. In spite of all the cash, he's a very simple sort of chap. A more generous fellow I've never met. Adores his old mother. I think you've been very lucky falling into that job, my dear Lucie.'

When Lucie intimated that she thought Mr. Ollivent rather 'terrifying', her one-time employer laughed at her.

Oh yes, Ollivent had no time for females, he admitted. Wrapped up in his job. Very much a 'man's man'. He believed there had been some disastrous love-affair, but he didn't know anything about it.

More than that Lucie did not learn about Adrian Ollivent. She was still in a daze when thirty-six hours later she found herself on the aircraft beside Ollivent.

She looked down at the Nile which threaded like a ribbon of blue silk beneath them ... at the fast-disappearing mosques and minarets and the tortuous streets of Cairo. Good-bye to Egypt.

Lucie peered downwards, her heart racing with excitement. Cyprus ... Cyprus at last! The enchanted Island lying down there like a jewel set in a blue sea.

'Oh, we're here!' she cried. 'Nicosia is the capital of Cyprus, isn't it?'

He grunted a 'Yes'.

Lucie simmered down. Mr. Ollivent had a horrid way of crushing enthusiasm.

She lapsed into silence.

He folded his arms and stared down at the Island which was fast coming into focus as they circled it.

Lucie decided not to speak to Mr. Ollivent again unless he spoke to her

It was a perfect May morning; hot, yet cool after the scorching heat of Cairo. And green ... so exquisitely green.

A car with chauffeur met them. She had never seen anything more inspiring than the distant mountains, purple against the blue sky; the fascinating road that wound through the mountain-pass along the coastal range. The nut trees, the pines, the glorious flowers, the radiant freshness of it all after Egypt.

They passed an old coaching house, rounded a bend in the road, and came within sight of the Kyrenian coast and the old Castle. It was a picture she would never forget. As they drove quickly down the steep road and she caught a glimpse of the white town, the tiny harbour, the picturesque cottages, she could not resist turning to Adrian Ollivent and exclaiming:

'Oh, it's all just as I imagined. *It's beautiful!* I understand now why they call it "*Love's Island*". I'm in love with it already...!' Then she broke off, her cheeks flushing, and turned away from the man, as though embarrassed.

He felt some surprise. This was an unusual girl, he thought and decided to tell her that Cyprus had been called '*Love's Island*' for quite another reason. Mythology had it that here, in Paphos, Aphrodite had been born of the foam, and had been worshipped as the Goddess of Love by the ancient Greeks. Once a year, even now, her feast-day was celebrated by the Cypriots.

They came now to the foot of the hill and just outside the village to some wrought-iron gateways and high white walls half hidden under clusters of flowering creeper. Over the gates, in ironwork, were the words VILLA VENETIA.

'This is my mother's home,' said Ollivent.

Lucie sat still and quiet while they drove up to the long, low-built white villa. White pillars encircled by flowers, green shutters, and a broad terrace which looked across a formal garden downhill to the harbour and the sea. Two tall cypress trees framed the portico. There were many trees here unfamiliar to Lucie but which she afterwards learned were pomegranates, juniper and quince. Here, too, there were sweet-smelling pines and flowing tamarisks; a miniature fountain, stone paving, an arbour graced by a white marble statue; beds of English roses spilling their petals in the heat of the sun.

A few moments later she was in a big cool dim salon, being welcomed by her new employer. Mrs. Ollivent was a small, fragile lady sitting in a winged armchair, with two ebony sticks at her side and silk cushions at her back. She had a delicate transparent face and snow-white hair beautifully waved, over which she wore, in Italian style, a small mantilla of gossamer black lace. It was a face much lined with suffering, but inexpressibly kind and gentle like her voice. The only resemblance to her son were those speedwell blue eyes, but even they held none of his hardness.

At once she made Lucie welcome.

'I had no idea my son would find me a companion in Miss Little's place so soon,' she said, 'but really, Adrian'—she turned to the man with a soft laugh—'you have brought me a young girl almost as small and weak as your old mother, and I need a strong arm these days!'

Lucie answered quickly:

'But I am strong, Mrs. Ollivent, I assure you. I am *much* stronger than I look and *never* ill. It's only my eyes that are weak. I can do anything for you, and I am not a child really. I'm twenty-four and quite independent. I held a most responsible post at the Embassy, and I'm very domesticated. I used to run the home and look after my own father until he died.'

Blanche Ollivent put out a hand to her.

'Well, well, dear ... we must see. I dare say you'll look after me very nicely, but you're rather young and pretty to be tied up to an invalid——'

'No, really I'm not!' broke in Lucie, her cheeks flaming with dismay.

Mrs. Ollivent laughed again and turned to her son.

'Don't you think she is, Adrian?'

Lucie dared not look at the man. She felt ready to sink through the floor with embarrassment. She knew that he would say something horrid—and he did.

'I'm no judge of pretty girls. And I brought Miss Gresham here not because of her face but because she seemed bent on coming and I thought you would need somebody at once to take Gertrude's place. But if Miss Gresham doesn't suit you...' he paused significantly. Lucie's heart sank a trifle lower.

But Mrs. Ollivent gave her hope.

'Poor Miss Gresham ... what an ungallant way of welcoming her to Villa Venetia! I am ashamed of you, Adrian. If she wants to stay and look after me, she shall do so. It will be delightful for me to have youth in the house. There are times when I feel very old and lonely.'

Then Lucie saw a new and unexpected Adrian. At once he crossed to his mother's side, lifted her hand to his lips, and said, in a warm voice:

'You'll never grow old, Mother you're ageless.'

Mrs. Ollivent pulled his hand against her cheek.

'It's wonderful to see you here again, my darling. How long can you stay?'

'I must go first thing tomorrow, I'm afraid. Urgent business in Athens.'

Mrs. Ollivent sighed, and looked at Lucie.

'I never see enough of my son—may I call you Lucie?'

Lucie gave a shy smile.

'Please do. . . .'

'Now you must let Nita, my maid, show you your room, which we prepared as soon as I got my son's cable. Then come down, and we will have lunch.'

Lucie followed the nice-looking Cypriot girl out of the salon and up the polished wood staircase. She had known as soon as she set eyes upon Cyprus why the urge within her to come here had been so strong. The place was entrancing. And the Ollivents' villa was one of the most beautiful homes she had ever dreamed about. Beauty was all here ... in the gracefully proportioned rooms ... the polished floors and priceless rugs ... the fine collection of pictures, marbles and bronzes, the Florentine brocades, the glittering delicate Venetian glass and china.

Downstairs, some of the furniture was antique Italian. Afterwards Lucie learned that Mrs. Ollivent had spent much of her early married life in Rome and Trieste, where Adrian's father had first inaugurated the now famous shipping line of Ollivent & Co. This villa had been her home since she was widowed, twelve years ago.

Lucie's bedroom (recently occupied by Miss Little) was extremely comfortable and thoroughly English with its rose and white chintzes and simple furniture, locally made and painted. Lucie looked down the hill towards the blue sea.

She wanted to stay here for ever. She was glad Adrian Ollivent was going tomorrow and she would be left alone in this paradise with the dear old lady. She was not going to let any of Mr. Ollivent's sarcasm destroy her pleasure.

She spent the rest of that day tactfully leaving mother and son together. She explored the grounds and later walked down the hill into the town. She was at once charmed by the friendliness and courtesy of the Cypriots. The brown-skinned, dark-eyed natives had a ready smile for the young English stranger. People abroad were always intrigued by Lucie's silver fair head and her passion for the sun. The only thing of which she gradually became aware even during those first few hours in Kyrenia was the gloom she cast on the villagers the instant she told them whence she came.

Mrs. Ollivent they knew and spoke of as 'the poor little sick lady who walked on sticks'. But at the name *Mr.* Ollivent, and when Lucie told them that *he* was here ... all smiles faded, and conversation abruptly ceased. Politely but quietly Lucie was shown that they had nothing more to say.

She returned to the Villa, intoxicated by the loveliness of

Kyrenia, but a little perplexed by the local people's obvious dislike of her employer.

Perhaps they all felt, as *she* did, that he was rather alarming and unfriendly ... yet she was sure there was something more than that about such antipathy. It gave her food for thought.

She did not see mother and son again until dinner. Nita told her that Madame always changed, even when she was alone, so Lucie put on a black skirt, and a white organza blouse with full sleeves and narrow collar, high at the throat.

Her silver hair was brushed severely back and twisted into a knot.

Mrs. Ollivent, wearing black, and with a fringed Italian shawl over her shoulders, jet in her ears and on her white hair, presented the picture of dignity. She had a friendly word of greeting for Lucie.

'Tell us all about your walk down to the town.'

Lucie started to speak, then looked up and met the full gaze of Adrian Ollivent, who sat opposite her, stiff and correct in a white linen coat with black tie. His sombre eyes were directed upon her with an expression which was quite hostile. It brought back the feeling of perplexity and even dismay that she had felt when she sensed his unpopularity in the town.

What *was* the matter?

THREE

HAD she but known it, Adrian Ollivent was, in that very instant, undergoing a strong mental conflict. ... Lucie's appearance at the dinner-table had startled him, to say the least of it. Hitherto he had seen her as an insignificant little person wearing glasses. Tonight she appeared without those glasses—revealing the full beauty of long-lashed golden eyes. Tonight she looked astonishingly pretty in that white blouse and short black skirt.

Miss Gresham ... Lucie ... was an attractive young woman.
He did not address a word to her during that meal. Gradually

Lucie was reduced to silence, although Mrs. Ollivent courteously tried to include her in the conversation.

Adrian spoke to Lucie only once again before that evening ended. He lifted his mother bodily up and carried her to her room. Alone with Lucie he said, icily:

'I shall be flying to Athens early tomorrow morning. I'm not quite sure whether I did right or wrong in bringing you here, but my mother seems to like you.'

Lucie flushed. He added:

'I would also like to repeat that I hope you will not start finding yourself a boy-friend and asking him here, or upsetting my mother in any way.'

Then Lucie went pink with anger. For all her tact, her desire to remain here, she was not willing to be spoken to like this and she told Adrian Ollivent so.

'I've accepted a post as your mother's companion, not a slave whose private life is to be directed by you, or anybody else. Please understand that.'

And she turned and walked swiftly out of the salon.

He heard the angry tap, tap of her heels on the polished floor. His gaze followed the graceful young figure, unwillingly admiring her pride and poise.

Suddenly he turned to the tall carved mantelshelf, leaned his arms against it, and hid a face which was suddenly convulsed.

'I'm becoming a monster,' he muttered the words. 'I've been abominable to that girl without the slightest cause. It's being back here in this place ... in this very room ... Oh God, *God*, if the past had never happened ... if one could go back instead of forward! ... maybe even Lucie Gresham would understand *if she knew....*'

But Lucie did not know, and found no excuse for Mr. Ollivent's boorish behaviour.

She came down to breakfast on one of those matchless mornings of blue sky, warm amber sunlight and sparkling sea. She saw Adrian on the verandah and he spoke to her—this time quite differently.

He had just bidden his mother good-bye and was about to drive to Nicosia. He looked down at Lucie, remembering the beautiful girl with the hazel eyes who had aroused such ill-feeling in him at dinner last night. He saw this morning the demure reserved Miss Gresham, wearing her glasses. He said:

'I want to say I'm sorry for being so bad-tempered yesterday.

I really owe you a debt of gratitude for consenting to come here and look after an invalid. I *do* thank you,' he added, as though the words were wrung out of him.

At once Lucie held out her hand.

'Please don't, Mr. Ollivent. I am so grateful for being given this chance.'

He took her hand. For an instant she felt the strength of his fingers, which were long, hard and powerful. Then he said:

'I'll fly over and see how you are getting on when I am less busy. If you think there is anything my mother needs ... or anything's wrong, kindly cable my head office at once.'

Then he was gone. With something of relief Lucie turned back into the Villa. Extraordinary man! She was amazed that he had bothered to apologize to her.

She went upstairs to see Mrs. Ollivent.

During the next few days she found that her life was to be tolerably easy, without any irksome duties, and those that were allotted to her she liked. Supervising the domestic staff; having care of the big oak press full of embroidered linen, lemon-scented and cool. Some mending, helping to dress Mrs. Ollivent and give her an arm as she walked painfully from one room to another. Shopping for her (it was easy to learn the local currency, for the Cyprus pound was equivalent to the pound sterling, and then there was the *para*, which was like the Egyptian *piastre*, with which Lucie was already familiar).

The Cypriot shopkeepers were always polite and attentive and Lucie found that their manner towards her changed the moment they knew that Adrian Ollivent had left the Island. They all seemed anxious to please the old lady at the Villa.

Except for these trifling duties, and an hour's reading aloud in the evening, Lucie had plenty of spare time.

Then there was the piano. A small rosewood Bechstein grand, which, the day after Adrian left, Lucie played for her employer. It had been kept in tune, and was a wonderful instrument. Lucie played for an hour. Blanche Ollivent was enchanted. The girl had an amazing ear and a sympathetic touch. She played Chopin, which Mrs. Ollivent adored.

'This will bring me the greatest pleasure I have had for years,' she told Lucie. 'I am charmed and I shall write and tell my son that you are exactly the right person for Villa Venetia.'

Lucie thanked her. Mrs. Ollivent added:

'I wish Adrian had heard you play, but next time he comes

down he will do so.'

Lucie did not reply. Mrs. Ollivent seemed to have a blind love of her son which excluded her from how other people regarded him. She was glad that she could bring pleasure to the old lady, whom she soon learned to respect and love. Blanche Ollivent was angelic in her kindliness towards others and her brave acceptance of pain and acute discomfort.

She talked constantly to Lucie about Adrian, praised his brains, the capable way he had taken over his father's business, his good work in the war, and his devotion to herself. No one, she said, could have a better son. But she hinted at some dark shadow which had destroyed his one-time love of Cyprus. But at the end of a fortnight Lucie was no nearer to solving the rather sinister mystery that surrounded him.

One perfect afternoon, after lunch while Mrs. Ollivent rested, Lucie put on a short cotton dress, sandals and a big hat of peasant straw which she had bought in Kyrenia, and taking her little camera, walked through the glorious sunshine on the road that led to the Abbey of Bellapais. She had been told by her employer to take a taxi at her expense. But Lucie preferred to walk.

She had heard so much about this marvellous fourteenth-century Abbey. It was supposed to have beautiful Gothic cloisters.

The breeze that blew from the violet mountains was scented with pine, and that curiously pungent perfume of the *carobs*, that strange vegetable that hung down in clusters from the trees, and was used by the natives for so many of their local industries.

Lucie stopped several times to take a snapshot. Then suddenly she came to a white inn of fair size standing on the hill, with a gay flowered terrace, on which there stood little tables and basket chairs. It was shaded by a trellis of grapevine which already bore magnificent clusters of the famous Cyprus grapes. From here one could look right down the hillside over the harbour at the blue-glass sea.

Lucie could not resist stopping for a rest and a cool drink.

She sat down at one of the tables, took off her hat and her glasses, and wiped her hot young face as she waited for the Cypriot girl who greeted her smilingly, to bring a jug of freshly-made lemonade.

A black-and-tan mongrel bounded out of the inn, saw Lucie and made a joyous leap at her. She loved dogs, and began to pat the comic-looking animal. A man's voice called sternly to the dog in a language which she recognized as Greek. It was now familiar to her. A slimly-built young man came out to chase the dog away. He had exceptional good looks, fair hair, bright blue eyes and a skin burned brown by the sun. He wore English-looking grey flannel shorts and a sports shirt. Lucie smiled at him.

'I don't mind the dog.'

He came forward and answered her in English:

'Oh, good afternoon! He'll put his dirty paws on your clean dress. He is a bad dog. Can I do anything for you? Do you want some tea?'

'Thank you, no. I've ordered lemonade. I'm on my way up to Bellapais but I couldn't resist coming in here. It's such a lovely place and has such a perfect view.'

He smiled at her and nodded, showing magnificent teeth. He had a fresh, radiant look of health and youth.

'I run this place for my grandparents. They are Greeks, but have been here in Cyprus for centuries. My name is Nicos Aliston.'

Lucie smiled and replaced her sun-glasses.

'And mine is Lucie Gresham. I adore this inn.'

He nodded. All the windows were framed in spotless white curtains. There were flowers everywhere, and the air was pungent with the strong sweet smell of grapes ripening in the sun.

'You must see our house inside, too,' he said. 'It is famous for the furniture, which is very old. Some of it is English oak which belonged to my mother. My mother was English,' he added with a touch of pride.

The maid brought a jug of lemonade. Nicos Aliston sprang forward—poured some out into a long glass for Lucie.

With frank admiration he looked down at the silver fairness of her hair. A moment ago when she was without her glasses, he had gazed into the most beautiful pair of golden eyes he had ever seen. Many English girls—tourists—came here to his inn. He had one or two English friends, Army officers on the Island and a few English and French ladies with whom he played tennis, swam and danced. But there was something about the slim sedate English girl which he found intriguing.

He asked if he might be permitted to stay and talk to her

23

while she finished her drink. Lucie said, 'But of course'—and sipped the ice-cold lemonade and listened to the young Greek talk—mainly about himself and Kyrenia. He was rather vain, but in his way ingenuous and respectful.

She learned that he spoke English so well because he had been educated in England. He had intended, he said, becoming a big *hôtelier*, but the war had stopped all that. Before he was twenty he had fought with the Patriots' Army in Greece, and had received a wound which had kept him in hospital a year. Then his father and stepmother had died together in an air accident, and he had come back to Cyprus. His grandparents were still running this inn, but they were both too old and tired to attend any longer to the business. So Nicos took it over for them.

'I feel sometimes I am wasting my time,' he confided in Lucie, sitting on the edge of a chair, swinging a leg thoughtfully, 'Next year, perhaps, I shall close down the Inn and go back to Europe. My chief worry is my sister, whom I do not wish to leave here alone.'

'So you have a sister?' murmured Lucie, interested. Heavens, she thought, how handsome the boy was, with the sun making his hair burn like gold! He had a lot of natural charm, too.

'Yes, I have a sister,' he said.

And then she noticed that his eyes darkened, and a cloud came over his sunburnt face.

'Young Aphra is a great responsibility,' he added. 'Ah—here she is!'

A young girl strolled out of the Inn and joined them. She was as dark as Nicos was fair, short, black curls framing one of the most exquisite faces Lucia had ever seen. She had enormous velvet dark eyes and a figure of voluptuous grace. She was, perhaps, eighteen or nineteen. Her beauty was spoiled by a sullen expression and a downward curve of the pouting mouth. She wore a floral cotton shirt and peasant blouse which had been embroidered locally. Nicos slid off the table and beckoned to her.

'Come, Aphra, and say "hello" to the English lady, who is a new arrival in Kyrenia. Her name is Miss Gresham.'

Without much interest the girl came forward and held out a hand to Lucie. When she spoke it was with a strong Greek accent. Lucie said:

'You are not at all like your brother.'

'Aphra is pure Greek,' said Nicos. 'She is my half-sister. I am twenty-five and she is seven years younger. Since the death of my father and stepmother I have been father and mother as well as brother to her,' he added with a pride which Lucie found delightful. But he looked at Aphra scowlingly and added:

'She is a great anxiety to me.'

The girl shrugged her shoulders and pressed her lips mutinously together.

Lucie laughed.

'She is so beautiful, I suppose she has too many boy-frinds for your liking, Nicos.'

'It is time she settled down with a good husband,' said Nicos.

'Oh, be quiet, I do. not want to get married!' the girl exclaimed.

Nicos curled his handsome lips and turned back to Lucie.

'Where are you staying, Miss Gresham? At which hotel?'

'I am not in a hotel. I am living at the Villa Venetia,' she said.

The name seemed to electrify both brother and sister. The young Greek's face went blank. He froze visibly, just as Lucie had seen other Islanders freeze. It filled her with strange consternation. She added:

'Mr. Adrian Ollivent brought me here from Cairo a week ago. I am looking after his mother.'

Again silence. But this time Lucie saw the young Greek girl's face go bright crimson and then an almost ashen hue. Her eyes dilated. Her lips quivered. She darted forward and spoke to Lucie in a panting voice:

'He is *here* again? He is on the Island? He is down there *now*?'

'Not at the moment . . .' began Lucie, somewhat startled.

Then Nicos cut in. He addressed his half-sister in a fierce voice.

'How dare you ask such questions! Go back indoors, Aphra! Go back at once, I say!' To which he added a stream of words in Greek which Lucie could not understand but which seemed to crush the girl completely, for she burst into tears, turned and rushed away.

Lucie stood up. Her whole body felt hot and uncomfortable. Once again the mystery of Adrian Ollivent's unpopularity thrust itself like a sinister shadow into the peace and happiness of life on the Island. Lucie said:

'I'd better be going on to the Abbey.'

'Oh, please don't go away. I am so sorry about my sister. Forgive her. But I would like so much for you to stay a little longer and talk to me.'

'I think I'd better go.'

'I also much wanted to hear you tell me about life in England these days. I wish Aphra had never interrupted us.'

'Why should the name of Adrian Ollivent upset everybody? Why should it make your half-sister cry?'

Nicos drew a deep breath. His blue eyes burned.

'I could tell you,' he said darkly. 'There is a lot I could tell you if I chose. . . .'

Her heart began to beat quickly. She did not speak. But she wondered if up here in this mountain retreat she was going to hear at last the truth about Adrian Ollivent.

In the warm grape-scented silence she could hear the sound of muffled sobbing ... Aphra, the Greek girl, sobbing there inside the Inn.

FOUR

APHRA'S weeping began to distress Lucie but it seemed to annoy Nicos.

He doubled his fists and looked in the direction of the Inn.

'Please excuse me, Miss Gresham. I must go and tell my sister to stop. She shall not cry for *him*!' he said furiously.

For *him*! ... Lucie drew in her breath. For *Adrian*? Nicos could not mean anybody else. Lucie was about to ask him a question but he had vanished. On second thoughts, Lucie decided that she, too, would disappear. She would continue her pilgrimage to the Abbey. She felt a sudden aversion to the idea of hearing a story in which her employer was involved. She was a member of his household and to listen to scandal savoured of disloyalty.

Nicos said: 'Can I come with you? I know every inch of Bellapais. I could take you over it and explain its history.'

'By all means come along.'

'Oh, I want to very much, and Aphra shall come with us. I will tell her.' He rushed into the Inn. He found his sister bathing her reddened eyes and flung her a rapid order. She was to come and walk with him and the charming young English lady, and she was not to *mention* Mr. Ollivent's name.

Aphra turned her huge dark eyes on her brother sullenly.

'I do not wish to go. Leave me alone.'

'You shall do as I say, otherwise you will be sent to Aunt Caliope.'

That was an old threat, and one which always worked. Aunt Caliope was a nun in a convent in Athens. To be sent to her would mean that Aphra would be forced to lead a life of extreme austerity in a place in which she would never see a man from dawn to dusk. Aphra was unhappy but she loved life—and she liked to be admired by men. She muttered:

'Very well, I will come, Nicos, but what is the English girl doing in the Villa Venetia?'

'She is companion to the old lady.'

'She is not *his* new betrothed?'

There was such misery in her voice that Nicos, who loved this young sister of his devotedly, grew pitiful and gentle with her.

'No, no. He has no betrothed. And he is not in Kyrenia. Now please forget that he exists and come with us, Aphra. The English lady is charming and I like her,' he added naïvely.

All last winter Nicos had seen a lot of Mr. Ollivent too, his hobby was painting. Then he had asked Aphra to sit for him. Once or twice Nicos saw the biggest and best painting in progress—a three-quarter length of the girl wearing the attractive dress of a Cypriot woman, with gold coins round her throat and, great gold earrings. Nicos thought it a marvellous likeness and when it had been finished, meant to have the portrait framed and hung up in the Inn.

In those days Aphra was a gay laughing child of seventeen—much sought after by the young men in Kyrenia, but carefully guarded by her brother and her grandparents in the strict Greek way. Only as a great favour to the well-known Ollivents was she allowed to pose for Adrian.

If Aphra was becoming a little too fond of going to the studio and too warm in her praise of the Englishman, Nicos did not worry. She was a foolish child, but Mr. Ollivent would put her in her place. He had no fears.

Then came Christmas Eve. A cold frosty night with a keen wind blowing from the mountain peaks which were already white with snow. Church bells were ringing from the Greek Orthodox Church for midnight service. Nicos and his sister and grandparents had all gone down to the service. There were crowds of them—all friends—there in the candle-lit, flower-filled church that night, and it was only when they came out that he noticed that Aphra was no longer amongst them.

For the next hour Nicos angrily searched Kyrenia. Aphra was nowhere to be found. None of their relatives or friends had seen her. Then Nicos met a special friend of his, one of the Cypriot police, and he on his patrol had actually caught sight of young Aphra, he said, an hour ago, walking through the gates of Villa Venetia.

Incredulous and full of dawning suspicion, Nicos went straight to the Ollivents' residence.

At the back of the Villa a large light room had been built on, a year ago, to make a studio for Mr. Ollivent.

Some instinct led the Greek boy straight there.

That instinct was horribly right. He had not believed it possible . . . but Aphra was there. He saw her. The lights were full on and through an uncurtained window Nicos saw.

She had gone down to church neatly arrayed with a black lace veil over her head. Now the veil was off. She looked dishevelled, her black curls tumbling down to her neck. She lay on a plain *chaise-longue* which Mr. Ollivent used for his *siesta*; there was a cushion under her head, and Mr. Ollivent was kneeling beside her, holding her hand.

Nicos did not wait to think. What he saw spoke for itself. Adrian Ollivent was in love with his sister and had allowed her to make this clandestine visit . . . like this at midnight, careless of her reputation. He, who had an English fiancée of his own! Yes, at that time he was engaged to a young lady well known in London society—Miss Valerie Bright. Nicos knew her. She and her mother had come once or twice to stay in Kyrenia, and it had been rumoured that she would be married to Mr. Ollivent this summer.

White with fury, Nicos sprang into the studio and accused Adrian Ollivent. Heaven alone knew what he did not accuse him of, he was so convulsed with rage. As head of the family and protector of his young sister, he was justified in the scathing things that he said, whilst Aphra hid her face and wept.

28

Mr. Ollivent had looked startled and amazed. He had begun by assuring Nicos that he was making a grave mistake. Yet when Nicos turned to Aphra, she flung herself into her brother's arms and confessed that she was madly in love with Mr. Ollivent and said that he had asked her to meet him here. Scarlet and, it seemed to Nicos, confused, Adrian denied this.

'Tell him the truth, Aphra,' he had said.

But all Aphra could repeat was that he had asked her to come here.

Nicos waited to hear no more either from her or the Englishman. But he marched up to the half-finished portrait of his sister, pulled out a pocket-knife, slashed it to ribbons, then turned to the artist.

'My sister will never come here again. And it is well that you have not done her more harm, or I would have killed you,' he said. 'Our friendship is at an end.'

Adrian started to speak, but Nicos had shut his ears. In a hot rage, he took his sister by the arm and marched with her out into the cold night.

From that day onward no Aliston ever passed through the gates of Villa Venetia. Kyrenia soon knew about it, and the once popular Mr. Ollivent was avoided and looked at askance. Aphra had fretted ever since—strictly watched over by her brother and grandparents.

Then another rumour spread round the Island—that the English fiancée had got to know about the affair, and had broken with Mr. Ollivent. And after that Kyrenia saw little of him. Nita, Mrs. Ollivent's maid, told her friends that the studio was shut up and that Mr. Ollivent never painted now.

To the strict and conventional mind of the Greek boy and his family, Aphra had behaved badly, but Mr. Ollivent was responsible. That was the end of it.

That was the story as Nicos Aliston knew it. Five months old now but still fresh in his memory. But he respected Lucie Gresham's wish that nothing more should be said about Mr. Ollivent.

The rest of that afternoon was a delight to Lucie. Aphra had dried her tears and was prepared to be more friendly, although her English was far less fluent than her brother's, so he had to interpret between them.

He was an enthusiastic guide.

Lucie had never seen anything so beautiful as the Abbey, so

29

proudly outlined against the blue sky on the edge of a high cliff. They wandered through the ruins in the cool shade of age-old cloisters, up stone steps, through the refectory and the church. The pulpit was still standing. On the marble lintel of the main door a coat-of-arms of the Royal Lusignan was still to be seen, and there were two Roman sarcophagi near the main entrance. Everywhere the grass grew, and wild flowers.

Standing in the warm sunshine, Lucie looked up at the belfry and drew a deep sigh.

'It is so beautiful here, and so peaceful,' she said.

Nicos shrugged his shoulders.

'I have seen it almost too often,' he smiled; 'as a boy I used to come up here with my little sister and play.'

'When was it built?' she asked him, and dreamily watched a snow-white pigeon fly through one of the narrow Gothic cloisters up into the sunshine.

'In the fourth century, but the monks belonged to an Order which was founded in 1120 in France,' he said.

'So long ago!' she said, and stood ruminating on the ruined loveliness.

Nicos proudly aired more of his knowledge.

'In the year 1570 the Turks destroyed a good deal of the building. What was left was handed over to our Greek Orthodox Church.'

Lucis turned to Aphra.

'Doesn't it interest you?'

'No,' she pouted, and added in her quaint broken English: 'for me all ... too sad. I not like places of monks and nuns.'

'Neither do I particularly,' laughed Lucie.

Nicos echoed her laugh.

'Aphra is afraid that she will be sent to her Aunt Caliope, who is a nun.'

Aphra tossed her head and turned away. Now Lucie took out her camera.

'I want to take a snapshot of you both here. Stand by one of those pillars, please.'

The young Greeks were both incurably vain and Aphra especially loved to pose. They made a handsome pair. Lucie took several snapshots both of them and of the Abbey. Nicos insisted upon taking one of her.

Just before they went down the hill again Nicos left Lucie alone for a moment with his sister, while he went to say a word to the custodian of the Abbey. Lucie smiled at the girl.

'Perhaps you will come and see me one day, Aphra.'

The girl looked startled, then blushed red.

'I cannot go to the Villa Venetia,' she said in a whisper.

Lucie bit her lip. The shadow of the mystery connected with Adrian Ollivent fell across them both.

'I ... see....'

'*Mees* ... please, *Mees* ... do you see *him*? He is to be married?'

Lucie answered only the last one.

'He is not to be married so far as I know. *Has* he a fiancée?' she added a question in her turn.

The pupils of Aphra's enormous eyes dilated.

'He was affianced ... but now they say ... it is all over.'

'I see,' repeated Lucie.

She was stumbling upon some of the facts that were hidden from her. But certainly neither he nor his mother had suggested that he had a future wife.

Aphra spoke again:

'Please, *Mees*, will you tell him something from me?'

'What, Aphra?'

'Just that I ... I remember him....'

Lucie's ears burned. This was rather too suggestive of secret intimacy. She was thankful that Nicos appeared and Aphra could say no more.

Lucie went back to Villa Venetia.

'*Just that I remember him*...' Could it be possible that there had been some sort of affair between her employer and Nicos' half-sister? And what about this fiancée whom he was supposed to have had?

The plot thickens, Lucie reflected. She walked into the Villa, to find Adrian Ollivent himself sitting in the salon with his mother.

FIVE

MRS. OLLIVENT greeted Lucie warmly.

'Come along in, my dear. I think the tea is cold but you can ask Loucas to make you a fresh pot. Isn't this a wonderful surprise? My son has been in Cairo—flown down to the Island to see me before going on to Athens.'

Lucis stood shyly in the doorway, conscious that she must look hot and untidy after her walking expedition. She took off her glasses and murmured 'Oh, hello...' to Adrian. Then added, 'Excuse me, please, I must get tidy,' and vanished.

Adrian sat down again. He was faintly amused. The Lucie who had just appeared was not at all his conception of the neat, old-fashioned little creature he had brought here to be his mother's companion. She looked quite charming, with her fair wind-blown hair and that hot colour, and she was at least a shade more sunburned than when he had left her here three weeks ago.

He turned to his mother.

'So Miss Gresham's a success, is she?'

'A great success, my darling. Really an improvement on poor old Gertrude. She cannot do enough for me. She is an educated, interesting girl, too.'

'The pain not too bad these days, Mama?'

'It doesn't get much better, my darling, but I have so much to be thankful for.'

'When you say things like that it makes me feel that everything is worth while,' he said in a low voice.

She leaned forward and touched his arm, an expression of sadness darkening her eyes.

'Haven't you found peace of mind yet, Adrian?'

He shied away from that question, from that look.

'I'm all right, Mother. It's good to know you're happily settled. That's what I hoped to find.'

The door opened and Lucie came in. Adrian turned back and watched her cross the salon and sit beside his mother. She was neat and cool again in a linen dress. He remembered her telling him that she had suffered from eyestrain while she worked at the Embassy, but it looked as though these three weeks down here had wrought a cure. Her eyes were clear and brilliant.

'Well—are you still liking the Island?' he asked.

'More and more. It's terrific, Mr. Ollivent.'

'Lucie is an indefatigable walker,' put in Mrs. Ollivent. 'I think she could write a pamphlet on Kyrenia.'

Adrian smiled faintly.

'You've seen Bellapais and St. Hilarion, I suppose?'

'I was at the Abbey this afternoon,' she said.

'Quite a fine old ruin,' he said.

Lucie had to confess to herself that she felt a trifle 'odd' about Adrian Ollivent, after the suggestive remarks which had been made about him by the Alistons, and she knew that nothing would induce her to give him that cryptic message from Aphra, the Greek girl. What kind of man was he really?

Dinner was quite a pleasant meal. Adrian seemed to make an effort to be amiable. And afterwards, while he and his mother drank coffee, Lucie entertained them at the piano.

Loucas had put out the lights except for two heavy silver sconces in which six tall candles were burning.

As Lucie began to play, Adrian's gaze wandered quite often towards the young figure on the music stool. Almost gratefully he listened, for she was playing as he had always wanted someone to play: with delicacy of touch, deep feeling, a real talent.

Gradually a sense of peace stole over him. With half-closed eyes he watched the girl who was playing.

Chopin ... an air or two from Schumann's *Dichterliebe* then some Debussy which seemed to fit in with the moonlight, the candles, the fragrance of dying roses.

Then suddenly the music became unbearably sentimental. Adrian hated it. Suddenly he interrupted her.

'Thank you, but that is enough. I'm going out to get some fresh air.'

Lucie got up. She blushed to the roots of her hair.

'I'm terribly sorry. I played for too long...' she stammered.

'Not at all, my dear—it was quite delightful and I am sure my son enjoyed it,' put in Blanche Ollivent, and threw Adrian a reproachful look.

He flung the stump of his finished cigar out into the garden.

'Miss Gresham plays extremely well. Forgive me if I say good night, but I need a walk.'

Then he was gone. Lucie walked slowly to Mrs. Ollivent's chair.

'I'm afraid I *did* play too long. I didn't notice how the time

33

was passing.'

'You couldn't play long enough for me, my dear. And take no notice of Adrian. He is a strange being . . .' the mother smiled sadly—'hard even for me to understand sometimes, but he has had a lot of trouble.'

Lucie bit her lip. Another mysterious allusion to Adrian's '*past*'. When would she know some facts?

On a sudden impulse Lucie sat down on the stool at Mrs. Ollivent's feet and said:

'I . . . don't like to hide anything from you, Mrs. Ollivent. I want you to know that somebody in Kyrenia told me today that Mr. Ollivent was engaged . . . will you think it impertinent of me if I ask you if that is true?'

Blanche Ollivent was silent a moment. She had been working on a piece of tapestry. Now the hand that held the needle paused.

'You have every right to ask me, now that you have become part of our household. Of course, people in small communities like Kyrenia like to gossip. However . . . my son is *not* engaged. He *was*. It was broken some time ago.'

'Thank you for telling me,' said Lucie awkwardly.

To herself, she was thinking that *that* part of Aphra's story, at least, was true.

But what of the rest . . . the significance of those tears and that message which haunted her?

She rang for Loucas and helped the old lady up to bed.

When she came down again she felt restless and unlike sleep. She could not go to bed yet.

She sat down and closed her eyes. She must have dozed, because she woke with a sudden start to find Adrian Ollivent standing in front of her, looking down at her with a slightly sardonic grin.

Flushed and embarrassed, Lucie sprang off the chair.

'Oh!' she said breathlessly. . . .'

'What for?'

'I oughtn't to have fallen asleep like that.'

He gave a dry laugh.

'You aren't forbidden to sleep if you want to, my dear girl. But it's getting late. Half past eleven. I've been walking for an hour and a half.'

Lucie glanced at the ormolu clock on the mantelpiece.

'How awful—so late!' she said, shocked.

'I must say I'm ready to turn in now. By the way, don't imagine that I didn't enjoy your playing this evening. I'm afraid I was a bit abrupt, but I did like it very much. You play well, Lucie.'

She stood before him, tongue-tied. It was the first time that she could remember him using her Christian name.

'Tell me,' he spoke again, 'have you met many people in Kyrenia?'

'Some of your mother's friends,' she said, 'and an English girl whom I used to know at the Embassy in Cairo, who was here for a day on her way up to Platras.'

'Quite a nice place in summer,' nodded Adrian.

'And, of course, I begin to know some of the local inhabitants ... the Cypriots,' added Lucie.

'Well, I expect you'll need young company sometimes,' said Adrian in a grudging voice, 'you won't want to spend your whole time with my mother—but don't get too friendly with the islanders.'

'But I find them charming!' she said.

'They are apt to take advantage ... become familiar.'

Lucie felt compelled to argue.

'Oh, really, I don't find that at all. I think the Cypriots are most polite and respectful.'

Then he snapped:

'I think I know them better than you do. I shouldn't be too friendly ... that's what I say and that's what I mean.'

Lucie resented this tone and interference in her private life.

With tightened lips she said:

'I've already made a good "local" friend today. The owner of an Inn. He took me over Bellapais. He has offered to show me St. Hilarion. I don't see why I shouldn't allow him to do so. I choose my own friends.'

As soon as she had spoken she saw the red light of danger. Yes, she could *see* the look of dawning suspicion in his eyes. . . . He snapped again:

'And who is this fellow who is offering to act as your guide?'

Almost her courage failed her then, and she regretted having let herself in for this. But the desire to come into the open had become almost unbearable.

'He owns that inn on the way to Bellapais. His name is Nicos Aliston.'

Silence. It was as though she had cracked a pistol-shot into the quiet salon. He stood rigid a moment. Then he said:

'Under no circumstances are you to invite either Nicos Aliston—or his sister—or any of his friends to Villa Venetia. Neither will you mention their names to my mother. I quite see that I have no jurisdiction over your personal affairs, but I can and will dictate as to who you bring here.'

Or his sister, Adrian had added. The hostility in his voice when he had uttered the name Nicos Aliston was there, also, for the lovely little Greek girl.

'I had no intention of asking them here,' Lucie said hotly. 'Neither need I mention the name to your mother if you think it would upset her.'

'Well, it would.... What is more, I advise you not to have anything to do with the Alistons.'

'Why?' demanded Lucie, bluntly.

He looked down at her as though amazed that she should ask the question. Then he snapped.

'That is my affair.'

'No—mine,' she argued; 'you are telling *me* to keep away from these people whom I have found friendly and interesting.'

Adrian Ollivent opened his lips as though to speak again, then, with a gesture of angry impatience, turned and walked out of the salon, closing the door behind him.

She did not see him again. He had already left the Villa for Athens before she came downstairs on the following morning.

She had had a restless night and felt tired and disturbed when she woke up. She wished that she had never mentioned the Alistons' name to Adrian. He was beginning to disturb her peace of mind.

The more she thought about it, as she carried out her usual routine in the Villa on that cloudless golden May morning, the more inclined she was to jump to hasty conclusions.

And one conclusion seemed to be that Adrian Ollivent hated those two up in the Inn *because he had been guilty of hurting Aphra.*

But where did the fiancée come in? What about *her*?

It seemed fated that on this very day a little more of Adrian Ollivent's past should be revealed to her.

Just before lunch, whilst walking round the walled-in orchard at the back of the Villa—she came to the long low room recently built on, which was kept locked. Mrs. Ollivent described it as 'Adrian's private studio', and had told her that he

36

used to paint there when he lived in Kyrenia but had given it up since he moved his head-office. Lucie had been quite surprised to find the two striking little oils—mostly of the Island—which he had painted and which hung in his mother's bedroom. He had a strong artistic streak under the façade of 'hard business man'.

Lucie noticed suddenly that the shutters of one of the windows was wide open.

Lucie found the old butler and questioned him. He said that he, too, had noticed the opened shutters and presumed that the master must have gone into the studio this morning and forgotten to close the window again. Madame had another key, so far as Loucas knew.

Lucie then went to the old lady and told her about it.

'I had better go and lock the shutters again, hadn't I? The room is on the ground floor and rather tempting to a burglar?'

Mrs. Ollivent agreed and repeated what Loucas had said. Her son must have entered the studio before he left and forgotten to close the shutters. She handed Lucie the key.

'Go and lock up, dear. How I wish he had gone on with his painting,' she sighed; 'he had the makings of a real artist.'

A few moments later Lucie stood alone in the studio.

The window threw a strong light on white walls hung with pictures, a table spread with artists' equipment, an easel, a *chaise-longue* with a gay Spanish shawl flung over it. With a queer sense of excitement Lucie walked slowly round, examining everything. Strange and rather sad to think that Adrian Ollivent must once have been happy in this room, she reflected, spending much time with paints and brush and enjoying his labours.

Most of the framed pictures on the walls were portraits, she noticed. So Adrian was a portrait painter amongst other things. She even recognized old Loucas, the butler, with his grey hair and walnut-brown wrinkled face.

There were one or two big canvases standing against the wall with their backs to her. Something made her lift one and turn it around.

Then her heart gave a jerk. She felt suddenly hot and even dismayed. She carried the canvas nearer the window so that the light fell on it.

It was a painting of Aphra, the Greek girl.

Aphra, with that brightly-coloured Spanish shawl now on the

chaise-longue, flung across one shoulder, and those same big golden earrings in her ears which Lucie had noticed yesterday. Aphra, her big dark eyes full of laughter, her inviting lips parted in a seductive smile.

It was a brilliant piece of work. Lucie knew enough about art to recognize that fact. With strong bold sweeps of the brush, and rich colours, Adrian had captured all the ripe beauty and youth of the Greek girl.

Lucie stared at the portrait for a long time, then picked up another canvas, and another. All of Aphra; Aphra in different clothes and different moods—lovely and enticing.

So there *had* been something between them after all.

Lucie stood staring at the portraits, and suddenly, quite crazily, *knew that she was jealous*. Jealous of the Greek girl's beauty, of the interest that Adrian had once in her, of the hours she must have spent here in this studio, posing for him.

Jealous. But why, for heaven's sake, why? Lucie suddenly, horrified at herself, turned and ran out of the studio, locking the door behind her.

SIX

She found herself looking up into the face of Adrian Ollivent. He gripped one of her arms. She heard his voice, quiet, a little menacing.

'What were you doing in there? I left orders that nobody was to go inside that room.'

She gasped.

'I—I thought . . . you had gone!'

'So it seems,' he said sarcastically. 'Who gave you the key?'

'Your mother!' said Lucie, her cheeks flaming. 'You left one of the windows wide open and anybody would have been able to climb in. Someone had to go and lock up.'

Adrian's lips relaxed.

'So that's it.'

'Now say you're sorry,' said Lucie childishly; 'you really are *impossible*. You as much as accused me of stealing the key to pry into your studio.'

Her indignant eyes and red cheeks seemed to amuse him suddenly. He laughed.

'What a little spitfire it is. But you are quite right. I *am* impossible and I apologize. To tell you the truth, Lucie, I came back here from Nicosia meaning to apologize for my conduct last night. Oh no,' he added quickly as he met her incredulous gaze, 'don't imagine that I cancelled my trip in order to make the apology. I certainly did not. But when I got to Nicosia I found that the flight is indefinitely delayed owing to engine trouble, and so as I shall not be taking off for some hours, I decided to drive back home.'

Lucie sniffed quite audibly.

'Just to be rude to me again, I suppose.'

That brought another laugh from him, his whole face softened, more youthful. He said:

'I was angry last night because you had the poor taste to pick on the Alistons for friends.'

'Poor taste? A taste you shared in the past, didn't you?'

Calmly he lit a cigarette and replaced the lighter in his pocket. She thought that he might fly at her in his quick-tempered fashion but he seemed calm and even tolerant this morning.

'That is so. But I would like you to accept the fact that I had my good reasons.'

'Must you be concerned about the friendships I make on the Island? As long as I don't ask people here who you or Mrs. Ollivent dislike ... am I not free to associate with them? If not, please tell me, and I'll try to readjust my ideas about my position in your employ. But it is expecting rather too much from me. I'm used to personal liberty.'

Adrian frowned, then raised his brows and gave a slight shrug of the shoulders.

'A very dignified speech, my dear Lucie. You must be free to make friends. But I'm sorry you have chosen the Alistons—that's all.'

She stood silent.

'It's hot out here and you have no hat. Give me the key, Lucie. Come into the studio and talk to me for a moment.'

She turned and followed him, a sudden feeling of excitement

rising in her.

He unlatched all the shutters, and threw open the windows, filling the studio with the strong morning light. Then he stared around him. She saw that his eyes grew dark with secret memories. But he looked at her with an ironic smile.

'You stand, my dear, in the graveyard of a man's desire to become a great artist. He is now director of a prosperous shipping firm. You have been on the Island only a few weeks. Haven't you heard them whisper what a monstrous character I am ... or was? Isn't it so?'

She stayed silent and uncomfortable. With a long paint-brush in his hand, he began to beat a tattoo on the table. He watched the dust rise up and dance in a spectrum of sunlight.

'Well, isn't it so?'

'It's true that people talk,' she admitted ... 'but they always talk. Everybody is apt to come under criticism in a small community like this. Especially an important man like yourself.'

He turned round and faced her.

'For what am I important, Lucie? What have I done in the eyes of Cyprus? I have money and power because I am the head of a firm which my father made important. I meant to retire from business and become a painter. I wanted the goodwill of my friends and the love and trust of the girl I was going to marry. And what did I get? ...' He gave a laugh that Lucie thought the most unhappy sound she had ever heard. '*You* can tell me. *They* will have told you. You must know what I am said to have done in this place.'

He swept paint-brushes and blocks off the table with a sudden violent gesture. The objects clattered to the floor. Dumbly Lucie regarded them. She had not the least idea what to say or to do. She knew that she could have asked for the truth ... but it seemed indecent ... and quite irregular ... that she should pry into his life. She was his mother's paid companion.

She heard his voice, composed again. 'I frighten you, don't I, Lucie? You must forgive me. I think I'm a little "touched". We'll leave it at that, shall we?'

Then she found her voice. 'I wouldn't say that you were "touched". And I am not frightened of you.'

'That surprises me.'

'Do you want to frighten me?'

He seated himself on the edge of the table, staring down at the things he had thrown on the floor, then up at her. Certainly she did not look afraid.

'You're really very nice, Lucie,' he said involuntarily; 'you have courage, too.'

'And I think you're nice, too, when you want to be,' she said; 'but you can be...'

'A monster,' he finished for her.

'It's rather a strong word.'

'You are cautious ... you weigh up every word, don't you?'

'I suppose so.'

'But you still haven't told me what you have heard about me.'

'Do you really want to know?' she asked.

An instant's silence.

'No. It doesn't really matter a damn what they say or do not say in Kyrenia. I've finished with it, just as it has finished with me.'

'Oh, that can't be true! You could never finish with such a gorgeous place.'

'"Love's Island", eh?' He broke into a cynical laugh. 'Thanks. You may keep your illusions about Cyprus and about everything. For me it's damned.'

'You don't really think that.'

'I won't qualify my statement. We'll make a bargain. You choose your own friends. I'll say no more about it. One thing and one alone concerns me. I do not wish my mother to be made unhappy by any unattractive story that you may hear about me.'

Indignantly, Lucie exclaimed:

'I wouldn't *dream* of repeating any gossip to dear Mrs. Ollivent.'

Adrian's lips softened.

'You are fond of her, aren't you?'

'I think she's a *saint*.'

'So do I,' he said. 'The place suits her health and she has expressed a wish to stay here. She shall, no matter what it costs me to come back from time to time. And I am really grateful for the affection you are showing her. She has never been more content than in your care. I feel it is a sacrifice on your part. It can't be very gay for you here.'

'You know that I'm perfectly happy in Villa Venetia.'

He gave a sigh.

'Oh, well, I'll go in and see Mama. Forget this conversation,

41

Lucie. Come along ... I don't want to stay in this studio any longer. I think I'll have it burned down.'

'You mustn't! Oh, it's such a shame that you don't paint any more! Your wonderful portraits ...' She stopped, confused.

Hands in his pockets, he walked towards her.

'So little Lucie *has* been prying?'

'I ... oh ... I do hope you don't mind ... I did look at one or two of the canvases.'

'Natural feminine curiosity.'

She watched Adrian go up to a pile of canvases and kick them with his foot. One after another, they scattered on the floor ... face upwards ... the vivid portraits of Aphra in all her flamboyant, seductive beauty. He said:

'An ex-girl-friend of mine. Isn't that what Kyrenia tells you?'

Lucie began to stutter, but he interrupted:

'Never mind. We agreed that I shouldn't probe into the past. I used to think these paintings were good. Aphra ... or Aphrodite ... the young goddess of love rising from the foam. All foam ... no heart ... no brains....' He gave another little kick to the canvas, laughing.

Lucie held her breath. Her confusion was complete. She could see that Adrian Ollivent hated the Greek girl in an almost brutal fashion.

Adrian picked up the portraits one by one and flung them in a heap in the corner.

'Don't destroy them, *please*,' Lucie cried.

'Why not? They destroyed me,' he said. 'I shall have a bonfire made of them next time I'm home for any length of time, and you shall come and watch it burn.'

'You're crazy!' she breathed. 'You have no right to destroy works of art.'

'Works of the devil, Adrian Ollivent,' he said, his mocking gaze upon her.

A single canvas which had remained against the wall—a larger one—slithered down suddenly.

Adrian did not move to pick it up. He was lighting another cigarette. Involuntarily Lucie moved forward and turned it over.

For an instant she stared down at it. This was not one of the Greek girl. It was a head and shoulders of another girl, a completely different type. A fresh, vital piece of work. The model had light brown hair waving down to her shoulders; long lazy-lidded eyes of greenish-blue; rather a long neck. She wore a blue polo necked jersey. There were pearls in her ears.

The next instant Adrian Ollivent pushed Lucie aside and put his heel straight through the canvas, ruining the paint, the beautiful face.

'Oh, you *are* mad!' exclaimed Lucie.

'I thought I'd already burned every one I had of *her*.... Aphra is one thing, but *she* ...' He broke off, his face congested.

'But it was lovely—the loveliest of them all!' wailed Lucie, carried away by her admiration of the portrait.

'Loveliest of them all,' he echoed—'yes, so I used to think. Aphra had no education, but Valerie was a cultured young woman. Aphra was a fool, but not Valerie. She was quite intelligent. No sense of loyalty. As treacherous as she was beautiful! For Aphra there was some excuse. For Valerie, *none* ...'

Adrian picked up the wrecked canvas.

'Meet Miss Valerie Bright—whom I was once going to marry. She is now the wife of an American with a hundred times as many dollars as I've got pennies. The dollars I hear console her nicely for her broken heart. Our engagement ended as soon as Kyrenia told her about the debaucheries with Aphra which, they said, took place in this studio.'

Adrian calmed down. 'I'm sorry, Lucie. I've upset you now as well as myself. One day perhaps I'll be able to discuss this thing calmly, without prejudice. For the moment don't be too quick to judge me—no matter what you may hear about me.'

She looked up at him timidly. What a queer, incomprehensible man ... and what a fascinating one!

He walked to the studio door and opened it for her.

'I'll follow you in a moment, Lucie,' he said. 'Tell my mother that I've come back and why, will you, please, and say that I'm just on my way up to see her.'

SEVEN

ONE month later—a hot morning in June—Lucie settled Mrs. Ollivent in her chair in what was her favourite garden retreat during the hot weather. An arbour shaded from the sun by a trellis of green grapevine, at the back of which two beautiful cypress trees added further shade. It faced a bed of English roses. Across a low stone wall, lay a vista of the mountains, pale amethyst through the golden-hued haze.

Lucie gave Mrs. Ollivent her writing materials. Nita brought a glass and a jug of iced lemonade to put on the little table beside her. Mrs. Ollivent smiled at Lucie.

'Do you know,' she said, 'you're just as brown as an Indian these days. And you were such a pale little thing when you first came to us.'

Lucie smiled back, and gave an extra pat to the cushions behind the old lady.

'I always feel so well here,' she said. 'In Egypt the sun is an enemy ... one shuts it out. But I simply adore to be out in Kyrenian sunshine.'

'Well, I'm very glad, my dear, only don't forget to wear your nice big hat at midday and *don't* forget those sun-glasses even though your eyes are so much better.'

Lucie went up to her room to collect her things together for her swim. It was her 'day off'.

Nowadays she was no longer such a solitary individual. She had two firm friends. One an American girl, named Carol Dexter.

Carol's husband Dex, a big chubby-faced American, was often away on business. Carol was glad of Lucie's company, and *vice versa*.

Mrs. Ollivent also liked the Dexters. They once or twice were guests for dinner at Villa Venetia wherein Carol vowed she was 'just crazy' about all the treasures.

Adrian had not been home for four weeks now. He had been to Athens then in Upper Egypt dealing with a crisis in his Khartoum office. She heard news of him regularly from his mother.

It had taken Lucie some little time to recover from the shattering moments spent in his studio, nearly a month ago now.

Afterwards he behaved towards her much as before . . . treating her with cool indifference. Yet on one occasion Mrs. Ollivent surprised Lucie by telling her that Adrian wished to be remembered to 'little Lucie'.

It was even more surprising to Lucie to find how often she remembered that message. He seemed to have an inexplicable hold on her imagination.

But she was determined not to be bullied or directed by him. Having made friends with Nicos Aliston, she continued to be friends with him.

Lucie was aware that Nicos at present had one ambition—to be considered her particular 'boy-friend'. He could not do enough to please her.

She upset him by teasing him when he became sentimental. But she was flattered. No man before had ever paid her such persistent attention.

Carol encouraged it.

'You're repressed, Lucie honey,' she had once said, 'much too inhibited. What you want is a good old love-affair . . . something to take you right out of yourself.'

'Not with Nicos, surely,' Lucie had protested, with an embarrassed laugh.

But Carol said: 'Yes, why not? He's a regular honey to look at and he's got nice ways, and dollars to spend.'

Lucie laughed. But she thought over these things.

Drifting from day to day, with nothing much to think about except her duties at the Villa, Lucie was all too conscious that she wanted something *more*. Something real and absorbing. Fulfilment of herself as a human being; *as a woman*.

Hazily, right at the back of her mind, lay the perpetual memory of Adrian Ollivent. His personality seemed to make itself felt in an inexplicable fashion.

But after all this time she was no nearer to knowing the truth about Adrian.

Today she was due to lunch down at the Dome Hotel with Carol after a quick dip in the sea. Then Nicos was fetching them by car. They had planned to take a picnic tea out at Hilarion Castle.

Lucie had already seen St. Hilarion, but she could not have enough of it. She thought it the most exquisite place in Cyprus. A fairy castle on a mountain peak, two thousand feet above the sea.

She had seldom felt happier. She really owed Nicos a lot, she reflected ... and Carol and Dex.... They were fast removing her old inferiority complex. Carol was even bent on making improvements in Lucie's appearance. An American glamour girl herself, she knew all the tricks of the trade. She revolutionized Lucie's ideas on clothes and make-up ... induced Lucie not to screw that lovely fair hair of hers into a severe bun. Now, when she was out of the Villa, she let it flow down to her neck in soft fair waves. At first Lucie had felt silly and self-conscious about it, but she got over that. Nicos admired the new hair-style enormously, and Dex said that it made her look 'cute'.

'Gee! I guess I know now who that fellow Adrian Ollivent reminded me of when we met him. He's the perfect type for Rochester.... Lucie is Jane Eyre.'

They had all laughed over that, except Nicos, who had not read the book. Carol had added:

'Heaven forbid that our Lucie should fall in love with that great morose Ollivent guy in the way that Jane Eyre fell for Rochester!'

Nicos remained sulkily silent as he always did when the name Ollivent cropped up. But it brought another laugh from Dex, in which Lucie joined. And only Lucie knew how her heart had jerked at the thought. She had echoed to herself:

'Heaven *forbid* that I should *ever* fall in love with Adrian!'

She finished dressing, took her big peasant hat and her sun-glasses—in accordance with dear Blanche Ollivent's advice—then with her swim-suit and towel in a small basket, made her way down the hill towards the Dome Hotel where her American friends lived.

Carol was waiting for her in the hotel lounge. She had been talking to another girl, but she rose and walked to the door to meet Lucie as the small figure appeared.

'Listen, honey,' said Carol, 'do you think there'll be room in Nicos' car for another person? If not, I can't come, because some folks have turned up. It's quite unexpected. One of Dex's business friends has just been sent to Cyprus for a conference. Bob Vanderlight. He's a big guy, and more or less Dex's boss. He has flown over from the States and brought his wife with him and they're staying in Kyrenia until the end of the month.'

'I'm sure Nic could squeeze one in, anyhow,' said Lucie.

Carol added, tucking an arm through Lucie's:

'Mrs. Bob Vanderlight's an English girl. She's cute. You'll like her. She knows Cyprus well, too. She used to come here with her mother. Unfortunately, she says it holds memories for her that are not too gay, as she had an unhappy love-affair here. But I told her she will darned soon forget it. We'll keep her laughing—won't we, honey?'

'*You* will,' Lucie smiled.

Then suddenly the blood rushed to her face. She had a suffocating feeling of excitement and shock. The girl to whom Carol had just been speaking, and whom she was now introducing as Mrs. Bob Vanderlight ... why, good heavens, *Lucie knew her*! ... That long throat ... the mane of light brown hair ... the tip-tilted nose, the lazy greeny-blue eyes. This was the girl of the portrait ... the portrait which Adrian had smashed to pieces.

It could be no other. Carol murmured the name now: '*Valerie*—this is my friend Lucie Gresham.'

Valerie! Mrs. Bob Vanderlight was Valerie Bright, she had married an American after breaking her engagement with Adrian Ollivent.

EIGHT

VALERIE VANDERLIGHT shook hands with Lucie without much enthusiasm. She had the limp kind of handshake which Lucie always found irritating. And Valerie thought:

'What a funny little person ... awful dress ... fits where it touches....'

Valerie wore perfectly tailored linen slacks. On her right hand there was an emerald which must have cost Mr. Vanderlight thousands of dollars.

Lucie turned to Carol.

'Are you sure you want to come on this party this afternoon ... that you wouldn't rather stay with your friend?'

'Of course not,' was Carol's answer. 'We'll go to the Abbey together. Valerie will be crazy about it.'

47

The girl who had been Valerie Bright, took a large expensive-looking white bag from the table, produced a mirror and a long gold lipstick pencil with which she outlined her large mouth, then examined her false eyelashes and the glossy hair which she combed back from her face. She was never 'crazy' about anything except her own beauty and the admiration of men.

She had not particularly wanted to come back to Cyprus. The beauty of the Island held no charm for her. She was far more interested in the big skyscrapers of New York. It had been a slight shock to her to learn that her husband had to go to Cyprus on a business trip, but she had come with him because she imagined it might be more amusing than being left to kick her heels in the Vanderlights' summer residence alone with her mother-in-law.

But a jaunt to the ruined Abbey which she had seen dozens of times before presented a boring prospect.

Suddenly she looked up sharply from her powder compact and said:

'What's the name of this Greek?'

Lucie answered, 'Aliston. He runs a lovely place up on the road to Bellapais.'

A very faint colour stole into the exquisite face of Mrs. Vanderlight.

'*Nicos!* Nicos Aliston! So *he's* still around.'

'Did you know him?' asked Carol.

'I did. *And* his little toad of a sister.'

Lucie caught her breath. What was she going to hear next? She had been right about Valerie.

'Say, what's wrong with Aphra? She's just a lovely little pagan. Where does the *toad* come in?' Carol laughed.

'Oh, that's a long story. I used to come to Cyprus with mama quite a bit after my engagement.'

'Were you engaged to someone in Cyprus?' asked Carol, who was the only one of the three of them who looked or felt cheerful and sensed no undercurrent.

'Sure! To a man named Adrian Ollivent. Ever come across him?'

Now it was Carol's turn to utter a whistle.

'Adrian! Well, imagine! *That* one! Holy smoke! I didn't think he had it in him to be engaged to anyone; he's a morose type. I thought he was a kinda confirmed bachelor. Did *you* know he was ever engaged, Lucie honey?'

Lucie's small face set into an expressionless mask. All the memories of the things that Adrian had said in the studio that day ... the bitter brutal things ... the way he had ground his heel through Valerie's portrait ... crowded back on her.

'Yes, I heard it.'

Now Valerie turned to the English girl.

'What else have you heard?'

Lucie looked at her squarely.

'Don't you think we'd better go and swim if we're going to get a bathe in before lunch?'

'Sure!' said Carol immediately. 'Come on. Would you like a swim, Val?'

'No, thanks. I'll be a looker,' said Valerie, and lit a cigarette.

Lucie did not enjoy this morning despite the freshness of the bright water and the sun. She kept thinking about Adrian and Valerie.

Once they were well away from the rocks, Carol—rubbing a hand over her wet, sunburned face—said to Lucie:

'I thought Val cute when I first saw her, but I don't know that I altogether take to her as time goes on. But as she's the wife of Dex's boss I'd better keep my opinion to myself. How does she strike you, honey?'

Lucie said:

'Marvellous to look at, but I wouldn't call her a charmer.'

'Oh, well—men like 'em like that, honey,' said Carol with a giggle. 'I have friends at home who know the Vanderlights, and they say Bob's crazy about his wife; she twists him round her little finger. Sometimes I think it's the right slant on life ... snatch what you can out of it and don't love anyone but yourself.'

'You don't mean that,' said Lucie; 'you've got a very big heart, Carol.'

'Sure, and it's always getting me into trouble,' laughed Carol. 'And what about you? Weren't you saying the other day that you feel things far too intensely?'

'Maybe,' said Lucie 'but I'd rather be that way no matter how much it hurts.'

After which remark she dived into the clear water and put and end to the discussion.

The whole afternoon threatened to be awkward. What would Nicos say when he saw Adrian's ex-fiancée? How much of the past would be stirred up?

Lucie's uneasiness grew and culminated into something approaching panic when Nicos arrived in his car. What would happen now?

When the Greek boy climbed out of the car and approached the three girls who came out of the Dome to meet him—Valerie deliberately moved forward.

'Well, *well*, Nicos. I didn't expect to see *you* ever again.'

Lucie, watching, saw Nicos start at the tall, slender girl in grey and yellow as though at an apparition. Then he gave a stiff and an entirely un-English bow.

'*Miss Bright!*'

'Mrs. Vanderlight's the name now,' she cut in smoothly. 'I married an American. My husband and I have just flown over from the States.'

Nicos went on staring at her. His eyes were full of amazement. There was not the vestige of a smile on his face. But he was polite and it did not seem to Lucie that he bore any particular grudge against 'Miss Bright'. He said:

'It is certainly a surprise to see you back on the Island.'

'I'm quite surprised to find myself here,' said Valerie languidly; 'and how is your sister?'

Lucie, her gaze still upon Nicos, now saw the muscles of his face tauten.

'Well, thank you. She did not come this afternoon as we had planned because my grandmother is ill and she has stayed behind to look after her.'

Lucie felt the tension break, and moved forward.

'Oh, Nicos, I'm so sorry your grandmother is ill. Ought we to take you away?'

His handsome face softened as he turned to her.

'It's quite all right. Aphra is looking after her. It is her old trouble. The doctor does not think she will live through another winter. But please let us enjoy our picnic as planned.'

He gazed at her with frank adoration. He was deeply in love with her. He longed to make Lucie Gresham love him. Lucie had captivated his mind as well as his senses. His dearest wish was to look after her, to give her everything he could. But she made fun of him when he became a little serious. It was depressing.

He was absurdly pleased when Carol insisted upon Lucie taking the place next to the driver, and seated herself at the back with Mrs. Vanderlight.

During that lovely ride along the precipitous road to Hilarion Lucie and Nicos exchanged little conversation. Through her dark glasses Lucie gazed at the wonderful panorama stretching below them. Now, in the clear afternoon light, the sea looked exquisite. The warm soft air was full of the queer strong scent of the carobs. All her life, she thought, she would connect that pungent nutty scent with Cyprus.

Valerie was not interested in classic Greek ruins or lovely scenery. She was annoyed because there were no men here to admire her when, after tea, she lay sunbathing on a grassy slope beneath the Castle walls. Nicos didn't count. There had been a time when she had thought she might have some fun with the good-looking Greek, but her mother had put an end to *that*, the first time they came across him, by reminding her that he had neither money nor position. Adrian Ollivent had had both. And Valerie tutored by a mercenary mother, was first and foremost a gold-digger.

Those days with Adrian seemed like another life to Valerie now. She decided to talk about it to the girl whom she now knew to be an inmate of the Ollivent household. And the chance was given her when Carol took Nicos off in search of a particular rare plant which grew out of the crevices of the ruins. Lucie would have gone too, but Valerie lazily called her back. Lying there in the warm grass with arms stretched behind her head, she looked at Lucie through her heavy curtain of lashes.

'Stay and talk to me. . . .'

Reluctantly, Lucie remained. She knew almost before Valerie started that the conversation was going to be about Adrian. It disturbed her. But Valerie, out of vulgar curiosity, was bent on raking the ashes of the past.

'How is the great Adrian these days?' she began. 'Carol tells me you are Mrs. O.'s companion. I wish you joy of it. Personally, I think it must be very dull. Mrs. O. is too good to breathe.'

'I'm extremely happy at Villa Venetia and I adore Mrs. Ollivent. I think she's a most wonderful person.'

'I didn't relish having her as a mother-in-law. She would have expected me to make a good wife. I'm not built that way. I have trouble enough with Bob's mother. . . .' She gave a tinkle of laughter.

Lucie plucked a handful of grass and rolled it nervously in her fingers. What a really unpleasant character! And Adrian had

51

loved her! Adrian of all men!

Valerie persisted:

'How *is* Adrian?'

'I don't see much of him,' said Lucie coldly, 'he is nearly always away on business.'

'He's taken over the shipping entirely nowadays, hasn't he?'

'I believe so.'

'And what about his art. That used to be the great craze. I spent my time sitting for him. Have you seen any of my portraits? Or has he stowed them all away?'

Lucie felt she could willingly have slapped Valerie's face.

'I've seen only one painting of you, but...' she grew suddenly malicious and totally unlike herself ... 'Mr. Ollivent burned it shortly afterwards.'

Valerie shrugged.

'Oh, *did* he! He must still be in love ... hasn't got over it yet, I suppose. Well, it's nobody's fault but his own. In fact, the whole thing was a frightful shock to me.'

Now Lucie felt that this conversation was a desecration of the grave and solemn beauty of St. Hilarion on this tender spring day. She spoke sharply.

'I think you ought to know at once that I don't know anything about Mr. Ollivent's private affairs. What you're saying doesn't mean anything to me.'

Valerie's big sensual mouth curved into a sneering smile. She was quick to jump to the conclusion that this dull sedate companion-help took a great personal interest in Adrian's affairs.

'Oh, then if you don't *know*, I'd better tell you. . . .'

Lucie started to protest, but Valerie pretended not to hear.

'I was engaged to Adrian for about six months. I was living in Cairo at the time. My father was in the Army and we were still stationed there. Momma and I used to fly down here for our summer holidays. That's how we met the Ollivents. I was young and credulous and thought Adrian the cat's whiskers...' (one of those tinkling laughs which grated on Lucie followed this remark) 'and he seemed to go quite crackers about me, I must say. He promised me the earth. He was a queer creature ... frightfully artistic and all that. I realize now that I would never have been happy with him, but I let myself be carried away. And he certainly made love very nicely. . . .'

Here Lucie interrupted, her cheeks on fire.

52

'Honestly, I don't want to hear ...'

'Oh, you might as well know what happened,' broke in Valerie. 'I dare say it's been hinted to you that I let Adrian down. But it was quite the reverse. *He* let me down. While I was away in England getting my trousseau and believing that Adrian was making all the preparations for our wedding, he was behaving disgracefully. Having an affair with a *peasant* ... Nicos' sister Aphra. Nicos found them in Adrian's studio late one night locked in a passionate embrace!' (Another sneering laugh.) 'Not very pretty—my future husband carrying on with a kid like that who was supposed just to be sitting for her portrait. These things get round. Nicos was naturally upset on his sister's behalf and nearly killed Adrian. Kyrenia simply buzzed with the story. And I heard that the Islanders would have made it too hot for the Ollivents to go on living here except that they liked old Mrs. O., who had done a lot of good amongst the poor, so they took no action. But nobody decent amongst the Cypriots ever spoke to Adrian again.'

Lucie sat still. She could feel her hands shaking in her lap. The story might be true ... perhaps the whole unhappy mystery was unravelled at last. It all connected up. It made Lucie feel sick deep down within her.

On the face of it, Adrian had behaved vilely. Nicos was entitled to his anger and Valerie to her sneers. Yet it was Valerie whom Lucie despised in this moment. The girl went on talking ... as though gloating over the sordid details.

'Nicos' story finally reached the ears of friends of my mother's who live here ... General Gryder, now retired, and his wife. You may have come across them?'

Lucie nodded briefly. She had seen the General and his wife in Kyrenia but they were not on Blanche Ollivent's visiting list. Valerie continued:

'They thought it their duty to tell us about Adrian's behaviour, and of course I broke my engagement at once.'

Then Lucie, goaded by some innate sense of loyalty to her employer and by her queer mistrust and dislike of this girl, broke out:

'And your heart as well, I suppose?'

Valerie did not appear annoyed. She giggled.

'Not little Valerie! I wasn't going to let Adrian Ollivent shake *me*. And all his art and music and seriousness went right over my head, anyhow. I'd just met Bob in Cairo and was beginning to think *he* was more my cup of tea. Now really, Lucie, don't you think it would be grim being married to the great Adrian?'

Lucie went quite white. Her eyes behind the smoked glasses were dark with anger. For she could still see Adrian's tormented face when he had broken Valerie's portrait with his heel. Yet even if he was guilty of seducing Aphra, wouldn't a girl who really loved him have refused to listen to ugly gossip, and stood by him?

Lucie stood up.

'Haven't we talked enough about Adrian? I don't see any good in stirring up the mud. You're married to somebody else now. Anyhow, what happened between you and Adrian is of no interest to me.'

At that moment the other two members of the party joined them, Carol with a small plant bearing tiny star-like pink flowers in her hand. She proudly displayed it.

'I've found my treasure! Dex will be thrilled. He's crazy about *fauna* and *flora*!'

Nicos was quick to notice the look of distress on Lucie's face.

'Anything wrong?' he asked.

'Nothing, but I'd like to get home now, if you don't mind.'

In the car going back to Kyrenia, Nicos said:

'Something has upset you. Is it that girl?'

'*Ssh!* I'm all right, Nicos,' she said. 'They can hear what we say.'

'Once I felt sorry for her,' he muttered. 'I thought she was badly treated. But she has not a nice nature. I have since discovered it.'

Lucie did not ask him how he had discovered it. Indeed, she did not want to discuss Valerie. The whole thing was too disagreeable.

Nicos drove Lucie home.

'If my grandmother is better I wish very greatly to take you and Aphra to Larnaca next week. You know there is to be the Fair there—what we call the Feast of Cataclysmos. The people from all over Cyprus commemorate the birth of Aphrodite, the Goddess of Love. It will be wonderful—especially for me if you will come with me. There will be boating, and much dancing and singing on the shore. Ask Mrs. Ollivent for a holiday and come with us, Lucie, please!'

54

She dragged her thoughts from the shadows in which Adrian Ollivent persistently moved. She had been reading about the Feast which was held in honour of Aphrodite, who mythology said, rose from the foam in Paphos many thousands of years ago. Seeing her hesitate, Nicos repeated his request.

'Come with us, Lucie, do. We have friends with a beautiful Inn built right on the shore. You shall be our honoured guest there.'

'I will think about it and let you know. Thank you very, very much, Nicos.'

His face fell. He looked so childishly disappointed that she took off her glasses and gave him a smile.

'You're always so nice to me, Nicos,' she added. 'I do appreciate it.'

He seized her hand and kissed it. The touch of his fervent young lips was a little exciting. If at this very moment she let Nicos put his arms around her and make love to her in his charming fashion, could she respond, she wondered, half afraid? Would it develop into 'the real thing'?

She felt suddenly nervous, unsure of herself.

She drew her hand away from Nicos.

'I'll let you know about Larnaca,' she said. 'Good-bye, and I hope you will find your grandmother better.'

Then she turned and walked into the Villa.

NINE

NITA opened the door to Lucie. In her quick broken English she told 'Mees', as Lucie was called by the servants, how thankful she was that she had come back. Loucas had gone down to the village to look for her.

Lucie said quickly:

'Is anything wrong?'

Yes, it was Madame. Nita began to gabble rapidly, her pretty brown face worried. Madame had had some sort of heart attack when she was dressing after her *siesta*. They had telephoned for the doctor.

Lucie's heart seemed to miss a beat.

'Oh,' she breathed, 'and I was *out*! How dreadful!'

She ran up the staircase, her mind full of dread. The health of Adrian's mother was always an anxiety to her. It was not only the crippling arthritis, but Mrs. Ollivent's heart was affected these days. The English doctor said that leading her quiet and secluded life here, she might live many years. But she was not strong.

'The doctor asked that you should telephone him when you came in, please, Mees . . .' added Nita.

Lucie turned and ran downstairs again. In a panic, she put through the call. Dr. Arnold-Jones was an elderly man and not a particularly brilliant one, but he had a good reputation amongst the English in Kyrenia and old-fashioned methods which appealed to Mrs. Ollivent.

He was at home and answered Lucie. His first words were alarming. Mrs. Ollivent had definitely had a coronary and must not be allowed to leave her bed until he gave permission.

'But how bad is she? Ought I to send for her son?' asked Lucie, in distress.

The doctor explained that fortunately he had been on the spot and given her an injection and she had rallied. He had only left her an hour ago and she had been almost normal again. She had miraculous powers of recuperation. He did not think it vital that the son should be sent for. It would only alarm him and suggest to Mrs. Ollivent that she was worse than she really was.

He gave Lucie a few instructions . . . he had sent round tablets, and he would come in the morning. Meanwhile, his patient must be kept absolutely quiet.

Lucie washed and went into the old lady's room looking more composed.

'Dear Mrs. Ollivent. I hear you've had a bad afternoon. You shouldn't wait until I go out, to do these things. I'm *most* upset!'

She advanced to the bedside, smiling.

She gave Lucie a bright smile in return.

'I am afraid I startled everybody, my dear. But it was no-thing, just a little attack of faintness. And Dr. Jones put me right in a very short time.'

56

'If only I'd been here . . .' began Lucie.

'I'm glad you were out, and I hope you enjoyed your picnic. I assure you, I am all right.'

Lucie was far from being reassured. It seemed to her that Blanche Ollivent's breathing was too rapid. The hand she picked up felt dry and feverish. She wished that Adrian was here; yet, as Dr. Arnold-Jones had said, it might alarm both of them unnecessarily if he was sent for.

Mrs. Ollivent's blue eyes resting with tenderness on Lucie's anxious face seemed to read her thoughts. She said:

'Now, no sending worrying telegrams or 'phoning for my boy. I'm *quite* all right. This attack will pass. I shall just stay a few days in bed until I'm quite myself again.'

'Well, it's time Adrian came to Kyrenia. It may be this week-end, and that will do you good.'

'Indeed it will. Now tell me about your picnic,' murmured the old lady tranquilly. She showed no anxiety for herself.

Lucie did not mention Valerie's name. She had not the least idea what effect it would have upon Mrs. Ollivent to learn that the girl who was to have been her daughter-in-law had returned to Kyrenia. She did not even know how much Blanche Ollivent knew about either of those girls who had played such an important part in Adrian's life . . . Valerie or Aphra.

She stayed for an hour, reading aloud to the old lady. Later she went down to dinner which Loucas served in the candle-lit, dining-room. Lucie felt depressed and kept thinking about Valerie . . . wishing the Vanderlights had not come to Cyprus. And she was worried about the dear old lady upstairs. She wished that she dared telephone to Adrian and ask him to come. After all, he had expressed a very definite wish that she should communicate with him if his mother was ever taken ill. He might be furious if she did not do so.

She even toyed with the idea of wiring the Cairo office to-morrow. She was not sure whether Adrian was there or still in Khartoum, and she could not ask his mother without giving the show away.

She felt restless and curiously nervous. The Villa was very quiet tonight. Nita said that Mrs. Ollivent had fallen asleep soon after her supper. The night was warm and there was no sound from outside except the incessant chirping of the crickets.

Lucie tried to read a book, but she could not concentrate. Her mind kept reverting to the unattractive story that Valerie had

57

forced upon her up at St. Hilarion this afternoon. The story of Adrian's betrayal of Valerie; the affair with Aphra.

Disconsolately, Lucie wandered round the beautiful salon. Finally she picked up an album of photographs. She had seen it many times before and it always fascinated her.

Adrian ... nearly all Adrian ... snapshots and studio portraits pasted in the book, treasured by his mother. Adrian as a baby; and later as a small boy.

There were two blank pages in this album which bore marks of paste as though certain photographs had been torn out. Photographs, perhaps, of Adrian with his fiancée, Lucie reflected, and shut the book abruptly.

Suddenly she heard a car drive up to the gates, and a door slam. She ran quickly to the front door and opened it herself, anxious that there should be no noise to disturb the sleeper upstairs.

As the light from the hall fell upon the face of the arrival she gave a cry:

'Why, it's *you*!'

Surprised and delighted, she stared at Adrian.

He greeted her with more warmth and friendliness than usual.

'Hello, Lucie. Surprised to see me?'

'Very!'

He had no luggage, only a brief-case. He took her arm and walked with her into the Villa. With a sigh of contentment he said:

'It's good to be back. I must say it's not only nice to find my mother here, but you too, these days! You're quite a part of the family now, and a very nice part, too.'

She was speechless. She was so unaccustomed to any flattery from *him*.

'Well, how are things?'

'All ... right ...' she stammered.

She could not be so brutally frank, she thought, as to tell him at once that his mother had had a heart attack. Adrian drew another sigh.

'How peaceful it is in here. My flat in Cairo is becoming unbearable. The Cairo traffic is the noisiest in the world, and I've been working like the devil. We've only just settled the trouble up in Khartoum.'

'I see.' Lucie nodded.

He took a cigar from the long leather case now familiar to her.

'It isn't very late, only a quarter past nine. . . . I want a shower and then some supper. Ask Loucas to lay on something cold.'

Lucie nodded, still startled by his unexpected arrival. He seemed suddenly to notice her agitation. He noticed, too, that she was looking extraordinarily attractive. Beautifully brown. Adrian's gaze travelled up and down the girlish figure.

You look very attractive tonight. I *need* soothing. I'm worn out. All the way from Limassol I've been thinking to myself—I'll have a few minutes with my mother . . . then some food and a cigar and a glass of wine and then Lucie will play me some of her Chopin. Will you do that later?'

Her gaze fluttered away from his. She would have to tell him in a moment about his mother, she thought. It seemed such a shame . . . and he had come here to rest; he needed what he called '*soothing*' . . . and he was in such a much more agreeable mood than she had ever known.

Adrian continued:

'In fact, I've thought a lot about things while I've been away this time, Lucie, and reached the conclusion that I've been far too introspective. I'm going to be different. I intend to stay home longer this time—perhaps a couple of weeks. I shall take a real holiday. I shall make new friends in Kyrenia. Now, I wasn't very pleasant to your nice American girl and her husband when I was home last time, was I? Are they still here, by the way?'

Lucie, thunderstruck at what he was saying, nodded.

He added:

'Well, we'll go down to the Dome together and make up a foursome with them. It's a few years since I've been to Larnaca for the Feast of Aphrodite. We might go to that together. Anyway, I've got to go to the Dome to see a chap on business tomorrow. He came over on the boat with me today.'

Lucie went hot and cold. In any other circumstances, Adrian's sudden change of front, his desire to put an end to his habits as a recluse would have delighted her. But the very mention of the Dome Hotel and the thought of Valerie shook her badly.

He would be bound to see her. It would be an awful shock to him. In fact, she had two shocks in store for him now and she did not know which one to give him first.

TEN

It seemed to Lucie that the best thing she could do for the moment was to rush away from Adrian, find Loucas and order the supper. So to gain time she gave him a nervous glance, said: 'Your mother's asleep ... better not wake her ... I'll be back in a moment ...' then fled.

She fussed over his supper, giving orders, her mind whirling with thoughts. She did not know what to say to Adrian or how to say it. The Greek servants looked at her in surprise as she bustled around the big spotless kitchen. It was not like 'Mees' to be so interfering.

At last Lucie was forced to return to the salon. By this time she had made up her mind not to beat about the bush, and that the truth was better out.

She found Adrian standing in front of the open french window. He was gazing down the hill at the magic beauty of moonlight on Kyrenia Harbour. He turned and saw her.

'Come and look at this. One never gets tired of it ... what a view!'

She stood beside him, her dejected gaze following his to the silhouette of the Castle, dark and mysterious against the luminous sky.

Adrian said:

'I would like to have lived in the beginning of the sixteenth century. The Venetians came and made that old Castle what it is today. There is so much beauty and pageantry wrapped up in the past. Sad thought that today, when we could make so much progress, the world spends its time discussing atom bombs that could wipe out that glorious old Castle and the whole of Kyrenia with it!'

Lucie nodded.

Adrian added:

'You're very subdued tonight. Has my arrival cast a gloom over you?'

She said:

'I hate to have to tell you, but I have bad news for you.'

Immediately his expression altered.

'Why? What's wrong?'

'Your mother is ill.'

That wiped every vestige of good humour from Adrian Ollivent's face.

'How ill? Since when? What happened to her?'

She told him about the heart attack, repeating faithfully every word of Dr. Arnold-Jones' diagnosis.

'You say she has rallied,' Adrian snapped now.

'Yes, but it is essential for her to be kept quiet, and not get up until she has quite recovered.'

'Naturally,' said Adrian.

He questioned her further and she told him everything that she could. Then added:

'Please try not to be too anxious. The doctor is very hopeful that she will make a complete recovery.'

He gave a short sigh. 'Thank God for that!'

'Coronaries are not necessarily fatal.'

'I couldn't bear anything to happen to her,' he muttered, and turned his back on Lucie and flung himself into a chair.

She thought:

'How deeply he loves her. And how wonderful ... to be loved by a man like Adrian.'

Again her thoughts sped to that girl down in the Dome Hotel. He must have loved Valerie *that* way, once.

Now that she had got over the first stile, and told him about his mother, she was reluctant to plunge him into further gloom. She would not tell him tonight that Valerie was in Kyrenia. Tomorrow would be time enough.

'Please have your supper and stop worrying,' she said.

He drew a sigh and moved to a chair in front of the table on which Loucas had set a tray.

'Very well. As long as you are not holding anything back from me. I'm rather angry, you know, that you didn't telephone the Cairo office at the time.'

'I wanted to, but Dr. Arnold-Jones said no. There is nothing more to tell. I assure you I have kept nothing back.'

His brow cleared and now he looked at her with compunction.

'Sorry, Lucie. You know I arrived here with every intention of not behaving so boorishly. I am sure you have done everything within your power for my mother and I am deeply grateful. But naturally your news has shaken me.'

She walked towards the door. Adrian called her back.

'You're not off, are you?'

She glanced over her shoulder, her cheeks hot and pink.

'I . . . I thought I'd go to bed. . . .'

'Won't you stay and talk to me, Lucie?'

She wanted to stay, but she had a sudden childish wish to oppose him; besides which she dreaded being involved in any conversation which might include an account of today's picnic, when she would be forced to mention Valerie's name. She stammered:

'Please excuse me . . . I'm awfully tired. Have you everything that you want?'

'Everything,' he nodded, and now he gave her a friendly smile. 'You run this place most efficiently.'

'Thank you.'

'As I'm not hurrying away this time, I'll see how my mother is, then if all seems well I'll fix that trip to Larnaca.' He added: 'You'd like to have the experience, wouldn't you? The Cataclysmos Fair is worth seeing, if only once, and I know you love this countryside.'

'Thank you very much. Good night . . .' she said, and vanished before he could say anything more.

Adrian Ollivent finished his supper in silence.

He would not disturb his mother until the morning. She would be happy when she heard that he meant to spend some time in Kyrenia with her, he thought. And following that came the thought of Lucie Gresham. Why had she run away just now? Was it really because she was tired? Or did she dislike him? Had his loss of self-control in the studio that day completely disgusted her? He would not be surprised. He had behaved like a temperamental fool. He rather wanted Lucie to like him. He had really grown to rely on her these days. There was something very unusual about her. He liked her. And as he had told her when he first arrived, she was beginning to look quite attractive these days.

What a long time ago, Adrian reflected, since he had bothered to notice any woman's attraction. His mind winged back involuntarily to the memory of Valerie Bright! Valerie who, so far as he knew, was now married to an American—and thousands of miles away in the United States. He could never wholly banish that cruel haunting ghost. Wonderful to make love to . . . to adore . . . to paint. A beautiful body without heart, a being without loyalty.

He could feel the old bitter indignation against her welling up inside him. He knew that he could smash a dozen portraits of her with his heel yet could never entirely wipe out the memory of her. It was a deadly thing to realize how a man could hate yet want a woman at the same time.

But why remember Valerie tonight of all nights, he asked himself, when he had come back to Cyprus meaning to begin life again? He reverted to the thought of Lucie and decided to make plans to take her to the great Fair. He had come home just in time for it.

He went to bed and slept soundly. It was time the dead past buried its dead. He had brooded over it far too long already.

He had a habit of waking early. At six o'clock that next morning, before anybody else stirred, he was up and out of the Villa. It was a perfect June morning. Kyrenia was still sleeping except for the fishermen already setting out from harbour in their *caiques* in search of sponges—one of the main industries here. The sea looked exquisite, radiant in the amber light. Adrian had a sudden desire to go to the Country Club and bathe there in the big pool.

The Country Club was a pleasant place on the hill beside the Castle. One walked down the steps to the moat, then to the level of the sea and into the pale green water of the pool. The waves broke gently against the rocks beyond. The surroundings were perfect and in the old days Adrian used to enjoy swimming here. 'Tomorrow,' he thought suddenly, 'I'll bring little Lucie down with me.'

As he had hoped, he found nobody else here yet. It was too early.

He took off his towelling coat, and dived suddenly into the translucent water. He came up again shaking the drops from his eyes, threading his fingers through his thick black hair. The water was fresh, cold and exhilarating. He felt suddenly glad to be alive.

A tall girl with a white towel over her shoulders and wearing a scarlet two-piece swim-suit, and a scarlet bandanna tied over her hair, strolled out of the Club and down the steps towards the pool. She had a cigarette in a long holder between her lips. Adrian Ollivent blinked as he looked at her, hands shading his eyes from the sunlight. For a moment he trod water and stared dazedly at the lovely face and figure. His heart seemed to stop beating. The blood rushed to his eyes. He gave a gasp:

'*Valerie!*'

Valerie Vanderlight stopped dead and stared down into the pool. Slowly she took the cigarette-holder from her lips. She, too, looked dumbfounded. Then her full red mouth curved into a wide amused smile.

'Good heavens above ... it's the great Adrian!' she exclaimed.

The man felt his frantic heartbeats shake his whole body. The radiant blue sky, the Club building, the Castle, went out of focus for a moment. He swallowed some water, choked, coughed, then shook his head; swam rapidly to the edge of the pool and pulled himself up. He sat there, rubbing his hair with his towel and looking in a stunned way at the girl who had once been engaged to be married to him.

Valerie seated herself beside the man, kicked off her sandals and dipped her lovely slender feet with their red toenails into the greenish, clear water. She looked at him questioningly.

'Well, *well*, so you *are* in Kyrenia!'

With a shaking hand, Adrian went on wiping his face and arms, but he looked at her as though he could not believe his own eyesight.

She laughed.

'Lost your voice, honey?' she mimicked an American accent.

'What are you doing here?' at last he asked, hoarsely.

'I came for a bathe.... I was dragged out of my bed by my husband and our friends, Carol and Dex, whom I think you've met. They seem to think it a good idea to have an early morning dip.'

With the blood singing in his ears, Adrian stared at the wonderful face which he had so often painted and had hoped never to see again.

'What are you doing in Kyrenia?' he rapped out.

She put the cigarette-holder back between her teeth, smiling lazily at him.

'My husband is Dex's boss. We were sent over from the States here to Cyprus on a job. There's a lot of business doing between America and Cyprus nowadays. A coincidence, isn't it, Adrian, little Valerie coming back *here*?'

He did not answer. It seemed that his fascinated gaze could not leave her. She looked back at him boldly, interested. He had changed much with the passing of time, she thought. There were actually a few grey streaks threaded in that black hair of his. The silver wings suited him. But he had a harsher, sterner look than she remembered. Well, she thought, that suited him too. Made him more interesting. And he looked as though the sudden meeting with her had completely dazed him, which fed her insatiable vanity. She loved to be disturbing to men.

Valerie had at one time been very much in love with Adrian Ollivent. But he had gradually bored her with his honest adoration. He looked less easy to manage these days, she had to admit. Intriguing! And what a stroke of luck that she was alone. Bob, Dex and Carol had changed after their swim and gone for twenty minutes' brisk walk up the hillside. They were far too energetic for her. She had grumbled when they got her out of bed for this early expedition and had refused to go walking. She preferred to lie here and sunbathe until they came back. Bob had only returned from Limassol last night ... possibly on the very same boat that had brought Adrian. How amusing ... her husband and ex-fiancé travelling together, without knowing it.

'Well, Adrian,' she said after a pause, 'do we meet as friends or enemies?'

He seemed to find it hard to answer. The muscles of his face were working. Then at last he said in a low, concentrated voice:

'I don't think there can be friendship between us, Valerie. Quite frankly, if I had known you were here at the moment I would never have set foot in Cyprus.'

She gave a little laugh.

'Goodness! Is it as bad as all that? But why? I'm married to Bob Vanderlight and my home is in America, and you, I hear, are a big shipping magnate these days ... and very successful. Must we remember that we were once engaged?'

The blood ran up under Adrian's brown skin. His eyes narrowed. With a quick nervous gesture he smoothed the wet, dark hair back from his forehead.

'I don't particularly wish to remember it, but facts remain. You did me a great deal of harm, Valerie, and I don't find it easy to forget.'

She stared at him, took the cigarette from her lips and then exclaimed:

'I did *you* harm! Well, I like that! It was you who did *me* harm. It was *you* who broke up our lives.... Why, good heavens, have you forgotten that Greek girl and the scandal on the Island, and all the rest of it? *You* were the one who behaved badly.'

He clenched his teeth.

'I did nothing that I am ashamed of. The whole thing was a damnable fabrication. I told you so at the time. I wrote you a full explanation and you refused to believe it. I doubt now if you or your mother ever read my letters.'

Her long lashes fluttered. She looked away from him down into the pool which reflected her own lovely face. Then she shrugged her shoulders.

'I had only your word against Aphra's and her brother's. Besides, you can't expect me to believe that you would invite that pretty girl up to your studio in the middle of the night just in order to listen to Christmas carols with her.'

For an instant Adrian felt his vision cloud over again in a mist of shock and rage. The old pain seared his heart at the very sight and sound of this girl. What she had just said was unforgivable ... and typical of her. He said:

'You have no right to say such things. They are utterly untrue. I loved you and I thought that you loved me; that you of all people would believe *me*, no matter what anybody else thought. Nicos had no proof ... I tell you it was Aphra's word against mine. ...'

'Oh, please, don't let's go into it all again,' she broke in with a beseeching look; 'it can't do any good now.'

'I deserve a hearing,' he said in a passionate voice; 'you didn't give it to me at the time. You wronged me bitterly ... Nicos and the whole of Kyrenia wronged me. And what could I say or do without denouncing that little fool of a girl for what she was ... an hysterical child who lied to save her own reputation? And in doing so she ruined mine. It was abominable. But if you had listened to me I could have told you the truth. You *should* have listened. We were going to be married. You *should* have believed that I would not stoop to common seduction of a village girl just before our marriage.'

Valerie felt some slight excitement. Really, she thought in her shallow fashion, this was terrific ... after all this time, that the great Adrian should still feel so intensely about her (as obviously he did). She was delighted. And she took all the feeling to herself, and put second the man's burning sense of injustice, his wish to vindicate himself. She thought:

'I hope the others don't come back too soon ... Thank goodness I came to swim. This was worth getting up for. He really is very attractive ... I like him better now he's older. He could

66

play lovely 'embittered-hero-parts' in films.'

Suddenly she turned towards Adrian and, giving her foot a little shake, splashing the water, said in a soothing voice:

'Now don't look so violent, Adrian. You take life much too seriously. You always did.'

He looked at her with angry eyes.

'And do you never take it seriously? Did you find it easy to throw me over without even hearing my side of it?'

She shrugged her shoulders.

'Everybody in Kyrenia believed the worst. Why shouldn't I?'

'Because you were my future wife.'

She pursed her lips and looked through her lashes provocatively.

'Why be so angry with poor Valerie? If the Greek girl let you down, you should be angry with *her,* not me.'

'Angry with Aphra? Good God, I was so mad at the time I wanted to murder her! But she knew no better. She was a semi-educated peasant type with primitive instincts. I don't suppose she realized what harm she did. But you, Valerie, with a little trust and faith, could have helped to put things right.'

'Well, I still don't know the real truth, do I?'

'Then I'll tell you . . .' he began fiercely.

'Adrian, really,' she broke in, 'it's all such old history. I'm married now. Why must we drag up that sordid affair?'

He stared at her unbelievingly.

'Are you absolutely without understanding? I loved you. I never let you down. I swear it.'

No answer from Valerie. Then Adrian said in a low voice:

'You are damned well going to hear the story whether you like it or not. You owe it to me, even if we never see each other again after this morning.'

She bit her lip with a half-smile and threw him a really wicked glance from under those long lashes. She was quite sure that Adrian Ollivent could be brought back to her feet again without much difficulty. She enjoyed this new violence in him. All that was feminine and pagan in her rose to it. Bob admired her, showered her with presents, spoiled her like so many American husbands spoil their wives. But the novelty of being married to a rich man had worn off a little, and was not the only spice in life to a girl of Valerie's temperament. It would be quite interesting to see whether she could get Adrian back. It would be a piquant amusement during her short stay in what

67

she thought this boring Island.

So she let him talk, her limpid gaze fixed on him.

The story poured out in a torrent as though let loose from the man's very soul after long months of bitterness. Valerie listened, half prepared to believe that he told the truth and that she *had* wronged him. He spoke with such passionate sincerity. But she was not really interested in whether he had, in the past, been disloyal to her or not. She was much more interested in the future ... speculating as to what it would be like to feel Adrian's arms around her again, to see that proud harsh face soften into the old tender passion which she had roused in Adrian the artist, Adrian the man who had loved her. ...

ELEVEN

Adrian, at the time of his engagement to Valerie Bright, had eyes and time for no other woman. He was utterly in love with her. The Greek girl, Aphra, had come into his life as a model. He looked upon her as any painter would—dispassionately—as a particularly beautiful example of young Greek womanhood which he wished to paint.

Unfortunately for Adrian, Aphra fell in love with him; eventually became a nuisance, although at that time he had not regarded her adoration as a real menace. He treated her as a silly child and thought no more about her once the 'sittings' were over.

Just before that fatal Christmas Eve they had a slight 'scene'. Aphra became amorous and difficult, and he told her that if she could not be more sensible he must stop painting her. It was then that she became quite wild and, leaving the family at midnight Mass, had come to his studio, where at that time he used to keep his big radio gramophone and enjoy orchestral concerts (he had hundreds of fine records) which he could play out there, no matter how late, without disturbing his mother.

Aphra flung herself into his arms. He protested, argued, grew angry and then tried to reason with her. She implored him to love her. She threatened suicide. She worked herself up into such a state that she fainted. When her brother Nicos came in search of her he found her like that, lying on the *chaise-longue,* with Adrian kneeling beside her, chafing her hands, imploring her to be sensible and to let him take her home. Nicos sprang at him. The two men almost came to blows.

Nicos questioned his sister and the girl sullenly refused to give the true facts. Then, to save herself, she lied. She maintained that the Englishman had seduced her and made love to her many times and inveigled her up there to his studio that Christmas Eve. Nicos believed her, refused to credit any of Adrian's explanations. He repeated Aphra's libellous story to everybody in Cyprus. So started the infamous scandal in Kyrenia which had ended in Valerie's desertion of Adrian. Every effort he made to induce Aphra to tell the truth failed. Nicos refused to allow her to see him.

'So I went away—my character blackened,' Adrian finished. 'I came back here only to please my mother, who—dear old soul—knew nothing about the incident with Aphra. The local people were at least kind enough to spare *her* the story. But you ... *you* could have stood by me and that would have made all the difference, Valerie. Aphra ruined me with her lies. But you confirmed them—by your very act in walking out on me.'

Valerie had listened half-heartedly. Now she looked at him with soft velvety eyes.

'Dear Adrian,' she murmured. 'What a dreadful affair! If it is true, I do indeed beg your pardon and I'm sorry that I did not trust you. But it's all so long ago and much too late—isn't it?'

He gave her a feverish look.

'Do you believe me now? Do you? Late or not. *Do you,* Valerie?'

She found nothing moving in his profound wish to vindicate his honour. But she put out a hand and lightly touched his, which was shaking.

'Adrian dear, don't get so worked up! What does it matter now whether you were a good boy or a bad one? It's all so out of date.'

He stared at her as though stricken. He seemed to realize more than ever before how utterly shallow and frivolous she was; that her perfect beauty was the mask for a petty, worthless nature. He could see that his story had made little impression, and his burning desire to be believed, still less. He sprang up, white as death under his tan.

'You shall believe me,' he cried, 'even if I have to find that girl and force it out of her—you shall hear the truth from *her*!'

Valerie also rose. She was beginning to be bored by Adrian.

'Oh, don't fly off the handle this way, my dear. Do pipe down and leave things as they are.'

His brilliant eyes burned down into hers.

'I absolutely refuse. You shall be made to believe the truth.'

Now she took a step nearer him and with a coquettish gesture whipped off the scarlet bandanna and shook back the flowing masses of her hair. She smiled lazily, invitingly, up at him.

'Why, Adrian Ollivent,' she said with her slight newly-acquired American accent, 'I guess you still want *me* to think you are marvellous. Like I used to. Is that it? Is that why you are so upset? Do you still care for me, Adrian?'

He knew, then, that he hated her. All that he had suffered through her disloyalty, her callous indifference to his heart's anguish, coupled with her incredibly egotistical reception of his explanation now, flung him into a blind rage. He seized her bare arms and shook her.

'Shut up. *Shut up!*' he almost shouted the words.

Valerie closed her eyes luxuriously. For an instant she contemplated throwing herself into his arms. She was seized with the mad egotistical desire to conquer him again and break through his furious rage. But at that moment she heard a familiar ringing laugh and voices. Her husband's nice boyish laugh and the voices of Carol and Dex; the trio returning from their walk up the hillside. She grew cool and wary. She drew back from Adrian, releasing both her arms, although her large eyes continued to shine with that cruel, selfish invitation to him. She murmured:

'Careful, Adrian. The others are here. Pipe down, my sweet. I'll see you some other time.'

Adrian's hands dropped to his sides. With a quick, blind gesture, he seized his bathrobe, put it on and tied the girdle, his hands shaking, his temples hot as though on fire. He was conscious of nothing but rage and his new hatred and contempt for Valerie.

He had no time to make an exit. The others were here, strolling out to the bathing pool, laughing and chatting. Carol in slacks and jersey. The two men in shorts and sweaters. Adrian's hot gaze raked them and recognized Lucie's friends, the Dexters. The other man, whom he remembered seeing on the boat, must be Valerie's husband—older—a typical American, with a chubby, youthful face, and thick upspringing hair streaked with grey. He wore rimless glasses.

As the three approached, Valerie's quick feminine brain decided on the course she would take. Quickly she sprang forward and seized her husband's arm.

'Hi, Bob! You're back! Did you enjoy your walk? I've had a swell time sunbathing. Came across an old friend, too. Meet Adrian Ollivent. Adrian, this is Bob Vanderlight, my husband.'

Carol and Dex exchanged glances. Carol thought:

'For mercy's sake . . . here's a situation!'

The smile was wiped off Bob Vanderlight's chubby good-natured face. He took a cigarette from his mouth and looked through narrowed eyes at the tall, dark-haired Englishman. Adrian stood frozen, steadily returning that look.

Then Vanderlight said, with a strong Yankee drawl:

'Say! Doesn't the name Adrian Ollivent ring a bell? Where've I heard it before, Val?'

She crinkled her long limpid eyes in a mischievous smile, sending a silent wicked signal to Adrian.

'Oh, he's the guy I used to be engaged to. He lives in Kyrenia. And he once painted wonderful portraits of me.'

Vanderlight put his tongue in his cheek.

'Oh yez?' he drawled.

Adrian clenched his hands at his sides. He could imagine exactly what was running through the American's mind. A dawning suspicion, coupled with the contempt he would naturally feel for the 'chap who had once let Valerie down'.

Adrian knew, as he stood there, writhing under the older man's half-curious, wholly-withering glance, that he would not rest now until he had cleared his name and made both Valerie and her husband apologize to him. He gave a short nod.

'Hello,' he said. 'Please excuse me. I have a date. . . .'

'Sure!' drawled Valerie's husband.

Valerie said:

'Don't run away, Adrian. . . .'

'I have no intention of running away,' he said quickly and

meaningly. 'But I want to have a chat with the Alistons. Afterwards ... I would like to see you again. Good-bye.'

She shrugged her shoulders. He bowed to the Dexters and walked quickly away.

As he disappeared from view, Vanderlight turned to his wife and slipped an arm around the tall, graceful body.

'Say, honey ... so *that* is the fellow who had the bad taste to seduce one of the local beauties just before you were going to get married?'

'That's the one,' she said thoughtfully. But she felt a sudden twinge of uneasiness foreign to her. What an awful look Adrian had had in his eyes when he shook her just now! Was it possible that his long explanation was the real one; he really *had* been misjudged and was innocent of wrong? Oh, well, what if it *was* so ... she was bored by the old drama. She would much rather have had an amusing interlude with him whilst Bob conducted his business tour of Cyprus. She wouldn't have minded being painted again by him either ... as Mrs. Bob Vanderlight. He used to be really good at portraits. She would like to find that head he had once done of her and give it to Bob. She must stop all this nonsense, anyhow; she would go up to Villa Venetia and see Adrian alone one day and tell him not to be so stupid. She would advise him to develop a sense of humour about the affair, even if he didn't find it as funny as she did.

Bob was saying something about Adrian being a 'heel' to have let her down, but that he was only too pleased since it had left her free for *him*. She answered lazily. But she was still engrossed with the thought of Adrian. The man had a peculiar fascination for her. He always had had it. He was a successful man in the shipping world these days, too. She might have had quite a lot of fun as his wife. It wasn't always a hundred per cent amusing with Bob, rich though he was ... because of that mother of his. She grimaced at the thought of Mrs. Vanderlight Senior. ('Mother's Day' in America!) ... Old Blanche Ollivent had been easy compared with *her*. But Bob's mother! *Gee!* And he himself was dull at times. But Adrian ... well, he had a latent force in him, both mental and physical. Now that she was older and more experienced, she was even more fully aware of these things.

Up in Villa Venetia, Adrian Ollivent and Lucie came face to face for the first time that day, on the sunlit verandah where old Loucas had laid a breakfast table for two.

Adrian appeared to be quite composed. He had put on grey flannels and a white silk open-necked shirt. But Lucie saw at once that the lines of his face were granite hard. There was nothing left of the smiling, would-be friendly Adrian of last night.

She looked at him with some perplexity. She began to pour out coffee.

'You have seen Mrs. Ollivent?'

'Yes. Thank God she seems almost herself.'

'Yes. She was so surprised and delighted to know you had arrived last night.'

Adrian nodded and sipped his coffee. His brooding eyes looked beyond Lucie's fair head at a mass of brilliant cerise-coloured bougainvillaea twining around one of the pillars. It was vivid and exotic against the blue Kyrenian sky. He said:

'I'm going for a walk after breakfast. By the way, Lucie, are your friends Nicos and Aphra Aliston at the Inn just now . . . or in Athens?'

Lucie's heart missed a beat. She gave him a quick scared look.

'N-Nicos and A-Aphra . . . oh, they are here,' she stammered.

'Thanks,' he said, and continued to eat his omelette in silence. Lucie, much disturbed, sat watching him, wondering what this was all about . . . and why he had mentioned those names which hitherto had been taboo in this house.

The telephong rang. Lucie rose and answered the call.

It was from Carol. She said:

'Lucie honey . . . I'm afraid there's been a spot of bother. Is the great Adrian there?'

'Yes, he is here, just finishing breakfast.'

'So are we. But I just had to 'phone you. You know he came down to the Club for a swim and ran into Valerie early this morning?'

Lucie's hand flew to her throat. A small pulse throbbed there. She knew instantly that there was trouble ahead and that it was that meeting which accounted for Adrian's strange mood now. A few more hurried questions in a low voice . . . and she knew a little more.

Valerie had been gossiping with Carol in her frivolous way—taking nothing seriously—not even her meeting with the man she was supposed to have once loved. She had told Carol that Adrian had attempted to clear his name with what Valerie

73

called a 'garbled version' of the old story, and had threatened to go and wring the truth out of Aphra Aliston.

'I honestly don't know the details, but I scent trouble, honey,' Carol finished. 'It might be a good thing for you to try and stop the great Adrian from raking up the old mud. He's got this thing on his mind, apparently, poor brute.'

Lucie put down the telephone. The healthy colour had left her face. So *that* was it. Adrian had met Valerie ... already the bombshell had exploded without warning at his feet. What must he think of her for not telling him last night that Valerie was at the Dome? She had not dreamed he would go out so early and run into her. How peculiar he had been during breakfast. Perhaps that was why ... because he was cross with her, and because of Valerie. He had just said he was going out for a walk. He had wanted to know if the Alistons were at home. *Did he mean to go up to the Inn and see Nicos and Aphra?* But why, why? What good could it do? Lucie did not know the details of the case. She felt utterly confused. She could only put two and two together, and presume that the sudden meeting with his former love had awakened the old demons in Adrian ... that he still loved her ... that he wanted to clear his name ... justify himself, to *her*.

Then she remembered Nicos ... all that he had said about Adrian ... his hatred of him. Heavens, it would never do for those two to start a quarrel! Nicos was half Greek and hot-blooded. Adrian also was at times hot-tempered and uncontrolled.

Lucie, her heart pounding, turned and almost ran out on to the verandah. She must talk to Adrian ... openly ... she *must* get this thing clear and try to stop him going up to the Inn this morning.

But his chair was empty. His table napkin had been screwed up and flung on the ground. Adrian was nowhere to be seen. He had already gone.

TWELVE

APHRA, the Greek girl, was in the wash-house behind the Inn, washing linen, in company with a young girl of her own age. Bare-legged, with skirts tucked round their waists, they stood in a huge shallow pan of hot soapy water, treading blankets. They looked as though they were dancing quaint little steps, and they were both singing, stopping now and then to talk to each other and giggle.

Nicos had forbidden his half-sister to do this kind of work. He wanted her to be a lady and to undertake only the most refined tasks in the Inn. Because of his English breeding and education he deplored the fact that she was growing up like 'a little savage' as he termed it; like any uneducated menial of the country. But one could not get away from the fact that Aphra came of peasant stock and was really happier doing this kind of work than any other; like the old grandmother who was now bedridden and unable to supervise. The old Cypriot lady was cunning. She agreed with everything that Nicos said when he was present, but once he was out of the place she gave Aphra other instructions. The servants were not to be trusted, and as she could not work with them, Aphra must.

Nicos was in Limassol on business today, so the grandmother had sent Aphra to the wash-house. The girl was delighted. The laundry maid, Zita, was her friend. Zita was telling her about her new admirer, a young Greek sailor. They were going to be married when his ship next came to the Island. Zita, a pretty, plump little thing of eighteen, giggled and sang and whispered to Aphra, telling her how daring her sailor had been, and how they had kissed and clung in the orchard by Zita's home, while her father, who was a farmer, was busy on the farm. He was going to buy her a washing machine too.

Aphra listened avidly but pouted a little. Zita seemed to have so much more fun than she did.

She and Zita took one of the blankets, carried it out into the courtyard and stood in the warm sunshine wringing the blanket into a tight roll, squeezing out the water. Above them the sky was a brilliant blue. Through an archway they could see an old grey donkey, nibbling at some branches. A faint smell of the carobs mingled with the scent of peaches ripening in the sun.

It was beautiful and peaceful but there was unrest in the soul of Aphra. She longed to be loved like Zita, and always with her visions of love came the memory of Adrian Ollivent; even after his long absence.

Suddenly Zita said:

'*Sst!* Look, Aphra!'

She looked and her heartbeats shook her breast. For there stood the man about whom she had been thinking. He looked stern and changed from the gay friendly artist with whom she had fallen so madly in love.

She gave a little cry, unpinned the long striped petticoat, letting it fall to her ankles again, smoothed her blouse and shook back her dark tangle of curls. She was horrified that he should see her like this. Yet the man standing there in the sunlit courtyard for one dispassionate moment appreciated the primitive beauty of the little scene he had just witnessed. It might have been a painting ... those two young girls with their bare brown legs and arms, in their bright-coloured skirts and embroidered blouses ... engaged in the oldest of tasks ... hanging their washing out to dry.

But as Aphra slowly and timidly approached him all artistic appreciation faded. He remembered her only as the neurotic little fool who had helped to ruin his life.

'Is your brother at home?' he asked gruffly.

'No. Nicos in Limassol.'

He said:

'I wish to talk to you, Aphra. To Nicos also, but as he is not here it must be you alone.'

Aphra threw a frightened glance at the back of the Inn. Up there behind one of those windows framed in frilly muslin, and with pots of scarlet flowers on the ledge, lay her grandmother. Grandfather was there too, but he could walk about and might look out of the window and see Mr. Ollivent. Memories of her brother's furious rage on Christmas Eve somewhat overshadowed Aphra's surprise and delight at seeing Adrian again. She glanced over her shoulder. Zita, the basket of clothes-pegs over her arm, stood watching curiously. In her own language Aphra whispered:

'I shall take him into the olive grove. Keep watch for me and call me if my grandparents ask where I am.'

Zita giggled and wished her luck. Aphra's spirits began to rise. She was so stupid that she could scent no immediate danger. She gave Adrian an arch look through her curly lashes. The fact that he was a rich English gentleman had always excited her and it still did. She murmured:

'We go little walk. I take you. . . .'

He went with her unwillingly. But he realized that they would be better out of sight. He followed her through a gateway up the mountainside to an olive grove. It was hot and fragrant there. Aphra was all smiles now, walking close to him. What a long time since she had seen him. Why had he been so angry? What had she done? A spate of words. He let her go on until they were out of sight and earshot of the Inn. Then he arrested the foolish chatter.

'Be quiet, Aphra,' he said. 'I want you to listen carefully to *me* and try to understand every word I say. It is of greatest importance to me. You understand the word *"important"*?'

She looked at him sideways, lips pouting.

'Yes.'

'Then you must understand what a lot of harm you have done,' he said patiently. Indeed, he felt none of the almost murderous rage towards this silly child that he had known in Valerie's presence earlier this morning. It was so much easier to be gentle with somebody who was so young and misguided as Aphra. He reasoned and argued with her gently.

He told her that he had lost his future wife, his good name in Cyprus, his friends and his peace of mind, because of her lies. He said that he knew she was at heart a good girl and religious and that the Mother of God to whom she prayed so often would not like her to do such a wrong to any man. He said that she ought not to let another day go by without making amends . . . confess what she had done . . . tell Nicos how wickedly she had distorted the truth about her visit to his studio that Christmas Eve.

Again and again he put the facts before her. But the longer Aphra listened, the more silent she became and the more mutinously her lips curved downwards. She kept looking away, then darting sulky, angry glances at him. She was bitterly disappointed. She had hoped he had come up here to tell her how beautiful she was and say that he wished to paint her again. He was crazy if he thought she was going to let Nicos know that she had lied. He would only send her to Aunt Caliope in Athens.

She was wholly concerned for herself. Adrian, his earnest

gaze fixed on that beautiful olive-tinted face, exquisite as a Murillo painting of the Virgin, felt his heart sink to its uttermost depths. He could almost read her mind. He did not see one spark of real understanding or contrition. Suddenly he broke out:

'Can't you see what a wicked thing you've done, Aphra? I never did make love to you. You know it. I never touched you except to push your curls away from your face when I was trying to draw the curve of your cheek one day. You *can't* let this go on ... you *can't* make me suffer for the rest of my days in the eyes of other people!'

To his dismay, Aphra burst into tears and poured out a flood of Greek which he did not understand. But she soon made her meaning clear, for she caught his hand and drew it up to her lips, covering it with kisses.

'Little fool! Do you suppose I want to touch you *now*? Oh, you don't *begin* to understand!'

She cried more loudly, hiding her face in her hands. She was frightened, and resentful because of his rejection of her. She had no interest in his appeal to her to clear his name. Her half-brother had never really blamed *her* for what had happened on Christmas Eve. He had blamed Adrian, and she was not going to alter that now.

'So this has all been for nothing. I am exactly where I was ... *Oh God!*'

It was a cry of despair wrung from Adrian's heart. And Lucie Gresham heard it. Heard, and was hurt by it to the depths of her own sensitive soul. She came walking quickly through the olive groves where Zita, the laundry girl, had sent her. She had been afraid she might find Nicos here and the two men would come to blows.

Aphra stopped weeping and looked at the English lady whom her brother liked so much.

'What the devil brings *you* here?' Adrian asked Lucie, amazed.

'You forgot to pay my salary last month, and I ... I need some money ... I ... want to do some shopping...' she broke off lamely. She was not a good liar and her face was scarlet.

But she was thinking:

'*Nicos isn't here! Thank the Lord!*'

A moment's silence. Adrian stared at Lucie. Slowly he took a packet of cigarettes from his pocket.

'Oh,' he said slowly, 'you came up here to get some money! How very odd! And how did you know I was here?'

Lucie laughed nervously. One could never get away with a lie with *this* man, she thought. And heaven knew why she had bothered to come. He was a strong man and he could fight his own battles without *her* feeble protection. Yet she knew that her heart sang, knowing that he was not mixed up in a brawl with the hot-blooded Nicos.

And other thoughts tumbled through Lucie's mind in this moment. That cool, orderly young mind which had hitherto never imagined that any man could be a flaming torch to set fire to her heart as Adrian fired hers.

She loved him. With all the strength and power of her being she loved him and wish that she could help. But she was less to him than Valerie Bright had been; less than this pretty Greek girl whom he had so often painted and must have once admired. Not for the first time in her life Lucie felt insignificant, wished idiotically that she had been born with great beauty, or with the gift of overwhelming magnetism which would have brought this man to her feet. Instead, she felt that he was eyeing her with cold indifference . . . even dislike . . . because she had followed him here. He interrupted her reflections.

'Let's get the hell out of here!'

Turning, he marched down the pathway through the grove back towards the Inn. Lucie turned to follow him. Aphra darted after her with a little cry.

'Plees, *plees*, Mees Lucie, tell him not to be angry with me.'

Lucie whispered, 'Aphra, what is all this? What have you done?'

Aphra shook her head.

Lucie had a sudden burning wish to know all the facts . . . *all* of them. It was beyond her. Aphra was beginning to cry again. Sharply, Lucie said:

'Be sensible, Aphra, and tell no more lies or there will be worse trouble. There *is* something you have not told your brother, isn't there? Something you *ought* to tell, Aphra?'

The Greek girl shook her head, sobbing. In exasperation Lucie turned and followed Adrian down the hill.

THIRTEEN

LUNCH at Villa Venetia was an awkward meal.

Adrian had remained perfectly silent on the subject of his personal affairs when he returned with her from the mountain Inn that morning. She kept wondering what he was thinking.

During the rest of the morning he stayed in his studio. She did not know what he was doing. But just before lunch old Loucas whispered to her:

'The master is very angry about something. He has ordered me to find a man and sell everything in the studio—all the furniture, his worktable, and the paints and canvases he used. It is sad. The room is to be left empty and unused.'

Lucie thought over this while she ate her lunch with Adrian. He addressed her once or twice politely, passing her the salt, or offering her wine. He commented on the perfect weather. And always when her gaze met his he looked away, as though either oblivious of, or indifferent to, the embarrassment which she felt. She was quite glad when the telephone rang so that she could get up and go and answer it.

Carol Dexter's gay voice was a relief.

'How's things, honey? Are we going to see you at all today? What about the Fair in Larnaca? Nicos said something about us making up a party.'

Hurriedly Lucie replied:

'I'm not sure now about the Fair. You know that *he* is at home and I think he wants me to go with him.'

'I wish you joy,' said Carol with a laugh.

Lucie stayed silent. Carol added:

'It's all rather awkward with Valerie in our party. We can hardly ask the great Adrian too.'

'Naturally not,' said Lucie, and was surprised to find that it irritated her because all these people kept alluding to him as 'the great Adrian'. It savoured too much of contempt. Why should any of them be contemptuous of him? What did they really know of him? In her estimation it was Valerie for whom they should feel contempt.

Carol added:

'Well, come down and see us when you want, honey. We're always pleased to see you.'

Then Lucie said:

'How long are . . . the Vanderlights staying in Kyrenia?'

'About a month, I guess.'

'Thanks.' Lucie put down the receiver, wishing Carol had said they were leaving Cyprus tomorrow.

She joined Adrian in the salon, where Loucas was serving coffee. When they were alone again Adrian gave her a peculiar searching look. He stood stirring his coffee thoughtfully. Then he said:

'In case you want to make other arrangements, I've changed my mind about going to the Fair. I may not even stay as long as I intended.'

Lucie felt suddenly nettled, and being a courageous person she aired her grievances, even to 'the great Adrian'. She said in a resentful voice:

'I wish you'd told me that before. I've just refused to go with the Dexters.'

'I may as well admit that I heard you doing so. One can't help hearing what is said on that 'phone.'

Lucie picked up her coffee-cup. Her expression was a little grim.

'As you invited me, I expected you'd take me to the Fair,' she blurted out the words.

A look of astonishment suddenly crossed Adrian's hard face. He stared at Lucie. He had been feeling deadly ever since he came back from the fruitless discussion with Aphra Aliston. As always, he admitted Lucie's spirit. It really was quite intriguing the way the girl retaliated on occasions. Most certainly she had a mind of her own. And as if she could possibly *wish* him to take her to the Fair! He said:

'My dear Lucie, one of your wisecracking American friends would be far more amusing than I in Larnaca—or even your Greek boy-friend. I'm scarcely in the mood to dance at the Cataclysmos Fair.'

'Very well,' said Lucie, flinging back her head. 'But remember you issued the invitation. As for being amusing . . . you don't *try*, do you? You just let yourself get into one frightful mood after another.'

Now Adrian opened his eyes very wide indeed. Seldom, if ever, had he been spoken to quite so plainly. He was really quite amused. Suddenly he burst out laughing.

Lucie scowled at him.

'Glad you find me so funny,' she said.

He stopped laughing, shook his head and took a cigar out of the box which Loucas had laid on the table.

'Well, well, you *do* surprise me, Lucie. I know you think I'm a surly, difficult fellow. You don't hesitate to let me know it at times. How, therefore, can you possibly want me to take you out?'

She felt horribly embarrassed. She wished she had never said anything. And she would have died rather than let him guess that she would enjoy the Fair with him more than with any of that crowd down at the Dome Hotel—or with Nicos Aliston, to whom Adrian had somewhat scathingly alluded to as her 'Greek boy-friend'. What was there, she asked herself, about Adrian that drew her like a magnet? She did not know. But she felt her heart beat ridiculously fast as she looked up at his sardonic face.

'Please forget it. I don't suppose I shall go to the Fair at all. Now, is it true that Loucas is to take everything out of your studio and hold a sale? If so, I must help. Loucas is growing old and forgetful. I must go round the town and find somebody who might make an offer for your things.'

Adrian looked down at her reflectively.

'You are quite cross with me, Lucie.'

'I have no right to be. I'm only a paid employee in this house,' she said sullenly.

He met the full gaze of her flashing eyes ... quite unlike the soft eyes of the Lucie he knew.

'Now don't say things like that or I really will be bored. I wouldn't like you to feel you are nothing more than a paid employee in this house. You have been so very kind to my mother.'

Lucie, her heart still pounding, turned away from him and walked across the salon towards the door. Adrian called her back.

'Really, Lucie, there is no need for us to fight. There's quite enough trouble in the world as it is. I've behaved very badly about the Fair, but quite candidly it never entered my head that you would mind whether I took you or not.'

She turned and made a gesture with one hand.

'Oh, if it comes to that, I *don't* care. But it just seems you *will* give up at the first fence. Why, because something upset you very much this morning, do you forget all those things you said to me when you first came home this time? ... how you were going to change and go out and be more sociable and not let life get you down? Well ... I *know* that it does. I know you have something serious on your mind. I know, for instance, that this morning you met that girl you used to be engaged to, and that *she* upset you. I understand it. I think she's *hateful.* I think it's awful to allow her to upset you. She isn't worth it!'

She stopped, horrified at her own temerity, and crimson to the roots of her hair. Quickly she added a breathless apology.

'I really do beg your pardon. It's no business of mine, I was crazy to say such things.' She turned again and would have fled from the room, but Adrian marched across the salon and caught her arm and detained her.

'You can't run away after all *that,*' he said, 'you must tell me more.'

Lucie was now panic-stricken.

'No ... please ... I'd better go ...' she stuttered.

But Adrian kept a firm hold of her arm.

'You've said a lot of things which have hit the nail on the head,' he said; 'there's no need for you to run away and think I'm offended. I'm not. You've got considerable nerve, you know, and you're a bit plain-spoken. But that's a fault on the good side. But just let's get down to a few more facts, Lucie. You say that I give up at the first fence ... is that how it appears to you? Am I a defeatist?'

Lucie shook her head. Adrian continued:

'Lucie. I fought pretty hard at the beginning and went on fighting until it seemed I'd lost everything I believed in. And then I saw no use in fighting any more. Until I met Valerie again this morning. Some of the things that were said between us shook me badly. I had an insane wish then to go on fighting the old battle and prove that I was right and that she was wrong. But even then, the fight was uneven. The fight with Aphra. What can you do if the person whose name has been linked with yours holds to a lie ... an infamous lie? I came back home this morning in what you call "one of my moods" ... "*one frightful mood after another*" I think is how you put it. Well, it strikes home, Lucie. It's too damn' near the truth. But if you knew all the facts you might be a bit more tolerant.'

Lucie regained some of her self-confidence and courage.

'Adrian, ever since I've been in Villa Venetia I've heard all sorts of rumours and hints. Perhaps you don't realize how difficult it's been for *me*?'

'I think you're very loyal, Lucie, and you have no cause to stand by *me*.'

'After that day in your studio, I formed my own conclusions.'

'For or against me, Lucie?'

'I just don't know. I don't begin to understand any of it.'

'But I want to know,' he continued. 'These impressions you've formed. Have they convinced you I am in the right or in the wrong?'

'I believe you're okay. I don't know much about it. But I *do* believe in you. That's all.'

A moment's silence. Adrian Ollivent's heart gave a twist. This girl whom he had brought here to look after his mother's home meant nothing to him. Yet that plain frank declaration of belief in him stirred him. He had not felt so profoundly moved for a long time.

'Thank you, Lucie. Thank you,' he said.

'I ought to go up to your mother. I always chat with her before her afternoon nap.'

'Very well,' he said, 'but after she has settled down come back. I'd like to put an end to all this rumour and scandal. I'll tell you my story from *my* angle.'

She raised a flushed face.

'You needn't, really!'

'It's time you heard it from me, Lucie,' he said, and for a long, extraordinary moment, held her gaze.

Earlier that morning, after Adrian and Lucie had left, Zita and Aphra began to gabble to each other excitedly.

What did the Englishman want? Zita asked, and Aphra, not wishing to appear rejected and foolish, told a few more lies. The Englishman had returned to ask her to go back to his studio and let him paint her again. Paint her or *kiss* her? asked Zita with a giggle. He was a fine handsome gentleman. Aphra shrugged her shoulders and pretended that she knew all about love-making. Then when Zita said that Nicos would be angry, Aphra grew frightened again and told Zita she must say nothing about this affair. Zita swore it.

But the laundry maid went back to the farm and excitedly related this morning's events to her sister Irene, who promised not to tell, then went down to the village and recounted the news to Jicko the fisherman, her boy-friend.

Jicko, drinking in a café that evening, having had a little more strong Cyprus wine than usual, forgot that he had promised Irene to say nothing, and repeated the news. The rich gentleman from Villa Venetia was after Aphra again. How would Nicos like that?

A burst of laughter, followed by a few sallies, greeted this question.

Nicos Aliston, having just returned from Limassol, stopped at the same café for a drink, and entered just in time to hear the laughter. Cheerfully he asked for the joke to be repeated so that he could hear it. The little company of men, nice fellows, mostly Cypriots, greeted him awkwardly then melted away without answering. Nicos was perplexed. He scented trouble. He was sure that the joke had been at his expense since none of them would tell him.

Being vain he felt a twinge of annoyance. He liked to be popular. He wondered what had happened. He had done good business in Limassol, too. He had made up his mind to buy a big hotel there, and work hard in future so that he could have something really magnificent to offer Lucie Gresham. For a long time now he had been in a state of mind which would allow him to think of little but the fair, reserved English girl.

He flung himself into a chair opposite Jicko and asked again for an explanation of the laughter, and the reluctance they all showed to repeat the joke.

Jicko, still fuddled with wine, gave a stupid laugh and leaned close to Nicos.

'They laughed because the gentleman from Villa Venetia is after your sister again,' he said.

Nicos turned white. He sprang up, sweeping the glasses off the marble-topped table. They went crashing to the ground.

'You lie!' he said in Jicko's language. '*You lie, you dog!*'

Jicko blinked at him foolishly.

'I do not lie. My girl's sister, Zita, was washing blankets at the Inn this morning and saw him there, taking Aphra into the olive grove alone.'

Nicos' bright blue eyes became like stones. Ice-cold rage possessed him.

'Zita said that?'

Jicko pushed his cap over one eye and picked up one of the fallen glasses.

'Yes, she said it. But perhaps it was in fun. . . .'

'My sister has nothing more to do with the Englishman now and he has not been up to the Inn,' Nicos said in a loud ringing voice which he meant all the others in the café to hear.

Then he turned and walked out into the starlit night. He got back into his car. He wanted no wine now. He was going home to see his half-sister. But on the way he meant to stop at the farm and question Zita; find out for himself if there was any truth in the infamous story.

FOURTEEN

ZITA, her sister Irene and their parents were at supper in the big kitchen of their farmhouse when Nicos walked in. The farmer and his wife greeted the young innkeeper jovially. They were proud to be considered friends of his. Nicos was a man of standing in Kyrenia and considered by Zita's family to be distinguished what with his English education and his wonderful capacity for making money without doing too much work.

They invited him to come in and sit down, have a glass of wine and share some of their meal—potatoes, vegetables and garlic sausage.

As a rule Nicos liked coming here and 'lording' over these simple people, although he never quite approved of his half-sister's friendship with Zita. But he had no smile on his handsome face tonight. He went straight to the point, turning his gaze upon Zita.

'I want a word with you,' he said.

The mother rose and wiped her hands nervously on her apron.

'Has my daughter offended you, Nicos Aliston?' she asked.

'No,' said Nicos coldly, 'but I would like to question her about an intruder who entered the Inn today without being welcome there. Zita was with my sister at the time.'

The family exchanged glances. Zita, her plump face scarlet, drooped her eyelids, but at a command from her mother rose and walked towards Nicos.

He looked down at her. She had never seen him in such a rage. Now she cast a furious look at her sister Irene, who smirked and turned from her. She realized that Irene had betrayed her confidence and that Nicos had heard about Mr. Ollivent. She was afraid ... because everybody in Kyrenia knew that Nicos Aliston had a terrible temper. As a rule he was amiable and easy-going, but when roused he was a demon. Indeed, Zita could remember a case in which the police had had to intervene—many years ago, when the young Nicos, in his teens, had almost strangled another boy who had insulted him.

Nicos questioned her in a low curt voice. She dithered and hedged but had to admit in the end that Adrian Ollivent had come to the Inn this morning while she and Aphra were washing and that Aphra had gone off into the olive grove alone with the Englishman.

'How long were they there?' demanded Nicos, and she saw that the knuckles of his clenched hands were ivory-white.

Zita began to weep and to say that she did not remember. The farmer, a consumptive-looking man with long black moustaches and melancholy eyes rose to his feet.

'Why does my daughter weep?' he asked perplexedly.

Nicos clenched his teeth and gave a curt nod.

'I am sorry if I have made her cry. *She* has done nothing wrong. Forgive me if I do not stay. Good night to you all.'

He went out and slammed the kitchen door. Zita's mother crossed herself and muttered that the devil had got into Nicos Aliston. Zita flung herself on her sister Irene and began to pull her hair in a frenzy, accusing her of mischief-making. The mother expostulated. An uproar ensued in the once-peaceful kitchen.

Nicos drove his car up to his Inn.

By now he was in an ice-cold rage. So—after all, Jicko's drunken revelation had not been the ravings of a bemused mind. He had spoken the truth. Zita had confirmed it. Nicos put his car in the garage and walked into the Inn. Several parties sat outside on the lighted terrace having supper. Many people—particularly tourists—drove up to this beautiful mountain retreat for supper on a fine summer's night. The view of the glittering harbour—miles below—was lovely, and the Aliston wine, home-made, and their special cheeses, were famous. The place had a tranquil, welcoming atmosphere. Aphra was nowhere to be seen. On questioning one of the maids, Nicos was told that his half-sister was upstairs with her grandmother.

He went to the foot of the stairs and called her down.

Aphra came down smiling and unaware of the trouble awaiting her. She had just put on a new silk dress and some blue earrings and stuck a flower in her hair. She looked beautiful, but that very beauty roused fresh rage in the heart of her brother. The scandal about Aphra and Adrian Ollivent had shocked him profoundly. Certainly he had not felt that same confidence in Aphra from that day to this. But to discover that Adrian and Aphra were still meeting was a terrible shock. Who was to know how many other times the two had seen each other, Nicos asked himself, or how often Aphra had slipped away from the Inn in his absence to meet this man who obviously had no respect for her.

The Greeks are fierce guardians of the chastity of the young women of their families and Nicos' mixed blood and English education had not eliminated that fundamental instinct.

'I wish to speak to you, Aphra,' he said, and beckoned her into the small sitting-room which was marked '*Private*' and reserved for the Aliston family.

At once Aphra changed colour ... her olive face took on a greenish tinge of sheer fright. The pupils of her eyes dilated. She recognized that note in Nicos' voice and his expression. *Nicos had learned about this morning.*

Then she was shut in the room with him, out of earshot of the crowd who were eating and drinking merrily on the terrace and the servants in the kitchen next door.

Nicos caught Aphra's wrist. He began to hurl questions at her, accusations. She was wanton and a cheat. Once more she had betrayed the good name of her family and put him, her brother, to shame. He had thought they had lived down the old scandal, but now her name was being linked once more with Adrian Ollivent's in all the cafés on the harbour. They were jeering at her and, because of it, at *him*, Nicos. It was insupportable.

How many times had she seen Mr. Ollivent? What had he said and done? She was to tell him or he would *kill her*.

Aphra, who was a coward, fell on her knees and began to grovel. She swore by the Holy Virgin and all the Saints that she was innocent and then, trying to save herself from her brother's wrath, babbled out a new tissue of lies. She was innocent, and

88

had never once tried to see Mr. Ollivent, but he had come up here to ask her to sit again, for a new portrait. That was all. By the Madonna she swore it.

Nicos, jaw thrust out, looked down at Aphra, listened and deliberated. He fancied that she spoke the truth. He preferred to believe that his sister was the lamb without guile, and Ollivent the wolf who ravened after her. *Wanted her to sit for a new portrait*, did he? That was rich! Long hours shut up alone with him in his damned studio! As if he had not learned his lesson, the scoundrel! He had not a friend left in Cyprus because of that Christmas Eve. Now he had the nerve to start it up again—driven, no doubt, by his passionate longing to get poor little Aphra back into his clutches.

Now Aphra was mentioning a name which interrupted Nicos' thoughts and made him take notice of her babblings.

'Mees Lucie ... Lucie ... she came to fetch Mr. Ollivent,' Aphra stuttered.

Nicos stared. *Lucie* had come up here to fetch Mr. Ollivent! That was news. By this time no doubt she realized what he was like. Anyhow, she seemed to have interrupted the lovers in the olive grove, for which Nicos must thank her.

He bent and lifted Aphra on to her feet.

'Stop crying now, and be sensible,' he growled. 'I believe you have done no wrong but Mr. Ollivent must be called to account. This time I swear he shall not go unpunished. He has money and power and position. But I am Nicos Aliston, and no sister of mine shall have her name laughed at because of his abominable designs.'

Aphra gulped and sobbed and remained silent and terrified. She was thinking only of herself. She whimpered:

'Do not send me to Aunt Caliope. I have done nothing wrong. Let me stay here with you, Nicos.'

'Go up to our grandmother,' he said abruptly. 'I will decide tomorrow what is to be done with you.'

She sniffed and gave him a scared look through her lashes.

'What are you going to do now, Nicos? You won't make trouble at Villa Venctia tonight, will you?'

He glared at her.

'Do you wish him to get off scot-free after insulting you with such a proposal? Do you think I'm fool enough to believe that he only asked you to go back to his studio in order to paint your foolish conceited face?'

Aphra averted her gaze. This was awful ... one lie seemed to lead to another and she could not help remembering that Mees Lucie had begged her, this morning, to tell the truth. And of course none of this was just ... or fair to Mr. Ollivent. But she *could not* confess the truth to Nicos. If he knew that she had lied right from the beginning, and that Adrian had merely come up here to seek justice, Nicos would half kill her and certainly plant her in Aunt Caliope's convent for the rest of her life.

His next words frightened her still further.

'I shall do what I think right so far as the man is concerned. But it is obvious now that our grandmother is always ill and you have no mother to guide you when I am away, that it is no longer good for you to remain in Kyrenia. We shall go to Athens at once and I shall seek the advice of our aunt.'

Aphra began to cry in earnest. Deep resentment welled up in her muddled young mind. Everything was awful and unfair ... she could not think straight. She only knew that life with Aunt Caliope would be all prayers and fasting and hard work in that Convent of the Greek Orthodox Church which was for the aged and bedridden. She would see no more men ... have no more fun ... not even a chance to laugh with Zita, or other girl-friends, in Kyrenia. And certainly she would never see Mr. Ollivent again.

She went weeping bitterly up to her grandmother.

Nicos, blind with fury and in reckless mood, drove his car at speed along the rough and winding road downhill leading to the town and all but ended his own life.

Earlier that evening, a lorry, which had run out of petrol, was left abandoned just around a bend in the road. The vehicle had no rear-light. Nicos drove his car straight into the back of it.

He was found an hour later, lying senseless in the road. His car had overturned in the ditch. He had been flung clear of it. It seemed a miracle that he escaped with only a dislocated wrist, and minor cuts and bruises.

He recovered consciousness to find that he had been picked up by a party of English people who had been dining at his Inn and were returning to their hotel. They wanted to take him straight to hospital, but he refused and asked that he should be driven home.

When later he staggered into the Inn, two strangers supporting him on either side, blood streaming down his ashen face, Aphra screamed with horror. She thought at first that he had been engaged in a fight with Mr. Ollivent and got the worst of it. She was tremendously relieved to hear the facts. Nicos told her to help get him into bed, then send for the old Greek doctor who attended his grandmother.

Aphra devoted herself to her brother, only too eager to be reinstated in his favour and hoping to avoid being taken to Athens tomorrow. It seemed quite certain anyhow, once the doctor came, that young Nicos would be confined to bed for several days. His wrist was set (it was the right one), his cuts bathed and bandaged, and once in bed he began to suffer from reaction and shock. In the night Aphra heard him groaning and muttering in fever. He uttered the name 'Lucie' several times.

Aphra, in her dressing-gown, sat beside him and asked him if he wished her to send for 'Mees'. He turned his fever-glazed eyes upon her, groaned as he moved the shoulder which was most badly bruised and then shut his eyes.

'Tomorrow I wish to see her,' he said.

Rather foolishly, Aphra turned the attention to her silly little self.

'Dear Nicos, I am so sorry that you have had this accident. But please say that you forgive me about this morning and believe in me.'

One of Nicos' eyes was half closed and swelling. With the other he gave her rather a malevolent look; his face wiped of good looks and youth in the sombre light of a small oil-lamp which cast huge shadows on the ceiling. He said:

'My visit to Mr. Ollivent has merely been postponed. Now go, Aphra, I will try to sleep.'

She crept away, asking herself in scared fashion what she had better do. She decided that she would telephone to the Villa Venetia first thing in the morning and ask Mees Lucie to come up and put Nicos in a better temper. After all, Mees could do her no harm; whatever she suspected, she knew nothing. She could not even deny that Mr. Ollivent had visited her, Aphra, with a view to renewing their old association.

That night, whilst Nicos tossed and groaned, a man with body and mind feeling sorely injured, he thought of what he had just said to his half-sister. Yes, his visit to Mr. Ollivent had only been postponed by this damnable accident. But the day of revenge would come!

FIFTEEN

LUCIE'S visit to Nicos on the morning after his accident was hardly a success from either of their points of view.

When she received the message that she was urgently wanted up at the Aliston Inn she was busy ordering the menu for the day. She was feeling extraordinarily happy for a variety of reasons. First and foremost, Blanche Ollivent seemed very much better and the doctor was confident that she would be able to get up and come downstairs and sit with them in the salon or in her chair in the garden, by the end of this week. Secondly, Lucie felt that she had cemented a real friendship with Adrian. He had told her his story. She had been the recipient of his confidences. She knew the whole thing now, from his point of view ... the unhappy history of his love for Valerie Bright, and of that fatal Christmas Eve on which he had been unjustly involved with Aphra.

He had told her everything, briefly, without frills, but two things were plainly revealed to Lucie. First, the extent of his love for that beautiful girl who had refused to accept his word and had so heartlessly jilted him. (It seemed pathetic, but all too obvious that the strong, clever man had been wholly enslaved by his adoration for Valerie.) And secondly, it was made clear that he had suffered abominably after Valerie broke with him. The knowledge that he had become an object of contempt in Kyrenia was insufferable for a man as proud as Adrian.

Lucie had always believed in him. Now that she had heard the story from his own lips she more than ever believed. When he finished telling her everything, he looked at her with a faintly apologetic smile and said:

'Of course there is no reason why you should accept my word. Even the girl who was once supposed to be in love with me refused to accept it.'

That remark had given Lucie food for ironic thought and hurt her not a little.

If only he knew that *she* loved him far more than Valerie could ever have loved. That in Valerie's shoes, she would never have doubted ... but would have stood shoulder to shoulder with him in that battle for his good name. She would have fought the scandal for him until she over-rode every doubt, every sneer directed against him on this Island.

'I believe every word you have said.'

His nervous fingers closed around hers in silence for an instant. Then he said:

'Thanks I'm grateful, Lucie...' and covered his momentary emotion by adding: 'It is fortunate my mother has remained in ignorance of that affair on Christmas Eve. She knew, of course, that Valerie broke with me, but being the wonderful person she is, she asked no questions and merely took it for granted that there had been some trouble between us. I told her, in fact, that Valerie discovered that she had made a mistake.'

Lucie had thought:

'And what a mistake! To lose the love of *this* man ... to exchange him for any other in the world!'

Then came the news of Nicos' accident. When she told Adrian, he was politely sympathetic and called it 'bad luck' but was obviously not interested in the sufferings of the young man who had for so long been his bitter enemy.

Lucie stammered.

'Do you mind if I go up and see him? He wants me to.'

Adrian at once seemed to draw back into his shell. With a rather tight-lipped smile, he said:

'My dear girl, you are free to do what you wish and go where you please.'

Her heart sank. What a moody, elusive creature Adrian was! Still, she assured herself, there was no need for her to be too downcast. He was always irritated when the name of Nicos Aliston was mentioned. He would get over it.

As she walked up the hillside in the warm sunlight she thought about Nicos with mixed feelings. He had always been charming and devoted to her. On the other hand, recent events had not endeared Nicos to her. She felt resentful of his treatment of Adrian. Naturally, he was fond of his sister and anxious to defend her honour, but he seemed to behave with unnecessary antagonism.

She felt uneasy when she reached the Inn. Aphra saw Mees Lucie, with her big straw hat on her head, and came out to meet her. Aphra looked sullen and her eyes were red-rimmed. She burst out crying again as Lucie greeted her. Between the hysterical sobs, Lucie gathered that Aphra had had a bad night with her brother. Nicos was ill. This morning he was in what Aphra described as 'a dreadful mood'.

93

'He means to take me to Athens for good as soon as he is better,' Aphra wailed. 'Oh, Mees Lucie, he will listen to you. Plees, plees, tell him not to make me go away from Kyrenia.'

Lucie felt no pity whatsoever for the girl this morning. She was just a self-centred, vain unscrupulous little creature, incapable of telling the truth. Lucie said:

'Now, Aphra, I do not intend to plead for you with Nicos, and I'll tell you frankly why. A convent and some hard work is just about what you do deserve.'

Aphra stopped weeping and stared at Lucie, stricken. How stern she was . . . the little 'Mees' who was usually so sweet and sympathetic. Aphra snivelled.

'Why are you so cross with me?'

'Because you don't tell the truth,' said Lucie, 'and you have done a great deal of harm to somebody who was once good to you and a friend of your brother's.'

Aphra lowered her lashes. Lucie saw immediately the way that the lovely young face 'buttoned up'. The maddening girl! She was determined to support her outrageous lies. But being angry with her was certainly not the line to take, thought Lucie. She must think of another way.

She went upstairs to see the injured Nicos.

He lay in bed under one of those exquisitely-embroidered linen and lace spreads for which the Cypriot women are famous. The bedroom was neat and clean.

He was a pitiable sight this morning, lying there with a bandage round his forehead, only a tuft of golden hair showing, one eye closed and his right hand lying uselessly on top of the left. He tried to grin at her.

'Thank you for coming . . . oh, thank you so much!' he said in a husky voice.

Lucie, ever tenderhearted, felt a rush of sympathy for him and sat down at his side and took off her hat.

'Nicos, I really am most frightfully sorry about this,' she began.

He half raised himself on one elbow.

'I've been in hell,' he said with a gulp—'in hell, Lucie. You don't know what I've suffered.'

'Surely you should be in hospital.'

'It's not my injuries . . . I am not concerned with physical pain. It is my mental torture,' he said, his breath coming unevenly.

Lucie felt embarrassed. She said with a smile:

'Come off it, Nic, don't lose your sense of humour.'

'I've lost it. Do you know what has happened, Lucie? You, who are so cool and composed, living down there in Villa Venetia . . . do you realize that you live beside a *scoundrel*?'

'Steady, Nicos,' broke in Lucie. Her lips tightened. There was no smile on her face now.

Nicos burst into denunciation of Adrian.

'He came up here after my sister again. After all this time . . . not content with what happened before. . . . Mother of God! . . . whatever you think of the man . . . however correct and circumspect *you* find him . . . can you blame me for wishing to protect my young sister?'

Lucie went crimson.

'Oh, Nicos, don't be so dramatic! So . . . so exaggerated!' Lucie said in a cross voice. 'You don't really know the facts. You never have known them. You've only heard Aphra's side of it.'

This seemed to throw Nicos into a fever. He began to rave. What did *Lucie* know of the truth? Hadn't he, Nicos, seen that Christmas night with his own eyes, Aphra lying on the sofa in Adrian's arms . . . and he had dishonoured her.

Here Lucie interrupted:

'Rubbish. He was kneeling beside her trying to bring her back to her senses. She had fainted with sheer hysteria.'

'That is what he says,' Nicos exclaimed hotly.

'Why shouldn't I believe him?'

'Why shouldn't I believe my poor little sister? And in any case, why did he come up here after her yesterday, taking her into the olive grove alone?' Nicos broke off with an indignant gesture and lay back on his pillow panting, groaning from the pain in his shoulder.

Lucie stood up. She felt an enormous loyalty towards Adrian.

'Nicos, you've got the wrong end of the stick.'

'But poor Miss Bright . . . Even she walked out on him. She believed he had wronged my sister.'

Lucie gave a cold smile.

'Poor Miss Bright, as you call her, did not know the facts.'

'Then everybody has lied except your Mr. Ollivent!' exclaimed Nicos.

Lucie shrugged her shoulders.

'I don't think there's much use us arguing so childishly.

Nicos, I thought we were friends, but naturally you'll want to end it now.'

Nicos sat upright again, his teeth clenched, his face ashen.

'It is you, not I, who are trying to end our friendship, Lucie. As for Aphra ... I will never believe that she has lied to me so absolutely. Why *should* I take Mr. Ollivent's word against hers?'

'Quite so, Nicos. Why should you? I don't blame you for believing her.'

'And you ... why should *you* give your loyalty to Mr. Ollivent? Is it just because you work for him that you turn against me ... when I love you ... adore you with all my soul?' burst out Nicos in a passionate voice.

Lucie coloured and pushed a strand of hair nervously back from her forehead. This was becoming extremely awkward, she thought. And, of course, she could not begin to explain to Nicos Aliston that she defended Adrian because *she loved him*. That was a secret which no one, not even Adrian herself, must ever guess.

'I think I'd better go, Nicos,' she said.

Then he made a grab at her hand and carried it to his bruised lips, kissing it wildly.

'Don't leave me when I'm so ill ... so much in pain. Lucie, this affair of my sister is between me and Mr. Ollivent. It cannot concern you. I love you, Lucie. You know that.'

She tried to draw her fingers away. She had never been more embarrassed. There were actually tears welling into Nicos' eyes. She could feel them wet against her hand. She had never really understood until now what passion she had awakened in the heart of this young Greek. She was not used to people feeling violently about *her*. And it roused no answering emotion in her heart. She could only be sorry for Nicos, and slightly irritated because he was making things so awkward.

He raised his bruised face.

'Lucie, Lucie, don't let this come between us. You mean my whole life now.'

She shook her head.

'Oh, Nicos, you're so ... so ... oh, I don't *know*! ... but if you really want to please me, you'll give up this unreasonable attitude towards Mr. Ollivent. He came up here yesterday to ask Aphra to help clear his name ... not because he is "after her", as you put it.'

'You are wrong!' Nicos almost shouted the words and dropped her hand. 'He tried to get her to go down to his studio again.'

'Nicos, that is just her word against his all over again.'

'And you . . . you are his defender!'

'That is my affair.'

'And you, do you not care for me at all?' he asked sullenly.

'Nicos, I am not in love with you. You *know* that.'

'But there is no reason why you should not fall in love one
day,' he said with a return of his old youthful arrogance.

'Please, you are making things so difficult.'

'But you mean everything to me now.'

She stood silent, began to put on her hat. This seemed to
throw Nicos into a fresh frenzy. He began to rant again.

Was she so attached to Adrian? Must she break his heart?
Was she walking out on him just because of her belief in
Adrian? Was he guilty not only of the ruin of Aphra's good
name in Kyrenia, but of coming between him, Nicos, and the
girl he loved? They had been happy together until Adrian's
return home.

'He is a dangerous man. He should be exterminated!' Nicos
shouted.

Lucie turned and walked towards the door. She felt hot with
anger. She was bitterly disappointed in Nicos and she was not
flattered by his mad passion for her. She regretted the breaking
of their friendship, certainly that had been happy and carefree
in the past. But she could not and would not stay here and hear
Adrian abused.

At the door she turned and said:

'I'm going now, Nicos. I don't think you are quite yourself.
When you are better and feeling less violent about things, maybe
we can have another talk. Good-bye. I hope you will soon be
well again.'

He called to her frenziedly:

'*Lucie!*'

She did not answer, but walked downstairs and out into the
courtyard. Aphra was there. She had just been picking flowers
and her arms were full of magnificent roses. It was her custom
to decorate the Inn, and sell flowers to the tourists. She gave
Lucie a scared look and was still more scared when she heard
her brother shouting through the bedroom window upstairs.

Lucie put a hand on Aphra's shoulder.

'I advise you, Aphra, to be very careful what you say in

future. With your terrible lies you are hurting everybody around you, and I do not think you can go to your church with an easy conscience until you have confessed the truth about Mr. Ollivent.'

Aphra did not answer but threw Lucie a look of dark hatred. Lucie saw that look and her heart sank. She had gained nothing. In her anger, she had even lost what slight affection and confidence she used to have from this girl. This was certainly not the way to help Adrian.

The shouts from Nicos had died away. Upstairs on his big bed he was lying on his pillow, shaking, convulsed with passion, his fingers plucking at the embroidered sheets. And now he hated Adrian Ollivent a thousand times more than he had hated him last night. He had taken Lucie away from him. Nicos said aloud:

'When I'm better I shall see you, Mr. Ollivent. And this time, whether your old mother is there or not, I shall pick my friends and we shall go to the Villa Venetia together and make you pay. . . .'

SIXTEEN

THE next three days at Villa Venetia were largely concerned with the convalescence of Blanche Ollivent.

The fragile old lady was carried down the stairs in the arms of her son and every morning now enjoyed sitting in a chair in her favourite place in the garden. She declared that she was quite well again and that there was no further cause for anxiety. But Lucie was never deceived by the fact that Mrs. Ollivent always made light of her infirmities and smiled when she suffered most. Lucie spent more time than usual sitting with her. Or playing the piano.

Mrs. Ollivent's chief delight she told Lucie towards the end of that week lay in the fact that Adrian seemed to have changed.

'He is quite like his old self, and seems really pleased to be back in Kyrenia. I believe he might even start painting again with a little encouragement.'

'He might indeed!' said Lucie.

The two women were sitting together in the garden. It was one of those matchless Kyrenian mornings, gold and sparkling, the heat tempered by the fresh breeze from the sea. Lucie sat mending a pair of nylons while they talked. Adrian had gone down to the town. He had told Lucie in confidence that he meant to take her advice in future and go out and about everywhere. Even though Aphra refused to admit the truth, he was determined now to ignore it.

'I agree with you, Lucie,' he had said, 'my best method is to let all these people in Cyprus see that I don't care what they think. I am, in my own mind, an innocent man. All this avoiding Kyrenian society—the Cypriots themselves—and rushing away from home at every opportunity, does rather suggest that I might be guilty and ashamed.'

And he had further declared that ever since he had talked to her and told her about things he had felt an urge to look at life from a new angle; had reached the conclusion that it was a declaration of weakness to allow himself to be so embittered by injustice.

Equally, he concluded that to burn or sell the contents of his studio would be a stupid and futile act which would gain him nothing. Aphra's portraits and Valerie's could be destroyed, but nothing else. Why shouldn't he make up his mind to paint again in the near future?

'Shall I paint *you*, Lucie?' he had suggested with a faint smile.

Lucie, threading her needle in and out of the nylon, felt her cheeks flame at the memory. It was wonderful to feel he might take such an interest in her. She had stammered a reply to the effect that she was not worth painting, and was flabbergasted when Adrian denied this. He looked at her with cool, critical gaze and said:

'That bleached hair of yours, your sedate delicate face and figure, and those golden eyes have their own charm, my dear Lucie.'

She shook her head vehemently.

'You should get somebody else to sit for you, someone who is really beautiful.'

He answered her with irony:

'I've had enough of what *you* call "real beauty". You have more. Full-stop.'

There the conversation ended. But the studio remained intact. That seemed to Lucie an indication of Adrian's rehabilitation.

There were other good signs. He renewed his invitation to take her to the Cataclysmos Fair. He arranged to drive her to Larnaca the day after tomorrow, and he did not care, he said, who they met whilst there. As for Valerie, he was even prepared to come face to face with her and her husband again. It would be a pity to give Valerie the satisfaction of thinking that she still had the power to disturb him. He had been a fool to suggest it after the shock of meeting her again.

All this, coupled with Adrian's new air of almost defiant good humour, gave Lucie, as well as his mother, great satisfaction.

He did not even bother to ask Lucie what had been said between Aphra and Nicos when she visited him the day after his accident.

'Nicos has the makings of a good chap but he is misguided,' was Adrian's opinion of the young Greek, and Lucie was inclined to agree. But she could not entirely wash her hands of the Alistons. She had a definite wish to make that maddening girl Aphra own that she had wronged Adrian.

Meanwhile, she knew to her secret cost that every day she spent in Adrian's company she fell more deeply in love with him. Now she had seen behind that 'iron curtain' (she remembered her employer in Cairo calling it that). He was so often charming these days, and always interesting. His attitude towards her remained completely platonic, however. She would never be anything more to him—of that she was quite sure. She just wasn't 'his type'. She did not dream of even trying to enter into another sphere with Adrian. But her passion for him was the most profound thing of her whole life, and something she knew, from which she would never recover.

Mrs. Ollivent looked over the rim of her dark glasses at the neat young figure of Lucie sitting there, sewing diligently, and thought, not for the first time, how very fortunate it had been when Adrian discovered Miss Gresham in Cairo and brought her to Cyprus. She had grown to love Lucie as she would her own flesh and blood. The old lady said:

'You haven't been down to see your American friends lately,

dear. Are they still at the Dome?'

Lucie knew that Mrs. Ollivent had no idea that Valerie was in Kyrenia.

'I've seen Carol and her husband when I've been shopping. But they have ... friends staying at the moment, and are rather tied up,' was Lucie's answer.

Mrs. Ollivent looked dreamily towards a pomegranate tree which was her special favourite.

'I wish some nice young man would come to Kyrenia—a *special* young man for you, Lucie.'

'Heaven forbid, Mrs. Ollivent!' Lucie laughed. 'I'm not particularly interested in boys.'

'I'm just a romantic old silly, my dear, but I feel you are far too young and sweet to be wasted here as my companion and housekeeper, much as I thank God for your devotion to me.'

'I'm perfectly happy here with you—you know that. I look back on my job in Cairo, and the good times I was *supposed* to be having going out with this man and that, as empty and meaningless. My real life started the moment I arrived here in Kyrenia. You know what an urge I always had to come to Cyprus. Now I know why.'

Mrs. Ollivent shook her head and smiled.

'You're very sweet, Lucie, and quite unique. But I still think it's unnatural that you shouldn't have what you girls call a "boyfriend".'

Again the hot colour flooded Lucie's face.

'I ... I don't want one.'

'Have you never been in love, Lucie? I was younger than you when I first met Adrian's father. He was a wonderful man and greatly resembled Adrian in many ways. Seemingly hard at times, but with such a wealth of tenderness underneath! Have you never longed for that tenderness in your life?'

Lucie averted her gaze and accidentally jabbed the needle into her thumb.

'Bother!' she said and sucked the thumb, thankful not to have to reply to the old lady, who was unconsciously probing a wound. Mrs. Ollivent persisted.

'Most girls want marriage and a home. Are you an exception, Lucie?'

'No exception, Mrs. Ollivent. I would quite like to be married and have my own home and children. I adore children.'

'Hear, hear!' said Adrian's voice.

101

Lucie crimsoned and turned. He had come across the lawn and reached them, making no noise on his rubber-soled shoes. She gave him an almost terrified look and hastily resumed her darning.

Adrian flung himself into a basket chair beside his mother and put some mail on her lap.

'Two papers, darling, and what looks like a letter from our Miss Little. Isn't that Gertrude's painfully neat handwriting?'

Mrs. Ollivent exchanged her smoked glasses for her reading ones.

'Yes. It is from poor Gertrude.'

Adrian gave a quick smile at Lucie.

'Your predecessor, dear Lucie. A glamour girl for whom I had an insane passion which kept me constantly chained to Villa Venetia.'

Mrs. Ollivent eyed her son reproachfully.

'Now don't make a mock of poor Gertrude. She was very plain, but a good soul in her way. She always writes to me faithfully.'

Adrian kept a sardonic gaze upon Lucie, whose head was bowed over her work.

'Oh, well,' he sighed, 'since our Lucie suits you so well, Mother, I must put up with it. But my heart belongs to Gertrude. I shall have to take Lucie to the Fair.'

Now Lucie had to smile.

'You needn't take me if you don't wish to,' she said. 'I can go alone and find myself a companion who would really appreciate me. You may have your Gertrude.'

'Now, really, I can't have poor old Gertrude made such a mock of,' said Mrs. Ollivent with mock severity.

Adrian smiled in a friendly way at Lucie.

'No, I don't think I'd better let you go alone,' he said. 'Gentlemen, including Cypriots, prefer blondes. We should never get you back, and what would Villa Venetia do without our Lucie?'

She bit her lip. Always when Adrian spoke of her the inference was on her usefulness as a companion to his mother. Oh, *always* his attitude towards her was maddeningly imper-sonal, even when it was friendly! They had never reached a real point of contact. They never would, she told herself, with a feeling of hopelessness.

'One of these days, a handsome unknown will waft me away

from the tyranny I put up with in your employ.'

'Tyranny be hanged! You're thoroughly spoiled in Villa Venetia—isn't she, Mother? It is *she* who tyrannizes over us. We all have to do what we are told by her.'

'Nonsense, dear,' said Mrs. Ollivent vaguely and only half hearing what the two young people were saying, for she was in the middle of reading Miss Little's dull letter.

Lucie rose to her feet.

'It's time I went in to see about lunch. It must be one o'clock.'

'Come back and tell me more about this "handsome" unknown,' said Adrian, his blue eyes fixed on her full of good humour. 'And don't forget that I expect to be consulted when the time comes as you are living under my roof and protection, I must "vet" your future husband.'

Her heart seemed to sink to its uttermost depths. She gave a tight-lipped little smile.

'You shall be consulted in due course.'

As she walked away, he called after her:

'We shall require a month's notice. Don't spring it on us, Lucie.'

She heard but did not reply. She was horrified to find that her eyes were stinging with tears; her heart beating fast with resentment. Oh, she loved him so much but he loved her not at all. Fool, *fool*, she thought despairingly, to give one's heart to a man who neither wanted it nor asked for it!

SEVENTEEN

At lunch time, Adrian said:

'I want to try out my new camera. I bought rather a fine one when I was last in Cairo, and I've learnt a bit about light filters. What about a visit to St. Hilarion?'

'Lucie has already been there,' said Mrs. Ollivent.

'I have,' said Lucie quickly, 'but I was dragged away from all the things I really wanted to see when I was with Carol.'

Adrian looked at her.

'Didn't you get right up to the top?'

'No. . . .'

And again she remembered how annoyed she had been at the time, when she had wanted to devote herself entirely to the joy of seeing the beautiful old ruin which had once been the stronghold of Richard Cœur de Lion; the background for so many historic battles of long ago—and how Valerie had insisted upon talking to her.

'There's nothing I'd like to do better than to see Hilarion again, with you as a guide, Adrian,' she said frankly.

'Then that's settled, we'll go soon after lunch.'

Lucie went up to her room to put on slacks and a cotton shirt. Forgotten was her depression when Adrian had been teasing her about her future husband.

She was to see St. Hilarion through new eyes that afternoon. He was so extraordinarily well-informed, she thought. The young man who was custodian of the Castle greeted Adrian with none of the coolness directed at him by most of the Cypriots in the district.

'Mr. Ollivent knows as much about the Castle as I do— indeed, I think much more,' he told Lucie.

The three of them were standing outside the cool, vaulted room which the custodian used for an office at the entrance to the Castle. It was full of booklets and postcard views of the place. But the Cypriot was not commercially-minded. He was heart and soul in love with his job and imbued with the romantic history of the place. Adrian told Lucie afterwards that he lived up here alone with his dog, and went only once a week down the mountain-side into the village to buy his food. Sometimes the whole of the countryside below was blotted out for him by cloud, and he looked down only upon the soft billowy masses which had the appearance of snowfields. He was utterly alone and lost to the world within the ruins.

'It is too long since you have been up here to see me, Mr. Ollivent,' the young Cypriot observed.

Adrian turned to Lucie.

'Come along—we'll climb up to the top.'

The guide did not follow them, and they went alone, walking slowly up the narrow steep path . . . climbing right up into the very skies, it seemed to Lucie. Down below everything was still and hot, but up here there was always a wind, and it blew deliciously against Lucie's hot young face. Adrian looked back at her over his shoulder and laughed.

'Warm work! Can you make it?'

'Yes, indeed.'

He stopped now and then to point out objects of exceptional beauty. There were three keeps; as they passed through each one into another stronghold Adrian explained that during the historic siege of St. Hilarion, when Richard Cœur de Lion held the Castle, each of these strongholds had their own separate defences and portion of food, its well of drinking water and the deep wells were still there to be seen, although dry at this time of year.

At one time there had been monks in occupation of the Castle and they came to the ruined chapel of the old monastery. There were little sunken courtyards, overgrown by long grass and flowering herbs. Arched empty windows from which Lucie could lean and gaze thousands of feet down to the sea. At one point Adrian showed her the smooth green sward which had been used for the knights' jousting. Through this arch, and on this terrace, he said, Richard and his Queen once sat to watch the tournaments.

'Oh!' breathed Lucie, 'How lucky they were! We are so high up, we seem to have reached the stars. It's so quiet, so *very* beautiful.'

Adrian nodded. He adjusted the lens of his camera.

'I couldn't agree more. I've often thought I'd like to take the place of our young friend the custodian, and bury myself up here away from civilization.'

'I'll come too,' said Lucie with a laugh.

He focused the camera upon her, thinking how charming she looked standing there by the arch, with the sun slanting through upon her hair, making a nimbus of light about her head. She had a slim waist and perfect small breasts.

'I think you'd grow a bit sick of it and want to get back to civilization again,' he said.

'I don't think I would,' she said.

'King Richard brought his Queen and her waiting-women to live in the highest tower, and sometimes the poor woman was left to languish in boredom for many months while he went forth to the Crusades.'

'That wouldn't have been so amusing.'

'Don't move for a moment,' he said.

He was directing the camera upon her. She stood very still, but her heart beat with quick, strong throbs. She was immensely happy up here with Adrian. They seemed so absolutely alone; cut off from the rest of the world.

'I'm a fool,' she thought, 'but I could think of nothing I would like better than to live here, on this mountain-top, and in this fairy castle, with *him*. I would ask for nothing more.'

They climbed to the highest peak. Once when Lucie, in an excess of enthusiasm, took a step too near the edge, Adrian pulled her back ... and his arm lingered about her shoulders. He told her another story of the Castle and the Crusades. She listened, conscious of his arm around her ... his nearness.

Reluctantly she descended the steep pathway and stone steps down through the three keeps again, realizing that she must return to Kyrenia. The spell of St. Hilarion was still upon her when she drove away. She was so silent that Adrian became aware of the change in her.

'You didn't stay in the sun too long?'

'No, I'm just bewitched. I didn't want to leave St. Hilarion.'

He looked at her face, and saw how genuinely she had been moved by the extreme beauty of St. Hilarion. He was grateful for her appreciation Here was a girl in a thousand.

He said:

'I think I've taken some good photographs. One or two of you, anyhow.'

'I hate photographs of me,' said she, smiling, 'but I'd adore to have some copies of the Castle.'

'You shall have them all.'

It was one of Lucie's red-letter days. Adrian's good mood persisted, and the concord between them had not been broken by the time dusk fell and dimmed the blue and gold splendour of the summer's day. At half past six Adrian invited Lucie to take yet another walk with him.

'You'll tire my Lucie out,' Mrs. Ollivent complained, secretly delighted to see Adrian renewing his old enthusiasm for life. For far too long he had sat silent with a book when he was home.

'I thought I'd take her for a drink in the Club on the harbour,' he said.

Lucie, who had not yet really come down to earth after her perfect experience this afternoon, was only too ready for yet another outing with the man who was fast becoming the great, the only, thing in her life.

It did not seem to her that she had ever fully realized or appreciated Kyrenia until now. First of all St. Hilarion. This evening a perfect walk along the harbour, with the deep violet of the sea on one hand and the quaint white houses and cobbled streets on the other. The fishing-boats had all come in; far out from shore a sleek grey cruiser lay anchored on the calm sea. Lights twinkled in the dusk, glittering from her portholes and reflecting goldenly in the water.

'Perfect, isn't she?' observed Adrian, stopping to light a cigar and looking out towards the cruiser. 'If a bit of an anachronism when one remembers the old Castle.'

'I hate cruisers,' said Lucie defiantly. 'They remind one of wars. I want to go back to St. Hilarion.'

Adrian smiled.

'I really do believe you are under its spell.'

'I know I am!' she said fervently.

The fervour was so unlike her, he thought, She had seemed such a calm, reserved little thing; one never knew what she was thinking or feeling. But this long day's association with her had shown him the intense love of life and beauty which lay under her reserve. He was intrigued.

He took her into the Harbour Club, a charming old house facing the water and exquisitely furnished, run by an English officer's wife. One or two people sat at high stools at the little bar, and there was an intimate warm atmosphere there which Lucie found attractive.

She hoped they would meet nobody who knew Adrian. The proprietress greeted him in friendly fashion, but nobody else seemed to recognize him. Two of the men at the bar wore white uniform and were on shore-leave from the cruiser.

Adrian immediately entered into conversation with them. The three drank iced beer, ordered by Adrian. Lucie sat on a stool, sipping hers, content. Her gaze rested continually on him. The young naval officer, who was a good-looking boy, tried once or twice to capture her attention. He thought that smooth pale gold head of hers attractive ... But he was of no interest to her.

Never before had she seen Adrian more genial and at ease in a crowd. There were quite a few of them gathered together there, chatting and laughing, before the drinking session ended. By that time somebody had started up a gramophone, and at the first bar or two of dance music Adrian raised an eyebrow at Lucie.

'This is where we totter home, I think.'

'I'm ready.'

They bade everybody good-bye and walked out.

One of the women who had come into the bar during the last few moments looked after them reflectively.

'Jolly decent chap, that,' observed the naval officer who had been talking to Adrian. 'Wonder who he is.'

'I know who he is, but I've never actually met him,' said the woman. 'Ollivent's the name. Bags of lolly, and has an invalid mother up on the hill in Villa Venetia.'

'Was that his wife?'

'No, he isn't married. I don't know who she was, but he used to be engaged to one of the visitors who came regularly to Kyrenia. There was the dickens of a scandal once about his model. He paints when he isn't busy making money. . . .'

The Naval officer ordered another drink.

'I wouldn't have thought he was the type, but it sounds exciting. Artist's model, and all that. Tell me more. . . .'

It was as well that Adrian Ollivent could not hear what was being said after he left the Harbour Club. He was feeling in particularly good form as he took Lucie's arm and walked home with her.

It was dark now, and the moon was out. The sea was a sheet of silver. The night deliciously cool.

'I enjoyed that,' he said.

'I did too,' agreed Lucie.

'Pleasant fellow, the N.O.'

'He was all right,' said Lucie.

Adrian suddenly laughed and looked down at her.

'Isn't your heart beating fast?' he enquired. 'He was a good-looking boy, and seemed rather smitten by you, Lucie.'

'Did he? I didn't notice.'

The night had lost its magic for Lucie, and after a few moments she lapsed into a silence that he could not break.

But for him the long period of misery and reticence and that wish to withdraw from the world into a shell had ended.

EIGHTEEN

On that marvellous day of early June—Adrian took Lucie to the Cataclysmos Fair—there was no room in her mind for trouble. She was entirely happy.

Adrian seemed to share her youthful excitement. They both made Mrs. Ollivent laugh by rushing in and out of her room early that morning asking for her opinion upon what they should wear.

Finally Lucie chose a white cotton frock with a short skirt. She carried a light blue coat and her big peasant hat. There was no need for them to take their food. They could eat at one of the many cafés in Larnaca.

Then came the wonderful drive to Larnaca, forty miles from Kyrenia.

There were hundreds of vehicles on the roads today. The whole Island seemed to be going towards Larnaca to the Fair which commemorated the birth of the ancient goddess of love. A pagan feast which had endured through the centuries, appealing to the hearts of the romantic Cypriots.

Adrian recounted some of the Island history as they drove through the warm sunshine. She listened to him, her blissful eyes looking dreamily through her dark glasses at the beauty of the scenery through which they passed. They became part of a procession of carts drawn by horses or donkeys, and cars driven by Cypriots in their national costume; handsome bronzed young men wearing baggy trousers, heavy boots and white silk shirts. Lovely girls in long full skirts with full-sleeved embroidered blouses, their heads tied up in gay-coloured scarves.

When they almost reached Larnaca they found themselves in a traffic jam. There were not so many cars now as people and animals cramming the road which led down to the seashore. The air was full of shouting, merry voices. The spirit of the Fair had already reached Larnaca.

Suddenly Lucie saw a large American car with four occupants. As it came close, some of the bright colour left her cheeks. *The Dexters and their friends the Vanderlights!* An inevitable meeting, although she had prayed it would not take place. Last night Carol had telephoned to say that they were all going, and to ask if she meant to join them with Nicos Aliston as originally planned. Lucie had told her that, so far as she knew, Nicos was still laid up and that she was going to the Fair with Adrian. Carol was a good-natured girl and had no wish to be malicious to Lucie, whom she had made her friend. But she had not been able to refrain from remarking 'that would surely mean rather a gloomy outing for Lucie'.

But now Lucie, with a warm thrill of loyalty and pride, looked at Adrian and thought:

'How wrong they all are! They don't know him as I do. He is the last person on earth with whom one could *ever* be bored!'

She hoped that they would be able to drive on before the four Americans caught sight of them. And her wish was granted—just as Valerie was turning her head in their direction, the car moved forward. Lucie breathed a sigh of relief. But the moment they got down to the seashore and parked the car, they once more ran into the Americans. All six of them found themselves shoulder to shoulder in the seething crowd that was pouring down to the shore. The blue waters of the sea were already dotted with boats. Tents and small shops had hastily been put up along the beach.

But Lucie's personal happiness faded, Valerie at last caught sight of Adrian, and after a whispered word to her husband, who shrugged his shoulders to intimate that he did not care, moved towards her ex-fiancé.

'Hi! ... isn't this fun!' she exclaimed.

Dex had always been fond of his wife's English friend. He leaned forward and whispered to Lucie:

'Say, honey, couldn't you have gotten yourself a more amusing pal?'

Lucie reddened and tried rather unsuccessfully to keep her sense of humour.

'He's all right, thanks.'

Dex grimaced and glanced at his wife.

'Say, Carol, what's gotten into our Lucie?'

Lucie ignored this and looked at Adrian and Valerie. Valerie was doing all the talking. Adrian seemed indifferent. He was smiling. But on second glance she saw that his smile had the quality of ice. Those blue eyes of his were frozen. He was putting over 'an act'—determined to carry out his new philosophy. He talked to Valerie without apparent embarrassment.

Valerie was working hard on Adrian, and rather resentful of the fact that she was getting nowhere. What a glacier he had become, she thought. Yet she knew there wasn't another woman in this vast crowd to touch her for looks. She was all in white today, and wore a brilliant turquoise and gold collar around her long throat, and earrings to match. Her long hair tumbled to her shoulders, golden-brown, shining in the sun. Her lovely eyes looked up into Adrian's with sensuous appeal.

'Can't we be friends?' she murmured. 'I've forgiven you ... why be so angry with me?'

He lit a cigar.

Valerie seemed to remember what a passion Adrian had for cigars and it wrenched her rather uncomfortably back to the past when she had had this man at her feet. What an intense lover he had been! Bob could buy her the earth—and did. But as a lover he was feeble. All the glamour and excitement of this brilliant day stirred her blood suddenly. Later on this evening, when darkness fell and the moon came out ... what fun it would be to wander away from the crowd ... *with Adrian* ... make him thaw ... force him to admit that he had been mad ever to risk losing her. She said:

'Let's join up and go round the Fair ... all of us together. Don't be a bear, Adrian.'

He gave a cool smile.

'I apologize if I am "a bear". I did you no wrong, so need no forgiveness.'

She gave a quick look at the other four, made sure that they were talking together, and moved closer to Adrian. Now she gave him the full entreaty of her limpid eyes.

'Don't let's start up that old quarrel. It's so futile. What matters is the *present.* We were destined to meet again. Let us make the best of it.'

Once there had been a time when Adrian Ollivent would have thrilled to the invitation in those lovely eyes. He could look back and remember the torment of days and nights after she had first gone out of his life without giving him a hearing ... when he had been crazily in love with her ... crazy to get her back in his arms for a single hour, knowing that she believed him innocent of the seduction of Aphra.

But this morning she left him cold; more than that ... he recoiled from that insatiable vanity and love of conquest with him that made a wanton of her.

He took the cigar from his mouth.

'Thank you so much for wishing to include me in your party,

111

Mrs. Vanderlight. But Lucie and I have other plans. Now, if you'll excuse us.'

He turned and took Lucie by the arm.

'Shall we move on? There's rather a congestion here,' he said pleasantly, murmured a *'Good-bye, see you later perhaps ...'* to the others.

Carol grinned at Dex.

'Gee! We've had the frozen mitt from the great Adrian.'

'Aw! He makes me tired,' growled Vanderlight, and then joined in a laugh with Dex. But Valerie looked furious. To hide her chagrin she pulled her compact from her bag and rouged her lips.

'He makes me sick,' she muttered.

'What had he got to say?' asked Carol.

'Oh, a lot of nonsense about wanting me to forgive him,' said Valerie, 'but I told him I wasn't prepared to discuss the past. I'm not interested in artists who mess around with their models, and he's such a hypocrite! Anybody would think he was stainless. Lucie Gresham must be hard up for a boy-friend.'

'Poor little Lucie. She never gets a break. I was furious Nicos got smashed up in his car! He's swell for a party like this.'

But Valerie's restless, hungry eyes were watching Adrian thread his way through the crowd until the tall, powerful body and dark, familiar head were out of sight. And once again she knew that now, because she could not get him, *she wanted him.* She half believed that she had been a fool to let her mother persuade her to throw him over for Bob.

She was bored with Bob. He was a good business man and had the dollars all right, but not a scrap of imagination. In his estimation everything that she did was right. It was deadly and she was *bored.* She wanted someone to interest her. Adrian with that maddening, critical, penetrating gaze of his, and all the superiority of his intellect ... and the tenderness which she well knew lay hidden under that steely exterior. He gave her the 'kick' which she never experienced in Bob's company.

Adrian and Lucie joined the thronging crowd. He did not mention Valerie's name to her, and Lucie remained silent on the subject of their meeting with the Americans. She was far too happy to care about it anyhow. Her heart had swelled with pleasure when Adrian had taken her arm and walked off with her as though he hadn't a care in the world.

They stopped at a gaily decorated stall. Adrian bought her a box of sweets on the top of which was painted a gaudy picture of Aphrodite reclining in a large seashell.

'There's a work of art for you,' he grinned at her.

'Oh, *thanks*! I shall frame the cover long after I've finished the chocolates,' said Lucie, laughing.

They passed on from one stall to another, and stopped to see one of the Island dances. The peasants were handsome and charming and they moved swiftly and gracefully to the local music. Most of them wore gold coins around their necks and in their ears. The coins tinkled pleasantly as they whirled around. They danced enthusiastically—obviously enjoying themselves on this great day.

'We'll go out in a boat later, if you like,' suggested Adrian. 'Tonight it really is a most attractive sight when the shore is all lit up. Look, Lucie, they've strung up thousands of coloured lights right along the beach.'

They came to a stall behind which a big stout Cypriot woman stood selling trinkets. In front of this stall there hovered a small girl, about five years old ... a brown-skinned child of the Island, wearing a pink cotton frock too long for her. When Adrian and Lucie arrived they found that she had been having an altercation with the stout lady and had got the worst of it. The little girl was crying.

Lucie immediately took her by the hand and tried to comfort her.

'You mustn't cry on the day of the Fair,' she said. 'Why, everybody is happy today, darling. Cheer up!'

The child did not understand and shook her head. The woman burst into a flood of Greek. Adrian, who understood, interpreted for Lucie.

'The poppet is the daughter of some Kyrenian people. She was fascinated by one of those necklaces made of shells. Her father gave her a few pennies to spend, but, of course, not enough, and the good lady isn't parting with her wares.'

'Oh, poor little soul!' exclaimed Lucie. 'I'll buy it for her.'

'No, I will,' said Adrian, and quickly tossed some silver on to the stall, then proceeded to hang the necklace of shells around the small girl's neck.

'There you are, my poppet, and I swear you have all the makings of a pretty, vain young female!' he chuckled.

The child stopped crying and fingered the necklace delightedly. At that moment a brown-skinned Cypriot strolled up to the stall. Lucie recognized him as the keeper of a small café from the harbour in Kyrenia.

She began to smile at him. But the man had no answering smile. He looked at Adrian with narrowed gaze. He spoke sharply to the woman. The little girl, Lucie gathered, was his daughter, for she threw herself into his arms and kissed him. He kissed her back, then put her down on the ground, pulled a piece of silver from his pocket, threw it at Adrian, and tore the necklace from the child's neck. The shells broke and scattered on to the ground. The child began to scream. The man shouted at Adrian. Lucie, who did not understand what was being said, looked on in dismay. She saw Adrian's face grow white. His hands clenched. He seemed to make an effort to control himself. The Kyrenian then spat at his feet.

Lucie's heart began to beat rapidly; she drew closer to Adrian at once. The look in his eyes, now, was terrible.

'Let's go on, please ... please ... let's go on ...' said Lucie breathlessly.

The Kyrenian lifted the weeping child and walked away. The woman behind the stall chattered like a magpie, obviously upset. Adrian made an effort to pull himself together.

'Oh, Adrian!' exclaimed Lucie. 'What *was* that all about?'

He gave a curt laugh. As they moved away, he said:

'That, my dear Lucie, is an example of my popularity in Cyprus. The gentleman who spat is a bosom friend of Nicos. He tore the necklace from the child's neck, maintaining that he never would allow presents to be given to his daughter by an Englishman who was a betrayer and seducer of young girls.'

Lucie gasped. She felt her whole body grow hot.

'Oh, Adrian!' She whispered his name.

He bit at his lip.

'So,' he added, 'you see why I've never cared to go around Cyprus. That is the sort of thing that is apt to happen. And if you are with me, things are also apt to be said about you. Don't you think we'd better go straight home?'

NINETEEN

LUCIE stood silent a moment.

Adrian added:

'It's rather a shame to spoil your day out. I suppose I ought to be big enough to suggest that we carry on, but it's rather put me off.'

'Naturally,' said Lucie in a small voice.

Now he diverted his attention from himself and his injured pride and saw that her face had changed—yes, quite changed since they started out from Villa Venetia this morning. It had not escaped his notice then that Lucie had looked radiant and quite pretty. Now her eyes were puzzled. The corners of her lips drooped with childish disappointment. It was that soft disappointed mouth that struck a chord in Adrian and made him feel sudden tenderness for her. She was such a dear, he thought, and so awfully good to his mother and to him. She rarely took a day off. She had looked forward to the Fair. Why should he drag her away just because an ignorant bigoted Cypriot had insulted him? But he thought of the man spitting and what he had said, full of the old sick disgust.

Lucie spoke.

'It's just as you like, Adrian,' he said. 'I'm perfectly ready to go home.'

'I've changed my mind. We won't go. We'll carry on.'

Lucie's spirits rose again, but she looked at him with an expression of uncertainty.

'Oh, Adrian, are you sure. . .?'

'Quite sure,' he snapped. 'Come on. We'll walk along the seashore, and to hell with all these people!'

That was what she liked to hear.

After an hour's walking, during which Adrian did not speak a word, he suddenly glanced at her and saw that her footsteps were lagging. She had taken off her big hat and was wiping her forehead. She looked exhausted. How thoughtless he had been . . . making her tramp like that without a moment's relaxation in the fierce midday sun.

'I ought to be kicked. You look dead tired. Do forgive me.'

Lucie was so tired that she could hardly move. She gave an

embarrassed laugh and said:

'It's been a bit strenuous, I admit. We've come quite a long way from the Fair, haven't we?'

Adrian looked back and was dismayed to find that he had taken her so far. The dancing, shouting crowd were now like dots in the distance. They had reached a deserted strand ... a sandy cove where the sun-warmed sand was smooth and golden, fringed with shells and seaweed left by the ebbing tide. An immense jutting rock, blue with mussels, cast a beckoning shade.

'This is just what we need. Half an hour's rest where it's sheltered and cool. The tide's going out. There isn't a soul around. Take off your shoes and lie down. You can have a nap before we walk back to our lunch.'

Lucie was beginning to feel better. It was thrilling to be alone with him on this beach which looked to her rather like the coast of Cornwall.

She flung herself down on the sand out of the sun and, lacing her hands behind her head, drew a deep sigh of contentment.

'Oh, this is super!'

He sat beside her—staring at the sea.

'When I come to think of it, I know very little about you,' he said thoughtfully. 'You don't show your feelings, do you?'

'I suppose not.'

'You're as cool and calm and unruffled as that sea,' he continued. 'What about your inner life? Girls of your age have love-affairs ... you must have had one or two.' He lay down near her now.

Lucie shut her eyes tightly so that she should not see the hard brown face which was so perilously close to hers. He had, of course, no idea of the effect that he produced on her. And he thought her 'cool, calm and unruffled' ... Heavens! she thought ... *if he only knew*! Her thoughts went round in circles before she could give him a sensible answer. Then she said, with apparent unconcern:

'Oh, I've had my moments, I suppose. There was one young man in Cairo I used to think I was fond of. But I was mistaken.'

'I think perhaps you are right,' he said. 'Keep away from love-affairs. They don't do one a ha'porth of good. You're a wise thing, Lucie. There are so many things in life of interest, besides human relationships—and the average girl is apt to put too much value on romance.'

116

'And men too little . . .' broke out Lucie.

He stared at her.

'Hey! Who's the cynic now?'

Scarlet with confusion, she added.

'I mean . . . I've met girls . . . worked with them . . . talked to them. Some who've been badly let down because the man was amused just for the time being, then found some more vital interest, and walked off.'

'Oh, I grant you . . . but it cuts both ways, my dear. Women treat men just as badly, and——'

'This is an absurd sort of discussion to have in these surroundings. Look at that white bird on the rock . . . his wings flashing in the sun. How proud and solitary he is and how happy.'

Adrian followed her gaze and looked at the bird.

She was thankful that she had diverted the conversation again. She was terrified of being too personal with Adrian. His own troubles were still so much in the foreground of his thoughts. They both watched the bird rise in the air then swoop down on to the sea with consummate grace and speed. Adrian said:

'He's lucky. Happy because of his liberty. No one can ever be as free as a bird. Man lives in perpetual imprisonment.'

'Oh, what a dreary thought!' she protested.

Adrian shrugged his shoulders.

'Isn't it true? His imprisonment begins in his childhood. Even the kindest of nurses is a gaoler. He mustn't do *this*. He mustn't do *that*. And so on until he passes on to school life. . . . More imprisonment. Then to a university. Fresh discipline, curtailment of his liberty. The business man is chained to his office, the underling is responsible to his employer . . . the employer, himself, has his liberty sequestered by every form of Government restriction. When can man ever spread his wings and fly into the unknown, like that beautiful bird?'

She turned her head on her arms and smiled at him. Seeing her face thus so close for the first time, he was surprised by the beauty of those hazel eyes; the gleam of small white teeth when her upper lip lifted in a smile. There was something warm and attractive about this girl, he thought.

'Anyhow,' she went on, 'physical liberty isn't the only thing. One can still be free to think. Some of the greatest epics have been written in prison—both in music and literature.'

117

'But one does not always feel free even to *think*. What man, in fact, is more wretchedly and effectively gagged and bound than by his private doubts and fears—the consequences of another man's injustice!'

She could feel the old darkness closing in upon him.

She kept silent, feeling the quickened *emotional* tempo of her heart. She moved suddenly a little further away from him.

'It's too hot for all this soul-searching. I could do with a nice long cold drink.'

'Go to sleep,' he said. 'Then I'll get us both a drink.'

She nodded and closed her eyes. But not to sleep. She could not begin to do so with that wild restless surging of her blood—the knowledge that he was there so close to her. Finally she lifted her lashes and looked at Adrian. *He was sound asleep;* breathing deeply and evenly. She stifled a laugh.

At length she too managed to doze. Adrian woke first. He lifted himself on one elbow and looked down at Lucie. Nothing was left of the prim, competent Miss Gresham. She was child-like and rather pitiful; her lashes glistening wet, as though she had been crying. It gave him a peculiar pang. Sitting up more straightly, frowning, he looked at her with concentration. It was as though he had never seen her before. The practical and agreeable girl who was his mother's companion-help had never appealed to the man in him so far. But now he saw Lucie as a desirable girl.

He could in that instant quite easily and naturally have gathered her up in his arms and kissed her. He noted the ex-quisite line of neck and curving breasts. Her bones were fragile —wrists and ankles delicate. Her skin was smooth, golden-tanned by the sun. He had never before realized that Lucie was physically so attractive.

He was surprised by his new interest in her.

Suddenly he drew his wallet from his pocket, searched for a sheet of paper, then a pencil. Quietly moving back a pace, he began to sketch Lucie's recumbent figure. He had just roughly outlined the charming contour of the small face and form when she stirred. Her lashes lifted.

Quickly he put the pocket-book away. He decided that he had thought enough ... too much ... about Lucie. He stood up, then reached down a hand to her.

'You've had quite enough shut-eye. Come along ... back we go to the Fair. I'm both thirsty and hungry.'

Immediately she put her hand in his and sprang up beside him. Her face was happy again. Her eyes shining. She was ready for the long tramp back.

TWENTY

THE long bright day—that first day of the Cataclysmos Fair—had almost ended.

Lucie and Adrian made their way to the place to their parked car. Behind them it looked dazzlingly beautiful with all the coloured lights twinkling like jewels and the lights in the ships. The sea had turned to a deep purple, milky with moonlight. The sky was studded with stars.

Adrian had been wonderful, thought Lucie, as reluctantly she took her place in the car. But it was nearly half past eight and they had the long drive back to Kyrenia in front of them. She knew that he had stayed here until after supper especially to please her ... so that she could see the festivities. They had lunched and dined together. The meal tonight had been excellent in a Greek restaurant overlooking the sea. Later he had even taken her to the '*Try Your Luck*' carts, where they had a mild flutter together; then they watched the local experts dancing in the moonlight.

They ran into the American party only once again. Valerie had made as though to walk towards them, but Adrian deliberately turned on his heel. So there had been no more 'incidents' to upset him.

As he drove the car up to the main road Adrian gave Lucie a quick look. She was tying a silk scarf over her head. He said:

'Tired?'

'A bit, now.'

'You must be more than a bit. You've been on your feet all day.'

She laughed and slithered down comfortably in the seat beside him.

'Oh, but it's been worth it! I've had a lovely, lovely day!'

'I almost believe I've enjoyed it too,' he said with a dry laugh.

'I do hope you have, Adrian,' she said, and felt hopeless, burning love for him in her heart.

She is an earnest little thing, he thought. *She ought to get married and have a lot of children. And she looked damned attractive when she was asleep on the beach this morning. I wonder if she really had been crying? I wonder if I behaved badly and upset her? I'm no companion for any girl these days. . . .*

He said aloud:

'I'm rather a dull sort of chap to go to a Fair with.'

'That's not true! You can be great fun when you let yourself go.'

He gave a short amused laugh as he swung the car around a bend in the road. The powerful headlights of the big car threw up the dusty whiteness of that road and turned the green trees and shrubs to an unnatural green. For some way along the route they could still look down on the shining sea. The moonlight was breathtakingly beautiful. He said:

'Well, well, and did I "let myself go" to your satisfaction, Miss Gresham?'

She coloured and suppressed a giggle.

'Adrian, *really*!'

'Well, I wanted you to have a good time,' he said in the kindest voice she had ever heard from him, then lapsed into silence. The beauty of the night caught her by the throat and hurt her. Just as Adrian's intrinsic indifference hurt. His very kindness was so horribly unemotional. If only he could have loved her . . . if only she could have meant to him what Valerie must have meant. *If only*, she thought desperately, *I was the most glamorous and beautiful girl in the world whom he could not resist, so that he would stop this car for one wonderful moment, and take me in his arms. . . .*

Suddenly he broke in on her reverie, shattering it rudely. He pulled up the car with a sudden jerk.

'Damnation, I believe that's a tyre gone! Hold on a moment while I look. . . .'

Lucie stifled an hysterical inclination to giggle. It brought her painfully back to earth.

The next few moments were spent in her watching while

Adrian changed the tyre.

They spoke little, until the dark silhouette of the Castle dreaming against the luminous sky came into view ... the landmark of Kyrenia. Then Adrian said:

'Well, here we are back again. Ten o'clock. That tyre held us up. Mother will probably be asleep. Did you leave any sort of message with Loucas?'

'I didn't know what time we'd get back, so I told him to leave sandwiches and drinks in the salon, and some coffee for me to heat up.'

She could at least feel that quite a solid understanding and friendship existed between herself and Adrian Ollivent nowadays. That was more than she had dared hope for.

Once back in the Villa, Adrian went upstairs to see his mother. He had seen a light in her bedroom window so knew that she was awake. She would want to know all about the Fair, and he also knew, although she never mentioned it, that she was always nervous about him driving at night on these curving coastal roads. She would be thankful to hear them return.

Lucie hastened into the kitchen to warm up coffee which she wanted. Adrian would probably have a glass of wine with sandwiches. Her feet ached after the long day's walking but her body glowed with health and she felt more than pleased when she thought over the fact that she had spent that long day alone with Adrian, and that he had seemed content and had twice, deliberately, turned his back upon Valerie. That gave her a feminine satisfaction.

Suddenly she heard the sound of a car coming up the hill. It stopped outside the Villa. Surprised, she opened the door and walked out into the garden. Who could be visiting them at such a late hour? In the moon-drenched garden she now saw, plainly, four men walking towards her. She knew only one of them. Nicos Aliston. He carried a stick in his left hand. The right arm was in a sling.

She watched the men approach. Halfway to the Villa they saw Lucie and stopped. Nicos said:

'Good evening, Lucie. It is a long time since I have seen you.'

'Not so very long,' she said slowly, and her brows drew together. 'What do you want at such a time, Nicos?'

'I am always delighted to see you, Lucie,' he said in a curious voice, 'but it is with your employer we have some business. We

121

heard that you were in Larnaca, we waited for you to come back.'

A sudden chill struck Lucie's heart. In the moonlight she saw that Nicos' handsome face looked granite-hard. His eyes like blue stones. The other three men she recognized now—she had seen around the place at some time or another, although she could not put a name to any one of them. They were all young, strong and brown-skinned. Each carried a thick stick in his hand. She said under her breath:

'What have you come for? Why do you want to see Mr. Ollivent?'

'He has an account to pay with me,' said Nicos. 'I was on my way to settle it some weeks ago when I had that accident. I was going to show Mr. Ollivent once and for all that he cannot chase after my young sister or any young Island girl. My wrist has taken rather longer to heal than I expected, but I can still use my left hand, and I have three good friends who can use both!'

Lucie's blood seemed to turn to ice in her veins. Now it was all clear to her. Nicos, during his illness, had been brooding over imaginary wrongs, and had decided to bring his 'thugs' and beat up Adrian. Her first thought was not so much for *him* ... for he was a man and strong ... as for his mother. The old lady ... with the weak heart ... upstairs. Lucie cast a scared glance over her shoulder. She said:

'You can't do this, Nicos! You *can't*! Mrs. Ollivent is seriously ill.'

He waved a moment, then shook his head.

'I've heard that she is better. In any case our business is not with her but with him.'

'But, you fool,' exclaimed Lucie, 'don't you realize that she doesn't know anything about this misunderstanding over Aphra, and that if she gets to know of it, or hears a row down here and finds out what it's about, it might *kill* her? Do you want to be responsible for her death? Everybody in Kyrenia loves Mrs. Ollivent.'

Nicos spoke to the other three men, who murmured among themselves. Then he turned back to Lucie.

'We have no wish to hurt Mrs. Ollivent. You have my permission to go and tell Adrian Ollivent to come out with us. We will take him elsewhere *where she cannot hear*.'

The sinister implication of the words struck Lucie as though these four men had already fallen upon Adrian and beaten him to a pulp. She had a quick and awful vision of it. Adrian would defend himself. These brawny youths, misguided in their belief that he had attempted to seduce Nicos' sister would set upon him. Four to one ... the cowards! It would be bound to end in disaster for Mrs. Ollivent, as well as an undeserved pain and humiliation for Adrian. Lucie could not endure the thought.

Nicos took a step towards her.

'Go and tell him we want him,' he said, 'and if you telephone the police we shall act at once.'

'I thought you were my friend,' Lucie said, trembling now. 'I have always defended you, Nicos.'

His gaze softened as he looked down at her.

'You know what I feel for you, too, Lucie. But, nevertheless, I am defending my sister.'

'You idiot! You don't know the truth. Aphra has lied. I can prove it.'

He stared at her, wavering.

'*Prove* it ... you ... how?'

'I can prove that he is completely disinterested in your sister,' she exclaimed.

'How?' repeated Nicos.

'Because Adrian Ollivent went to the Inn at my own wish ... and I followed later, as Aphra told you, *to tell her that he is going to marry me.* Yes ... he wanted her to be the first to know of our engagement, and I meant to tell you and everyone later. He is in love *with me* ... not with your sister. He has never loved or wanted her ... she has lied all the way along. Mr. Ollivent is going to marry *me*. And you can tell everybody in Cyprus so, then they can't imagine that he is after your silly little sister——'

She broke off, almost choking, scandalized by her own importunate, hot-blooded method of averting disaster.

A shadow fell across the moonlit path. Lucie and all the four men turned. They saw the tall figure of Adrian Ollivent. He had heard the voices and come downstairs and into the garden to see who was here.

Lucie, the colour draining from her face, looked up at him, wondering if he had heard all that she had said in that moment of wild fear for him and his mother.

TWENTY-ONE

ADRIAN made it clear that he had not heard. When he reached the group he addressed Nicos:

'What the hell are you doing here and who are your friends?' he demanded.

Lucie cut in excitedly, before Nicos could answer:

'Nicos came to see *me*, Adrian, not you. I hope the ... voices have not disturbed your mother.'

'No,' said Adrian, 'she is not asleep actually.'

Nicos stood tapping the end of his shoe with his stick. His young bitter face looked suddenly white and tired, touched by the moonlight. He was deeply perplexed. He was still obsessed by the idea of vengeance. Yet what Lucie had told him had upset all his theories and left him astonished. If it was true Adrian Ollivent was going to marry Lucie, it seemed hardly possible that he would have made yet another effort to pull Aphra back into his clutches. The invitation to paint her again may have been innocent. Nicos did not know what to think, and yet he must believe Lucie whom he looked upon as a person of virtue and integrity.

Lucie, still at fever-pitch, recklessly put an arm through Adrian's and said quite brightly.

'Well, Nicos, I think I have made myself quite clear. Will you forgive me now if I go in? It's getting late.'

Nicos shuffling his feet, stared at Lucie.

'I must admit that what you have told me has taken the wind out of my sails, Lucie,' he said in a grudging voice. 'Aphra misunderstood Mr. Ollivent's visit. I cannot be friends with *him* ...' he jerked his head in Adrian's direction, 'so I cannot be friends with you. Good-bye.'

She felt a surge of wild relief as she watched his retreat, followed by his formidable-looking colleagues. She had saved the day. She had saved Adrian. But at what a price! How on earth, she asked herself with dismay, was she going to explain this evening away to Adrian?

Already he was beginning to question her.

'Well, what was all that about, Lucie? What did Nicos want? You say he came to see *you*. What about?'

They were back in the lamp-lit salon now.

'Come on, what's all this about? What the hell *was* that young man doing down here? He isn't trying to threaten *you*, is he?'

'No ... just ... he wanted to know why you had been up to the Inn and spoken to Aphra.'

'What did he want to bring an armed guard for ... merely to question you about his sister and myself? What did you say to him? And what the devil did Nicos mean about not being able to be friends with you because he wasn't friends with me?'

Then Lucie stuttered:

'I should have thought his meaning was obvious. You never have liked the idea of my knowing the Alistons, and now Nicos feels the same because I ... I am part of your household. Does that annoy you?'

'You're quite right. I *am* hard to please. And I'm most perverse because I told you, didn't I, when you came here that you were at liberty to choose your own friends. If Nicos appeals to you, my dear Lucie...'

She interrupted:

'Don't be silly! He doesn't appeal to me. But I see for myself it is impossible for me to go on associating with somebody who hates the very name of Ollivent. I must go to bed. Good night.'

She turned to go. But his hand on her shoulder detained her.

'Now I've really made you cross. Not at all like you, Lucie...'

She could not even bring herself to say good night to him, but ran up to her bedroom. Her anxious heart beat fast. She must get up very early before the rest of the household was awake and go up and see Nicos. Then what would she say? How could she tell him to keep the announcement of her engagement quiet, when it was exactly what he wanted in order to divert public notice from his sister?

What had she done? What new trouble had she started?

Needless to say, she did not sleep much that night. She let herself out of the Villa and walked quickly and breathlessly up to the Aliston Inn.

She *must* see Nicos and revoke what she had said last night. She would abase herself if necessary to the last degree ... admit herself in love with Adrian ... confess that what she had said was because she loved and wished to spare him; beg Nicos to try and understand and spare *her*, in her turn.

She found the Inn wrapped in silence, shuttered. It was very

125

early. Nobody was about. She tapped on the door. Nobody answered. She knocked louder. Now the shutters of one of the bedrooms upstairs opened, and a head was thrust out. The curly head of Aphra. She gave a little cry when she saw 'Mees' down in the garden. Lucie looked up at her.

'Aphra, I must see Nicos at once,' she said rapidly.

Aphra had no greeting smile for Lucie. She snatched a shawl, wrapped it around her shoulders and looked down at Lucie with a sullen air.

'If you wait I will tell him,' she said.

Lucie waited. She kept formulating in her mind the things she would say to Nicos.

After a moment Aphra thrust her head out of the window again.

'My brother is not here.'

'Not here!' repeated Lucie, dismayed.

'No. Last night some friends called for him and he went down to the town. His bed is not slept in.'

Lucie's heart gave a jerk. This was the *end*! Nicos and his supporters must have gone down to some tavern to drink and stayed there. Drink would have loosened Nicos' tongue. No doubt what she had told him was all over Kyrenia by now. The damage was done.

She wasted no more words on Aphra. She turned and walked away.

By the time she reached Villa Venetia again Nita had already taken her lady's early cup of tea, and it was Nita who delivered the first blow at Lucie.

She came upon her in the salon, where Lucie had started gloomily and without enthusiasm to arrange a bowl of fresh roses for the breakfast table. Nita approached, beaming from ear to ear.

'Oh, Mees ... may I please be allowed to offer my congratulations!' she exclaimed.

Lucie paled. She thought she was going to faint. She whispered:

'What do you mean, Nita?'

'Marko, the milkman, has just told me,' said Nita. 'He heard from some friend who saw Nicos late last night that you are going to be married to the master. It is such joyful news, Mees, and Madame is so happy. She has asked to see you as soon as you are up. I have been looking for you.'

Lucia stood motionless. It was as she had feared. The worst had happened! Already Nicos had spread the report. *And Nita had told Mrs. Ollivent!* Why had she ever said such a thing? And, having said it, why hadn't she confessed to Adrian? He should have been warned. His mother should not have been allowed to hear it through one of the servants. Adrian would never forgive *her* for that—never!

Lucie ran upstairs. But she was not even allowed to get her way and find Adrian. The door of Mrs. Ollivent's bedroom was open. The old lady caught sight of Lucie and called to her:

'Lucie ... dear *naughty* child. Come here at once.'

In an agony of misery and embarrassment, Lucie walked into Mrs. Ollivent's room. The old lady held out both hands.

'Come here, darling. How could you and Adrian keep such news from me?'

'Mrs. Ollivent, I ... oh, really I ...'

Lucie stammered and stopped, hopelessly. Mrs. Ollivent looked radiant ... sitting up with her blue lace wool shawl over her fragile shoulders, the sunlight silvering her white hair.

'You need not look so guilty. It's the best news I've heard for many years. The only thing is, I am sorry all Kyrenia heard it before I did. Of course I realized you and Adrian were becoming great friends. But I did not guess that you were in love. Nita tells me it is an accepted fact that you are to announce your engagement today.'

Lucie felt incapable of speech. She only knew that the catastrophic events which she had tried to circumvent last night were crowding down upon her now.

Then she turned and saw Adrian standing out in the passage. He was bathed and shaved in a bath-gown. She knew by the look on his face that he had heard what his mother had been saying. His face was white. His eyes dark with fury and astonishment. Lucie opened her mouth and tried to speak but no words came. He was beckoning to her, standing back where his mother could not see him. Twice he beckoned, with head and hand, ordering her out of the room. She made a great effort and pulled herself together.

'Please excuse me one moment ... just one moment, *dear* Mrs. Ollivent.'

Then she walked out of the room and shut the door and leaned against it, trembling so that she could hardly stand.

Adrian's long fingers gripped her wrist.

'In here . . . quickly!'

She stumbled with him into the little room next door . . . a tranquil, sunlit room, full of Mrs. Ollivent's personal treasures.

The storm broke over Lucie's head. Still gripping her wrist, Adrian said in a fierce voice.

'This wants some explaining, my dear Lucie. Out with it. *What is going on?* What does my mother mean? Kyrenia knows that you and I are going to be married! Since when? Who started such a story? Come on . . . *you* know. Let's have it!'

Lucie tried to pull her hands away.

'Please . . . you're hurting me!'

'Since when have you and I become engaged to be married? Who dared tell my mother such a story?'

Suddenly confusion fell away from Lucie, and with it her agony of anxiety. She went suddenly cold.

Now the whole thing was over and she must tell the truth.

'Let go of my wrist, please, Adrian, and I'll explain,' she said.

He dropped her hand, his eyes dark and furious.

'Go ahead.'

TWENTY-TWO

ADRIAN stood at the window of his mother's writing-room and stared blindly down at the garden. He knew everything now. He knew why Nicos Aliston and those three men had come here last night. He knew that those sticks had been intended for *him*, and that Lucie had saved him from the possible ignominy and pain of a brutal assault. She had saved him through her outrageous story of their engagement. And already it had spread through Kyrenia and reached his mother's ears. That upset him as much as the story itself . . . because he knew his mother's sensibility and how hurt she would be to think that she should be the last rather than the first to be acquainted with such a fact. He had no intention of getting married, either to Lucie or

128

any other woman. Once with Valerie he had contemplated marriage ... but after she had walked out on him he had said 'never again'—and meant it.

He knew Lucie had done this with the best intentions. But he could not be grateful to her. He felt humiliated by the idea that he sheltered behind a woman.

As Lucie's faltering explanations ceased, he turned and faced her, hands dug in the pockets of his bath-gown. She looked back at him miserably but without shrinking now.

'Of course, we must deny it ... we must think out some way of telling your mother it was a mistake.'

Adrian said under his breath:

'You little fool! Do you think it's going to be as easy as all that?'

She winced.

'No ... I don't suppose it will be easy, but it will have to be done.'

'Do you realize that *she* is waiting in there to hear our supposed confession of love, and give us her blessing. Do you realize that she is glad about this? She has always wanted me to get married. And she is devoted to you. Nothing could please her more than the idea of me taking to myself a nice reliable wife.'

The tone of his voice lashed her to protest.

'Oh, stop calling me nice and reliable! You can see now how unreliable I am ... what an idiot I've made of myself!'

'I agree, your action was idiotic—and dangerous.'

Her own anger mounted to meet his.

'I did it as a last resource. I didn't want them to beat you up. Your mother might have heard. It might have killed her. I said the first thing that entered my head that would *convince* Nicos he was barking up the wrong tree.'

As Adrian looked down into her blazing eyes and saw her trembling, his lips softened.

'I fully realize that what you did was to spare my mother. You were always thoughtful for my mother, for which I thank you.'

'Please don't thank me. I've made a frightful mess of things,' she said, near to tears.

He gave a short laugh.

'You've certainly started a nice new scandal about *me*.'

'Yes, an engagement to me would be very scandalous,' she broke out with childish impotent rage.

'Don't be silly. Scandal was the wrong word. It would be all the same if my name was linked with any other girl's. Better yours than most.'

'Thanks,' said Lucie bitterly.

'Oh, hell!' said Adrian under his breath, 'there is my mother waiting to see us. What do we do now?'

'Deny it,' said Lucie weakly.

'A denial won't alter the fact in her mind that our names are linked. Besides, I tell you she is pleased about it. That is what makes everything so much more difficult.'

Then Adrian added:

'But I'm not going to hide behind a woman. I shall have this out with Nicos, and the sooner the better.'

'Do that and you undo all the good I tried to do last night!' she cried. 'If Nicos thinks I lied to him and you two start a fight it will come to your mother's ears.'

'You see what a hellish mess your story has got me into,' he growled.

'Oh, you're ungrateful and beastly!' exclaimed Lucie.

Nita's voice sounded outside the door.

'Monsieur ... Mees ... Madame is asking for you, plees....'

Adrian and Lucie stared at each other. Lucie's body was shaking. Then Adrian pulled himself together. He put both hands on her shoulders.

'Listen, Lucie,' he said more gently. 'I am beastly, I know, but not ungrateful. I realize that what you did was for my sake. Naturally, sooner or later, we'll have to deny it. Leave me to manage it. We must go to my mother ... I'll see what she says. Leave everything to me, and please follow my lead. Later on I'll deal with Nicos.'

'But you aren't going to let your mother think ...'

'I tell you I'll see how the thing breaks ...' interrupted Adrian, harshly.

She followed him out of the room.

She was confused again and quite wretched when at length she stood with him beside Mrs. Ollivent's bed. The old lady gave them a radiant smile.

'My dear, *dear* children! I ought to be angry with you for keeping your little secret, but I'm sure you meant to tell me today. Oh, Adrian, my darling, I'm so happy! I do so warmly congratulate you and dear Lucie. It is perfectly wonderful for me to know that you are going to be married. I have grown to love Lucie and I know she will make you a splendid wife.'

Lucie opened her lips as though to speak, then caught Adrian's warning glance. One of his hands closed over hers:

'Now, Mama, aren't you a little previous? You haven't given us a chance to admit or deny the truth of what you have heard. And you know that this place is a hotbed of gossip.'

Blanche Ollivent's face fell. She looked up at her son.

'Oh, Adrian darling, isn't it *true*?'

He looked as he felt . . . disconcerted. But he laughed.

'To be quite frank, darling, nothing definite has been decided between Lucie and myself, otherwise I would have told you.'

The old lady's face took on such a woebegone look that Lucie wanted to throw herself down on the bed and burst into tears. It really was so sweet of her to *want* this thing. Adrian's hand retained its hold of her cold trembling fingers. He said, hastily:

'Now don't look like that, Mama. Would it mean so very much to you?'

'Of course, my dear. It has always been my great wish to see you happily married, and little Lucie is my favourite girl.'

She held out a hand. Lucie took it and bent and kissed the delicate fingers in all humility.

'Oh, dear Mrs. Ollivent . . .' she began, but Adrian, as though fearing what she might say, cut in:

'Well, don't let us take our fences before we come to them. It will all work out.'

The mother looked at him anxiously.

'There is every reason for this rumour about you two, isn't there?'

Lucie held her breath. Adrian answered:

'There's never any smoke without fire, Mother darling.'

'Then may I take it for granted that if the doctor lets me come down to dinner tonight we can open a bottle of champagne and you will let me drink a toast to a possible daughter-in-law?' asked Blanche Ollivent, smiling up at her son.

His face flushed. Such words sounded strange and rather frightening to him. He dared not look at Lucie. Yet he had not the heart to wipe that hope from his mother's heart. He bent and kissed her.

'We'll see, darling.'

She drew a sigh.

'Then if I heard any more of these lovely rumours I shall hope they are true. Lucie, give me a kiss.'

But Lucie could bear no more. She tore her hand out of Adrian's and ran out of the room, the back of her hand pressed to her mouth. The tears were pelting down her cheeks.

She rushed to her room and locked herself in and wept bitterly and profusely. She knew that this could lead to nothing but misery for *her*. I trying to save *him*, she had ruined even the remotest chance of friendship with him in the future.

She wanted to pack up and run away and never see Adrian Ollivent again. After a while she became imbued with the idea of leaving Cyprus—of trying to put this hopeless love for Adrian right out of her heart and begin a new life in a place where she need no longer be associated with him.

She did not see Adrian for the rest of that morning. She knew only from the servants' chatter that he had taken car and chauffeur and driven to Limassol to meet a business friend.

It was a trying morning for Lucie. Blanche Ollivent, to whom she was so devoted, unconsciously made it harder. Lucie dared not let the old lady see her with red-rimmed eyes and white face and she avoided her until it was absolutely necessary to be with her. That was at eleven o'clock, when they always used to drink coffee together after Mrs. Ollivent had been carried down to the garden. By that time Lucie, with dark glasses hiding her eyes, looked normal once more. Then the dreaded conversation began —about *him*, and herself.

'I know my son ... he takes a long time to make up his mind about something, but I can see he is going to make it up quite firmly about you, Lucie,' she observed.

Lucie's tired eyes closed, then opened again.

She forced a suitable answer.

'I don't want him to decide anything that is not for his happiness,' she said in a low voice.

'Dear Lucie, you will make him very happy, you know.'

Lucie bit nervously at her lips.

'Nothing is certain yet ...'

'But it will be,' nodded Mrs. Ollivent, 'I feel it in my bones, and you know what Adrian himself said ... there is no smoke without fire. ...'

After a pause Mrs. Ollivent added:

'You do love my son, don't you, Lucie?'

Lucie lifted her head. For an instant she felt that she was being racked; torn apart.

'Yes, Mrs. Ollivent, I do.'

'That's all I want to know. You realise, don't you, that there was once somebody else in his life ... a girl who didn't understand the meaning of faith or loyalty?'

Lucie swallowed.

'Yes.'

'But you,' said Mrs. Ollivent softly, 'would die rather than be disloyal.'

Lucie made a tremendous effort to be gay.

'Maybe Adrian has gone to meet a lovely blonde in Limassol and will have no time for me when he comes back....'

Mrs. Ollivent laughed.

'Not much fear of that, my dear.'

Nita came across the garden to announce that 'Mees' was wanted on the telephone.

Lucie answered the call. It was from her American friend, Carol.

'Say, Lucie, I've just heard the news.'

Lucie's heart sank.

'What news?' she asked, although she knew what the answer would be. Yes, Carol and the others at the Dome had already heard (from heaven knew where) that 'she was engaged to Adrian Ollivent'.

'If that's the way you want things, then I guess I'm mighty glad for you, honey,' finished Carol; 'and all this is the result of a day at the Fair, hey?'

Lucie remained silent.

'We all send congratulations,' went on Carol.

Then Lucie was driven to say:

'Does that include Valerie?'

'Sure,' said Carol; 'she's right here now and says she wants to speak to you.'

Then Lucie started to shake. She said:

'Please ask her to excuse me ... I'm just in the middle of a job I can't leave....'

'Say, what's come over you, Lucie? Aren't we going to meet any more?' began Carol.

'Yes, sometime soon,' said Lucie desperately, 'but I must go now.'

'Hey, wait a minute ... when's the wedding to be?'

But Lucie hung up the receiver, two red spots on both cheeks.

This thing was getting out of hand.

Nicos had certainly not been slow to spread the story around Kyrenia.

Once or twice during that long day which seemed to drag by Lucie with great bitterness decided to tell him, tonight, that she *must* go away—that he must find somebody to replace her—so —automatically this crazy story of their engagement would end.

Just before her son came back from Limassol, Mrs. Ollivent sent for Lucie. She handed her a little box.

'You have ordered a specially nice dinner for us, haven't you, Lucie?'

'Yes, Mrs. Ollivent.'

'Open your box, dear. It's a little present for you ... something I have always treasured. Adrian's father gave it to me on the first anniversary of our wedding.'

Lucie lifted the lid. She was being emotionally shattered again, and she wondered how much more of this she could bear. Involuntarily she gave a little 'Oh' of pleasure as she saw the present that she was being offered. It was a thing of great beauty: an antique cross of silver set with precious stones of many colours which sparkled exquisitely as she lifted the cross on its fine silver chain.

'I used to wear it with a black velvet gown. Adrian's father always loved it. Now you shall wear it tonight to please me— and, of course, Adrian. This pendant is one of his great favourites.'

Lucie's throat ached with a sob that made no sound.

'Oh, Mrs. Ollivent ... I can't take it ... not yet...' she began.

But Mrs. Ollivent would brook no refusal. Whatever happened in the future she wanted Lucie to wear the cross tonight.

The whole prospect of the evening appalled Lucie. It seemed such a farce. And she knew Adrian would feel the same and even more irritated than herself. She heard him come back and go into his mother's room ... afterwards heard the bath running and knew that he, too, was preparing for this difficult 'celebration'.

She finally chose a short dress of pale pink organza, which Carol had given her and which she had not yet worn. It was one of Carol's many lovely American models, exquisitely cut. Deliberately Lucie put a lot of colour on her cheeks and rose-pink rouge on her lips. She combed her fair hair into soft long waves. When she had finished, she looked almost beautiful and she knew it—for a moment she held the cross against her breast. The effect was dazzling. But there was something wrong with the clasp, so she carried the jewel with her when she went downstairs.

When she entered the salon it was full of soft light from the wax candles, and Mrs. Ollivent, looking like a duchess in violet silk with a black lace mantilla over her white hair, was already seated in her special chair, talking to her son.

Adrian stood leaning one arm on the mantelpiece.

As Lucie came into the room in her quiet way he looked up at her and seemed a little startled by what he saw. For she was a stranger to him ... this lovely girl in the rose-pink dress, and hair falling in gilt waves to her neck.

She gave him a quick scared look:

'Hello! ... I hope you had a successful trip....'

'Very,' he said, 'thanks.'

Mrs. Ollivent said:

'How lovely you look, Lucie! Why aren't you wearing my present?'

'I ... the clasp is difficult ...' Lucie murmured.

'Well, she must wear it, mustn't she, Adrian?' Mrs. Ollivent addressed her son. 'Look, dear, your eyes are better than mine. No doubt you can do the clasp up for Lucie.'

Adrian came up to Lucie. When he was close to her, and took the jewel from her hand, she began to tremble violently.

'Steady,' he warned her in a whisper—close to her ear. 'No use upsetting Mother now. She's set her heart on this ... besides you started the game, Lucie, you might as well play it.'

'You can't want it,' she whispered back in an agony.

'Never mind what I want, and I must say you're looking damned attractive. Any amount of glamour tonight,' he said with a short laugh.

She could not stop trembling. She felt his strong warm fingers against the back of her neck as he struggled with the clasp.

'There you are,' he said when it was done, and turned her round to face him.

All day at Limassol he had been thinking about Lucie and his mother and this sorry state of affairs. The thought had interfered with his business ... crept back into his mind again and again, leaving him angrily frustrated.

Now he saw her tonight as a new and quite exciting girl ... slender, virginal, seductive, with his mother's cross flashing on her breast. She looked frightened and helpless. Poor Lucie.

Mrs. Ollivent said:

'Aren't you going to give her a kiss, Adrian? I remember when I first put it on for your father he kissed me, you unromantic boy.'

Lucie found Adrian looking at her in a queer way. There was passion in his eyes ... the sudden hot desire of a man for woman. She did not want that from him.

Involuntarily, her fingers touched the gleaming cross and she whispered:

'*Oh, no!*'

But Adrian gave a low laugh.

'I must behave like my father did before me,' he said dryly, 'and salute this beautiful girl—Kyrenia tells—I am going to marry.'

Under her breath Lucie said:

'I hate you. ...'

But now he was past caring whether she loved or hated him. It was a long time since a woman's allure had gone to his head.

He caught Lucie in his arms and kissed her on the mouth.

TWENTY-THREE

THAT passionate kiss took Lucie by surprise and broke down all her powers of resistance. She loved him. This was something that swept her right off her natural balance and set her heart pounding deliriously fast. She yielded to Adrian with a hungry passion to match his own.

It was like a hot flame darting between them. Then they drew apart. Adrian was shaken. So there was fire beneath Lucie's staid exterior, he told himself. It was a revelation which shook and mystified him.

Carefully he wiped a smear of her rouge from the corner of his mouth.

'Delightful!' he murmured; 'and may I say how beautifully you acted your part.'

She felt that she died a small death of shame as she saw that ironic amusement in his eyes. She wished she had never surrendered to him.

Her lips were bruised from the fierceness of his kiss. Her heart felt bruised, too. She wished that she could turn and rush upstairs and lock herself in her room.

But Mrs. Ollivent—utterly unconscious of the little drama which was being played between her son and her 'dear Lucie'—spoke to them with affection and pleasure in her voice.

'Bless you both. That was very sweet.'

A low laugh from Adrian. He glanced at Lucie. How pale she was! What was the matter with the girl? Perhaps she hadn't taken that kiss as lightly as he had imagined.

He felt annoyed with this whole farce that was being enacted for his mother's benefit, and annoyed with himself for his part in it. His mood changed. He reached out a hand, took one of Lucie's and held it.

'Come along . . . let's keep a sense of humour, no need to take things too seriously.'

She could not answer. She felt choked; bitterly indignant. *No need to take things seriously!* From his point of view he couldn't care less, she thought. The kiss which had been of such vast importance to her had meant so little to him that he could laugh about it. She did not know when she had felt so ashamed.

He whispered against her ear:

'Sorry if I upset you. You didn't seem to mind. . . .'

She whispered fiercely back:

'Oh, be quiet . . . you don't know how much I hate you!'

Again he laughed but his eyebrows went up. He looked at her more critically. He did not want Lucie to hate him. What the hell *did* he want? He asked himself the question gloomily. He felt weary of the whole situation. *But*, he argued with himself, it was Lucie who had got them into this mess. She could not blame him for the consequences.

Old Loucas came in to announce dinner. Mrs. Ollivent was carried by her son to her seat at the head of the table.

The dinner was perfect, and for Mrs. Ollivent it was a dream in which she saw the beginning of real happiness for her son.

137

She knew nothing of what was going on in his mind, or of the storm that raged in Lucie's heart.

To Lucie the most trying moment was when Mrs. Ollivent proposed a toast.

'To Adrian and Lucie! ...' she said and raised her glass of champagne, smiling first at her son and then at the girl opposite him.

Adrian also raised his goblet.

'Come along, Lucie. ...'

His words were more of a command than a request. She lifted her glass, and, with a brief look at him, sipped the iced wine. Abruptly she set the glass down again.

Of course she had never for an instant imagined when she took this way out of saving Adrian from the 'thugs' brought here by Nicos that so many complications would arise. She could only blame herself. Once or twice during the dinner Adrian gently reminded his mother that the engagement was by no means yet a '*fait accompli*', but the old lady only smiled.

'It will come ... I know you two love each other. I am sure of it. I'm not anxious,' she said. 'I have no doubts.'

And each time Lucie caught Adrian's gaze it seemed to her that he smiled in a mocking way, and her own discomfiture increased.

She was thankful when the long-drawn-out dinner came to an end. Then in the salon, while Adrian lit his customary cigar and coffee was served, the old lady asked her to play the piano.

'Just a few moments more before I go to bed ... I love to hear you play and I know Adrian does.'

'I do indeed,' said Adrian, and walked across the salon to open the lid of the piano.

She steeled herself to carry on.

He bent over her and felt suddenly full of remorse. She looked so desperate.

'Lucie,' he murmured.

She gave him a sombre, resentful look.

'What?'

'Are you very furious with me for kissing you? Did I offend you?'

'Yes,' she said sullenly.

'I didn't know you disliked me so much.'

'Please let's forget it.'

'Then you do dislike me?'

'I see no point in discussing our feelings for each other. The whole of this thing is a frightful mistake.'

'But you . . .'

'Yes, I started it,' she interrupted, and looked up at him with anger. Mrs. Ollivent, dreaming in her chair on the other side of the salon, could not hear what they said.

'I started it,' Lucie repeated. 'It seemed at the time a good way out, but it's been catastrophic.'

'I don't doubt you wish you had left me to be beaten up,' he said dryly, 'and I rather think I might have enjoyed a free fight with Nicos and his friends. Three and a half against one. We'll count Nicos as a half with his wounded arm. As for me'—he gave a short laugh—'You might have had a few bruises and cuts to attend to instead of kisses.'

She struck a wrong chord.

'Must you stand there annoying me? Why don't you go away?'

He felt suddenly surprisingly contrite again and moved to apology. He wanted the old Lucie back . . . the happy friendly Lucie of the Larnaca Fair. Her new open animosity hurt him.

'I'm sorry you are so upset,' he said. 'If it's my fault please forgive me. Both my mother and I owe you so much.'

She dared not meet his gaze. Her fingers shook so that she could scarcely play.

'Oh, *please* go away and stop talking to me!' she whispered.

He moved across to his mother's side. The old lady was dozing. He looked down at her fragile face—at the expression of complete contentment. It gave him a pang. Poor Mother! She had really enjoyed this evening with its special significance for her. She really wanted him to marry Lucie Gresham. She loved Lucie. . . .

A new idea began to formulate in Adrian's brain. An idea which he found suddenly fascinating, though accompanied by considerable doubts and fears.

Supposing he did in fact marry Lucie. She was not only good and capable, but charming to look at. Once or twice yesterday he had studied his half-finished sketch of her; remembering the slender, rather boyish grace of her limbs and that very fair hair. She had none of Valerie's exotic beauty. Yet she had considerable attraction. Just before dinner, when he had kissed her, he had realized that she was all-woman, waiting to be loved; that a man might want her very much. *He, Adrian,* could be that man. . . .

Then his mood changed. Lucie wouldn't have him. She disliked him now. It was all a ghastly muddle.

She rose from the piano stool and closed the lid. Loucas had come in to help carry his mistress up to her room. For Lucie the long-drawn-out torment of the evening looked like coming to an end. The old lady kissed her good night tenderly.

'You have all my good wishes for your future happiness and I look forward one day to the celebration of your official engagement to my son,' she said.

Lucie kissed her back but made no reply. She did not find it possible to answer those words. They seemed to tear her very heart out and leave an aching void where that heart had been.

She wanted to get out of any further encounter with Adrian tonight. But just before he went upstairs with his mother he turned to her and said:

'It's a lovely night . . . we might stroll down to the harbour before turning in.'

Under ordinary circumstances there was nothing she would have liked better than a walk in this beautiful summer moonlight down to the Kyrenian shore—with Adrian—but in her present state of mind she found the idea almost frightening. She had been hurt enough for one night, she thought. She was not going to lay herself open to any further injury. When Adrian came downstairs again, she spoke to him coldly, with her gaze averted.

'I don't think there's any need for any more play-acting between us. If you don't mind, I shall go to bed.'

He felt curiously disappointed. A new sense of frustration stole over him. He realized suddenly that he was used to Lucie falling in with his wishes in this house.

'Oh, come, Lucie . . . why must we fight? Change out of that long dress and come for a walk with me. I feel stifled indoors tonight and I'm sure you do.'

'Maybe, but I'm tired—too tired for a walk.'

'I don't believe it. You're just being contrary. What's come over you, Lucie? I told you I was sorry about that kiss. . . .'

She interrupted him . . . stung to a passionate retort.

'Oh, I don't want to hear any more about *that*! I assure you it didn't mean a thing.'

He gave a brief laugh.

'Come on, Lucie ... let's be friends again. Things are not as bad as they seem. I admit that we've got ourselves into a bit of a jam, but we can get out of it, in time. I just wasn't willing to disappoint my mother too abruptly. But perhaps I was mistaken and should have denied the thing right away.'

'I am sure you should,' said Lucie bitterly.

He gave a short laugh.

'*Hell is paved with good intentions!* Isn't that the old saying? And you found this evening hell, quite obviously.'

'Yes,' said Lucie in a rather sullen voice.

Now some curious instinct drove him to add:

'Would it be so distasteful if you thought you really were going to marry me?'

The direct question dismayed her. She went scarlet and caught her breath, but she had no intention of being emotionally exploited any further. She said:

'It's out of the question. I can't think of anything more stupid and inappropriate.'

Adrian lifted an eyebrow and pursed his lips.

'Than an alliance between Adrian Ollivent and Lucie Gresham?'

'Yes,' she said in a low voice.

'But I might want to settle down, get married—not only to please my mother but myself.'

She took it for granted that he was mocking her. Her eyes flashed at him.

'Then you must find a suitable wife.'

'And you think yourself unsuitable?' he persisted, smiling and more intrigued than he would admit.

'Quite,' she said in a strangled voice.

He was silent an instant. Then he bit his lower lip and laughed.

'In which case we must in time deny these rumours which are sweeping the Island?'

'Quite,' repeated Lucie.

His gaze narrowed, resting on her mouth, and then on the jewelled cross on the young curve of her breast. He had an irresistible desire to kiss her again but he controlled it. He gave a formal little bow.

'I'll go for my walk alone. Good night, Lucie. And you needn't look as though it is the end of the world. I intend to go back to Cairo on Monday. I've stayed here long enough. And before I come back you will perhaps have tactfully prepared my mother for her disillusionment about our proposed marriage. Good night.'

He turned and walked out of the room. She wanted to call him back, to tell him that *she* wished to leave Villa Venetia and the Island ... that she could no longer bear to remain here and be hurt ... hurt because she loved him so much that she wanted to die.

But he had gone. Now the tears gushed into her eyes; those tears which had been threatening to fall all evening ... they came pelting down her cheeks and would not be stopped. Picking up her long skirt, she stumbled out of the room and upstairs to her bedroom. She threw herself down on her bed and cried until she could cry no more, sobbing his name into her pillow.

'Adrian! Adrian! My one and only love!'

The old silver chain about her neck broke. She caught the cross in her hand as it fell and pressed her hot wet lips against it, drenching it with bitter tears.

TWENTY-FOUR

CAROL DEXTER decided that it was high time she saw something of Lucie. Their friendship, since the arrival of Valerie Vanderlight, had become almost negligible, for which Carol was genuinely sorry. She had grown fond of the young English girl and liked her a great deal better than the spoilt vain wife of Dex's 'boss'. On the whole she would be glad when the Vanderlights' stay in Cyprus came to an end.

This morning, after breakfast, she walked up the hill to Villa Venetia, full of excitement about the news which had reached the Dome Hotel. An engagement between little Lucie and Adrian Ollivent! *That*, as she had said to Dex this morning, was 'something'. And although Lucie had been so guarded about it yesterday on the telephone—even curt and uncommunicative—Carol determined to see her and offer personal congratulations. Lucie's seeming unfriendliness she generously put down to her resentment of the fact that none of them liked Adrian and had openly said so. But if he could make Lucie happy—well, that was enough for Carol.

The first person she ran into was the 'great Adrian' himself. Dressed rather more for town than country, she thought. Maybe business was taking him away.

Carol walked straight up to him and held out her hand, with her wide engaging smile.

'I'd like to say how real pleased I am about you and Lucie,' she said. 'I think it's O.K.—and Dex sends his good wishes, too.'

Adrian, who looked as harassed and frustrated as he felt, had no answering smile for Lucie's American friend. He barely touched her fingers.

'Thanks,' he said grimly; 'no doubt you've come to see Lucie. I'll let her know you're here.'

'Listen——' began Carol. But he had gone. She drew in her lips and shook her head. 'Gee! Falling in love or becoming engaged or whatever it was hadn't sweetened the great Adrian's temper any,' she told herself wryly.

Then Lucie came out into the sunlit garden. It struck Carol immediately that she looked pale and heavy-eyed and no more pleased with life than the man to whom she had become engaged.

'Oh, hello, Carol,' she said in a subdued voice.

The gay greeting Carol had prepared froze on her lips. For an instant she stared perplexedly at Lucie, whose eyes were hidden by the dark glasses so Carol could not see that she had been crying. But there was some mystery here and it baffled Carol. She put an arm through Lucie's.

'Say, honey, what's come over you? What goes on? I offered your boy-friend my congratulations and he thanked me as sourly as though I'd wished him a speedy death. What *is* wrong? I hoped that this was going to be the big thing in your young life and I came up full of good intentions towards you both.'

Even that pleasantry did not bring a smile to Lucie's lips. She drew a deep sigh, turned her gaze from Carol's searching eyes, and looked blindly through her smoked glasses at the little marble fountain which was one of the beauties of the garden. The sculptured nymph on her pedestal glittered as though with a million diamonds, sprayed by the iridescent water. But to

Lucie, this morning the marble was a figure of sorrow; Niobe bathed in her tears. All night long Lucie had been crying. This morning, with cold indifference, Adrian had informed her that he could not stay here a moment longer and, pleading urgent business, had told his mother he was flying to Cairo. The whole thing had, he said, 'got him down'.

He had not bothered to ask how far it had got *her* down, Lucie had thought. Typical. But she answered him with a chill indifference to match his own, determined never again to betray her true feelings as she had done last night.

She had not the least idea what to say to Carol. But she knew that she must say something. She walked with her friend, slowly, arm-in-arm, through the garden, neither seeing nor caring where they went. It was nice to have Carol up here like this on a friendly visit. She really was very fond of her. But what use was friendship now? Everything was spoilt. Everything lovely that had happened to her on this Island of her dreams.

At length she attempted to make some kind of explanation.

'It's a bit early yet for hearty congratulations,' she said with a forced laugh; 'our engagement is only a rumour, you know.'

'You mean it isn't true?' asked Carol, wide-eyed.

'Well ... not ... exactly.'

'Then how did it start, honey?'

Lucie swallowed hard. It was so difficult to talk naturally—to invest anything she said with a semblance of the truth.

'Oh ... I don't say there isn't some reason ... but it doesn't necessarily mean that ... Adrian and I will eventually get married.' The words stuck in her throat.

'You mean that you're having a sort of 'trial go'?'

'If you like to put it that way.'

Carol shook her head.

'You've got me beat, Lucie honey. It doesn't make sense. Either you and the great Adrian are in love with each other or you're not.'

Lucie made a gesture of despair.

'Oh, I dare say it's hard for you to understand. But one can't always explain one's private feelings and actions even to one's best friend.'

Carol shook her head again and then laughed.

'Beats me. I was hoping you'd found some real happiness, honey. But looking at you both this morning I should say

144

there's no future in it.'

And Lucie thought with bitterness: she's terribly right!

After a pause, she stopped walking, turned to the American girl and said:

'Don't think me unfriendly, Carol dear, but it's all rather ... rather a muddle at the moment. One day perhaps I'll explain. But I don't want any more gossip on the Island, and if anybody asks you ... just say that nothing is definite.'

Carol looked disappointed but she nodded brightly.

'O.K., honey, anything you want.' Then she added: 'Valerie was pretty staggered when the news reached *her*.'

Now the hot colour stole into Lucie's pale face and a gleam came into her eyes. To Valerie, of all people in the world, she did not want to deny the 'rumour'. That heartless creature who knew not love or loyalty and had so thoroughly spoilt Adrian's life. With compressed lips, Lucie said:

'Well, you can tell her that Adrian is certainly not interested in *her* any more.'

Then Carol gave a really merry laugh.

'I like to hear you talk that way. It makes you sound human, honey. You don't like Valerie, do you?'

'I think she treated Adrian vilely at a time when he most needed her support,' said Lucie in a low voice.

Carol took out her cigarette-case and tapped one against it, her gaze fixed upon her friend.

'You seem very sure that the great Adrian is a much maligned man and that none of that stuff Val told me about ... his affair with Nicos' sister ... is true.'

'I'm quite sure it isn't true,' said Lucie.

'Why? This interests me.'

'Well, it's just that Adrian isn't like that. He was crazy about Valerie at the time and he wouldn't have stooped to the seduction of a young and ignorant girl like Aphra just because Valerie was away.'

'But Nicos saw them ...'

'Oh, it's no good going into details,' interrupted Lucie. 'I don't know enough to argue about it. But I don't care what Nicos saw or thought he saw. I think Aphra is neurotic and she is definitely a little liar. And I think the whole story grew out of nothing and was fostered by the fact that Valerie jilted Adrian. It was horrible of her.'

Carol put an arm around Lucie's slender shoulders.

'You sure do love that guy, don't you, honey?' she said in a soft voice.

The caress and the words threatened to destroy the composure with which Lucie had started this new day. She could hardly endure it. Her heart beat fast with misery and the effort to control her feelings. She resorted to a cynicism which was foreign to her.

'Oh, I don't know that I really believe in *love* and it never lasts anyhow. Now, Carol darling, please forgive me. I've got so many jobs to do, and Adrian is just off to Nicosia. He's been cabled for from Head Office.'

Carol could see that she was being asked, politely but firmly, to go away and stop asking questions. She kissed Lucie goodbye and departed. She bore no malice. She was far too goodnatured and genuinely attached to Lucie. But the whole thing mystified her. And she walked back to the Dome with the decided conviction that all was not well with Lucie and that the marriage with 'the great Adrian' was not likely to come off.

She was, of course, set upon at once by Valerie, who wanted to know everything. But Carol had little to say beyond what Lucie had asked her to say; that 'nothing was definite'. That brought a cynical smile from Valerie, who, as usual, took a quick look at her face in the nearest mirror and was pleased with what she saw there. She said, laughing:

'I shouldn't think that will ever come off, my dear. I rather imagine it all to be a fabrication of dear little Lucie's mind. I can't imagine Adrian falling in love with *her*.'

Then Carol snapped—unmindful of the fact that this was the 'boss's wife':

'Well, there you're wrong. I see every reason why Adrian or any other man might fall for Lucie, once they got to know her. She's a honey and worth more than the pair of us put together.'

Valerie put her tongue in her cheek and hunched her shoulders.

'And did you see Adrian?'

'I did.'

'And what had *he* to say?'

'Why should *you* worry?'

A shrug from Valerie. She was eaten up with curiosity—and with annoyance. She had wanted Adrian back at her feet, to amuse her while she was in Kyrenia. The news of his engagement to Lucie had irritated her acutely. She said:

146

'I'm just interested to know how he took your congratulations.'

'He said, "Thank you",' returned Carol shortly.

'M'm,' murmured Valerie; 'perhaps I'll go up and add my good wishes.'

Then Carol said:

'If I were you, I'd leave them alone up there. It isn't very fair to do otherwise.'

Valerie smiled but there was an ugly expression in those wonderful eyes as she looked at Carol's unfriendly face.

'I'm sure your advice is well meant, dear,' she said acidly, 'but I don't need it.'

And there the conversation ended, leaving a somewhat strained relationship between the two.

There was an equally strained atmosphere up at Villa Venetia, and Lucie was almost relieved when he finally left for Cairo.

Their good-bye had been unemotional and with forced courtesy on both sides.

'I must thank you again for all you tried to do for me the other night,' Adrian had said politely, just before he went out to his car.

She had answered:

'What I did was pretty fatal. I really do apologize to you.'

'On the contrary,' he said, 'you saved me from a tough encounter which would probably have ended in gaol for Nicos and his friends. Don't worry, my dear Lucie. This thing will work itself out. I don't suppose I'll be back in Kyrenia for a few weeks. You can tell my mother bit by bit that you've changed your mind about me and that I feel the same. You might intimate that we both acted a bit hastily.'

'That is only too true.'

His final words had been touched with kindness.

'Don't let this get you down too much, and don't entertain any silly ideas about quitting my mother's employ. She needs you and I'll see as little of you as I can.'

Somehow she had managed to smile grimly and thank him.

Then he had gone and for her the whole world seemed empty and desolate. But at least some of the strain of the last twenty-four hours was lifted. And now all she had to do was to try and keep Adrian's mother well and happy and throw herself heart and soul into her job.

147

But during the fortnight that followed she found life increasingly difficult. She still liked her work but she no longer allowed herself any relaxation except an occasional walk or swim which she took alone. She avoided the Dexters because the Vanderlights were still with them there at the Dome. And she shied away from seeing any of the other friends or acquaintances she had made in Kyrenia. Everybody wanted to congratulate her on her rumoured 'engagement'. Each time she made a half-hearted denial or assent it was like being tortured all over again. She could no longer even be happy in her companionship with the old lady. For Blanche Ollivent was still innocently delighted at the thought of her son's possible marriage with Lucie Gresham. Unconsciously, she added to Lucie's torment and difficulty by showering her with affection, presents, a dozen and one little tributes of her pleasure in the supposed 'unofficial engagement'. She was never done talking about Adrian, or her hopes for the future. She deplored the fact that he had had to rush away on this urgent business and expressed every hope that he would rush back to his 'dear little Lucie' as soon as possible.

To all these things Lucie listened in silence, and suffered. She began to wonder how she could *begin* to disappoint Adrian's mother. It would be easy enough for her to say that Adrian had no real wish to tie *himself* down. But how in God's name she was going to bring herself to look Blanche Ollivent in the face and deny that she loved Adrian, she did not know.

Day after day she was forced to pay a fresh price for the false position in which she found herself. She had to explain the fact that Adrian never wrote to her.

'I should have thought he would have sent a little note to you every day,' said Mrs. Ollivent on one occasion when she opened her own mail from Adrian, who was now in Athens. 'His father was a great writer and I still have some of the beautiful letters he wrote to me both before and after our marriage.'

And Lucie had to laugh and say:

'We're not nearly so sentimental in this generation. . . .'

To which Mrs. Ollivent replied:

'But you're not a modern type of girl, which is one of the things I like about you. I'm quite sure *you* write to *him*.'

Lucie had no answer for that but reflected in silent bitterness how much she longed to sit down and put her thoughts into words—what wonderful letters she could, indeed, have written to Adrian.

She dreaded his next visit. She did not know what she was going to say to him. How she could explain the fact that the position here had not altered one fraction since he left. If she had had only herself to consider, she would have told Mrs. Ollivent the truth and run away from Villa Venetia at once, before she could see Adrian again. But each time she made up her mind to warn the old lady that the marriage was never likely to come off, Mrs. Ollivent made some fresh remark or sign that it was the one thing in the world she most desired. It was a hopeless position for Lucie.

She grew thin and began to suffer from perpetual headaches ... just as she had done when her eyes were so bad in Cairo. She looked and felt ill and unlike herself. She knew that she was growing morbidly introspective. She had made up her mind to one thing ... that she would tell Adrian as soon as she saw him that she could not and would not stay here any longer. Deeply though she hated to upset Mrs. Ollivent, she must go—or break. It was all too much of a strain.

The long hot summer days dragged by more and more slowly. Lucie began to feel ill and languid. She never allowed Mrs. Ollivent to see it, but Nita noticed and remarked that 'Mees' was looking very poorly.

'You do not like the heat?' she suggested.

'Yes, that's it,' said Lucie.

She no longer visited Bellapais or St. Hilarion. She no longer wandered up to the Aliston Inn. And she had not seen Nicos since that night he had come down to attack Adrian. Heavens, what a price she had paid for that intended assault! But she heard through the servants that Nicos had gone with his sister to Athens and the Inn was temporarily closed down.

It was the beginning of August before Adrian returned to the Island.

As usual he telegraphed to his mother and told her that he might be expected late on that Saturday afternoon—by 'plane from Cairo.

He seemed to have been on a long tour of all his branches.

Mrs. Ollivent showed the wire to Lucie and immediately suggested a 'little party' to celebrate Adrian's return.

'It's a shame that work has kept him away from you for so long. But tonight you will both be full of joy, my dear.'

149

Lucie stood silently before her employer. She had grown almost accustomed to these sort of remarks ... learned to accept them unflinchingly as though the lash of the whip had no power to hurt her. But today, at the thought that Adrian was on his way home, a shiver of apprehension went through her. She could not bear to face him. It was not so much that she minded his harshness, his indifference ... it was the memory of *that kiss* which bit like acid into her soul. She felt that it would always be between them, ruling out any possibility of friendship ... a memory of her deepest humiliation.

Then for the first time Mrs. Ollivent noticed that Lucie was losing weight. Blanche Ollivent felt a sudden thrill of anxiety.

'Aren't you much thinner than you were darling?' she asked with sudden concern.

'I ... don't know,' said Lucie.

'I think so. I don't know why I haven't noticed it before. Adrian will be cross with me for not looking after you. I'm a selfish old woman always letting *you* look after *me*. What will he say if he sees his darling grown so thin?'

Lucie turned her head away, her eyes stinging with hot tears.

'Oh, I'm all right. He won't find me changed at all,' she said.

She was thinking ... *I can't face another celebration like that last one.... I can't bear the thought of Mrs. Ollivent watching us ... expecting us to be delighted by our reunion.... Adrian must tell her the truth ... he must! And I shall warn him that I can't carry on.*

She had worked herself up into a fever by the time that the car brought Adrian from the airport to Villa Venetia.

It was a glorious evening. Darkness was falling as Adrian stepped out of the car. One lovely star hung like a jewel in the deep blue sky. A young new moon was rising. It promised to be a perfect summer's night.

But Adrian Ollivent found little pleasure in the exquisite and familiar scene. He was hot and tired. He had worked deliberately, like a lunatic, without rest during these three weeks—trying to wipe out the emotional side of life and steep himself in his job. But he had felt no less worried about the situation than Lucie. He often wondered what he would find when he got home again.

He also wondered what sort of mood Lucie would be in. He seemed to have been away from the Island for years instead of weeks. And he knew nothing about Lucie beyond the fact that in all of his mother's letters, which he collected from the Head Office, she was wholehearted in her praise of the girl, her pleasure at the prospect of having her for a daughter-in-law.

But there was one paragraph in the last letter that had come as a bit of a shock and given Adrian to think quite a bit during the journey home.

One thing I can assure you of, my dearest boy. You are deeply loved. This time will not be like the last. Love and loyalty with Lucie go hand in hand. And I put the question to her myself. 'Do you love my son, Lucie?' I asked. And she looked straight into my eyes and said—'I do!' So I know that it is true.

That had shocked and surprised Adrian. It seemed incredible that Lucie should do a thing like that. How could she have looked his mother in the eyes and declared her love for him? She *hated him*. She was afraid of him. He knew it.

And yet he remembered the complete surrender of her in his arms ... and her passionate yielding lips ... and he confessed himself mystified.

He would ask Lucie about that unnecessary lie.

He hoped that he might get a chance to talk to her before he saw his mother. As he stood by the garden gates he saw old Loucas on the verandah and called to him.

'Tell Miss Gresham I'm here, and ask her to come out and speak to me,' he said.

TWENTY-FIVE

LUCIE received that request with trepidation. So Adrian had come back and she must face him again! There was nothing more to be done about it.

She went out into the garden, her heart jerking as she saw the tall familiar figure. He threw her a brief critical look. Even though his mind was full of troubled thought, he could not help observing that Lucie had changed considerably during his three weeks' absence; although she remained tanned by the sun, her small face looked exhausted and thin. She had gone back to the old style of hairdressing with that severe knot in the nape of her neck, and she had put on very little make-up—as though she had decided to abandon her efforts to add 'glamour' to her appearance. He thought that she looked shockingly ill. He commented on the fact before he asked her any questions.

'Have you had fever or something?'

His voice held a note of concern. She had schooled herself to be firm and cool in Adrian's presence. There must be no more losing her head.

'I haven't felt too fit,' she admitted and seized this opportunity to add: 'In fact I don't think ... the summer in Cyprus is suiting me. I doubt very much if I shall be able to stay on. I meant to tell you so after dinner.'

He raised his brows and stared down at her. She was hardly recognizable this evening from the girl with the shining eyes and tumbled hair who had laughed beside him on the shore at the Cataclysmos Fair. It was only a month ago. But Adrian felt as though it was very much longer.

He said:

'I wanted to speak to you alone before we joined my mother—that's why I asked you to come out.'

'Mrs. Ollivent knows you have arrived.'

'*Maleesh*,' said Adrian with a grim smile, using the Egyptian word with its complete significance of '*never mind*' ... '*who cares*'.... 'No doubt my mother will imagine you have rushed out here to give me a rapturous welcome.'

Now he saw the red creep up under Lucie's skin and her eyes darken as though with anger.

'I'm afraid she'll be wrong to think any such thing.'

'My dear girl,' he said, 'you don't have to tell me that you have suddenly started to dislike me thoroughly, I'm not altogether surprised. But there are one or two mysteries which I would like cleared up before we go indoors. First of all, you say that Kyrenia no longer suits your health. Is Miss Gresham handing in her notice?'

His sarcasm made her grit her teeth. She thanked heaven that she had her emotions so well under control tonight. Somewhere

152

deep inside her she was so tragically glad to see him. Nothing that he could do or say seemed able to kill the attraction that he had for her. Nor that knowledge in her heart that, had she been given the chance, she could have loved him as no other man in the world had ever been loved—with all the power of her being.

It was rapidly growing darker. There in the beautiful garden, Lucie stood like a pale image, her face a mask. She said:

'Yes, that is exactly what Miss Gresham is doing.'

Adrian drew in his breath sharply. He felt dismayed. He snapped:

'So you're walking out on your job?'

'I've tried to do that job to the best of my ability during the time that I have been here. But if I have to go because of my health, you can't justifiably accuse me of "walking out".'

'If it really were a question of health, I'd agree. But I know it isn't. It's the result of this absurd situation between us.'

She shrugged.

'All right. Put it down to that if you wish. I take all the blame for starting it, mind you. I never made a greater mistake.'

'Lucie, we've had all this out and I thought we'd reached some understanding. Why this sudden unfriendliness?'

She twined her fingers together behind her back in the old nervous 'schoolgirl' way. Each time she had this kind of encounter with Adrian it was a fresh strain on her nerves. But she was determined to stay firm. She said:

'I don't wish to be unfriendly but . . . the whole thing has become too much for me.'

'Then may I ask why you told my mother such a barefaced lie?'

Her heart missed a beat.

'What do you mean?'

'She said, in her last letter, that she had asked you if you really loved me and that you had said "yes". She is now convinced of the truth of that statement. Did it amuse you to watch the poor old lady's pathetic pleasure and push us both a little deeper into the pond?'

She looked at him dumbfounded. She had not the least idea how to repudiate the statement she had made to Mrs. Ollivent without involving herself in fresh lies. While she stayed silent Adrian looked more closely at Lucie's face. It was scarlet. He added:

'It was a little unkind and unwise, even if you meant to please my mother. Surely that moment was just the opportunity for you to make some sort of denial—or at least a suggestion that you were unsure of your feelings for me.'

For the life of her, Lucie could not speak. He spoke again, irritably:

'Really, Lucie, you don't seem to have done a damn' thing about preparing my mother for a supposed change of feeling on both our parts.'

Then she forced herself to speak.

'Why put all the difficult work on to me? What have *you* done about it? You have written her. Have you suggested in any of your letters that you didn't mean to get married?'

Touché, he thought and felt exasperated. This girl always seemed to defeat him. Why did he feel so angry? Was it really because he found himself still 'unofficially engaged' to Lucie in the eyes of his mother, or, on the contrary, a sense of frustration because the whole thing was not true? He was so damnably tired and damnably lonely, too, he admitted to himself. Life would have had some meaning could he have walked through these gates and found a future wife who was both sympathetic and charming waiting to welcome him. Lucie said it was getting too much for her. Well, it was the same for him. He knew that while he was away he had not had the heart to tell his mother in black and white that she was going to be disappointed for the second time—robbed of her natural desire for a daughter-in-law—for grandchildren.

Lucie spoke again.

'You must tell her yourself, Adrian, I can't. You don't know what it's been like ... she's been so delighted, she's never stopped talking about us.... If you think my part has been easy, you're wrong.'

'I'm sure it hasn't,' he said and shrugged his shoulders. 'But the last thing I want you to do is to leave her. Her state of health is precarious—you know that. If you were to go away now she would be heartbroken. She is truly fond of you, Lucie. And you know damn' well that I am always grateful for the happiness you have brought into her life. You have given her something it wasn't possible for a woman like Gertrude Little to give. My mother could not replace you. I suggest you don't leave without serious thought.'

He was reduced to pleading with her now. Her heart ached at

the look in his eyes and at the sound of his voice. She could not bear to stay and yet neither could she bear to hurt Blanche Ollivent. As for Adrian—his solicitude for his mother was something that never failed to touch her. What a hopeless tangle it was! She gave a long sigh.

'Oh, I don't know what to do!'

'We'll find a way,' he muttered and took hold of her arm and began to lead her through the flower-scented garden towards the Villa. The touch of his hand made her shiver. It wasn't easy to maintain her attitude of cold hostility when he was so close. His kindness was more difficult to cope with than his sarcasm. She looked up at the darkening blue of the sky, then down towards the twinkling lights on the waterfront. What a lovely summer's night! Why must there be so much loveliness and magic in a world which, for her, held nothing but heart-break?

Just before they reached the portico, Adrian spoke to her again with that same note of pleading which she found hard to resist.

'Do nothing for the moment, Lucie. After my mother has gone to bed we'll talk again and see what we can work out. Nothing matters so long as we don't upset her too much.'

'Very well,' she whispered. But she drew away from his guiding hand as though it burnt her. He looked after the small sedate figure. She had shivered when he touched her arm.

'I seem to have made a real enemy of Lucie. God knows why she hates me so much. Am I so repellent?' he wondered.

Once again Lucie faced an evening of desperate effort—forced into that game of pretence in front of Mrs. Ollivent. But Adrian made it impossible for her to act otherwise—at least for tonight. And whether it was because of her threat to leave his employ or because she had said that she was not well, she did not know; but he was not nearly as sarcastic or provoking as usual. He was gentle—even charming at moments—so charming that she could have sworn it was not merely acting on his part. At times when he smiled at her she felt her very bones melting. Her nervous tension increased. She was so mortally afraid of making any response which might be misleading to him.

But Mrs. Ollivent was content. Her son was back ... they had had another 'little celebration', and she accepted Lucie's whispered excuse that she had 'a bad headache' when she commented on the girl's look of strain.

'Poor darling Lucie has been feeling the hot weather,' she remarked to Adrian, after dinner when they were back in the salon. 'I don't think we can even ask her to play to us this evening.'

'I'm very sorry to hear this, my dear,' said Adrian.

He was standing with his back to the empty fireplace, hands in his pockets, cigar in the corner of his mouth. Lucie looked at him and had an insane desire to laugh. He sounded like a sedate middle-aged man who had already been married many years. And now he caught her gaze and grinned back in a manner which transformed his face to boyishness—to a humour which she so rarely saw. She thought:

Oh, he could be such fun and how I wish I could laugh with him ... really laugh again, as we did at the Fair. If only I hadn't made that mad announcement to Nicos! Ever since then, friendship between Adrian and myself has been impossible!

Perhaps she was foolish to be so self-conscious—to take it all so seriously. But it was the way she was built. Having fallen so deeply in love with him, she was quite unable to fall out again or adopt a devil-may-care attitude.

She was thankful when Mrs. Ollivent retired for the night.

'You must both come in and kiss me good night,' the old lady said brightly. 'I never sleep until late. You will find me reading. You know I'm halfway through *The Forsyte Saga* for the second time. It's most interesting, Adrian.'

'I haven't had time to read it again,' he said. 'I'll try to dip into it while I'm home.'

'Can you stay any length of time, darling?' she asked.

'We'll see,' he smiled, without looking at Lucie.

After she had gone, Adrian said:

'Last time I asked you to go for a walk with me, Lucie, you refused. There is a lot for us to discuss, and I think it would be quite a good idea to get everything we want to say out in the open air. Let's go down to the sea, shall we?'

She wanted, yet did not want, to accept. It had been no untruth to say that her head ached violently. She had been neither eating or sleeping enough. But she could not resist the invitation. And because Adrian was being kind and considerate, she felt that she had no right to be disagreeable.

'Very well,' she said.

156

'You won't need a coat—there's hardly a breath of air to-night,' he said.

She turned submissively towards the door. Cigar in mouth, Adrian followed her out of the Villa and through the starlit garden.

TWENTY-FOUR

ABOUT half an hour later, a tall slim girl wearing a smart dinner-dress and pink and black tartan jacket walked through the gates of Villa Venetia and up on to the verandah. She peeped into the salon, found no one there, strolled in and stared round her with darting curiosity.

Same old salon ... not a thing changed! ... she thought, and drew a compact from her bag, made up her face, then combed back the long nut-brown hair. She looked beautiful—flushed after the exertion of walking up the hill from the Dome Hotel.

She stood a moment, listening for voices, but heard none. Where was everybody? Where would she find the great Adrian? It was Bob who had told her that he had seen Adrian at the airport in Nicosia.

Valerie Vanderlight had made up her mind tonight to force an interview with Adrian and under cover of offering him congratulations on his engagement find out exactly what was in his heart. It was her considered opinion that he had rushed into this affair with Lucie not because he was in love with the silly little thing, but out of pique because she, Valerie, had married somebody else. She could not forget his subtle fascination for her, and how much more attractive she found him, now that he had grown mature and hardened his heart towards *her*. Valerie was a creature of insatiable vanity. She always desired the un-attainable. Now that she had lost Adrian, she wanted him more than any other man on earth. She was determined to get him—if only for the pleasure of taking him away from Lucie

Gresham who so obviously disapproved of her.

Carol Dexter had told her to 'lay off', but what did she care for Carol's opinion? And, anyhow, none of them down there at the Dome would know that she had come here tonight. They had all gone to the local cinema. There was a film showing—an old one—in which one of Bob's Hollywood friends was playing lead. He particularly wanted to see it again, although it had been shown in America years ago. He had thought his wife would go with him, but at the last moment Valerie had cried off. She insisted on his accompanying the Dexters. She had had too much sun today and her eyes hurt, she had pleaded. She did not want to go to the pictures, but he must go. Reluctant though he had been to leave her, he had given in. She had got him safely away. Then she had come up here.

She did not for a moment expect a pleasant reception either from Adrian or Lucie—or that silly old mother of his. But the women didn't matter. She was interested only in the man. She was going to ask to speak to him alone on urgent business and then when she was alone with him would rely, on her fatal beauty, all her sex attraction which had never failed to conquer Adrian in the past.

She wandered round the salon for a moment, impatiently. There was not even a servant to be seen. Loucas, Nita and the rest of the staff were shut in the kitchen quarters, eating their supper.

'Perhaps Mrs. O. is upstairs and Adrian is with her,' Valerie reflected, remembering that rumour had it that the old lady was very much of an invalid these days.

She had no idea that as she had strolled up one road to the Villa that Adrian and Lucie had taken another route down towards the harbour.

Valerie was capable of anything. She had complete confidence in herself. Since her marriage with Bob she had enjoyed one success after another amongst the men she met in America. She had the firmest conviction that she could get anything and anybody she wanted—if she tried. And Adrian Ollivent included.

Without doubting that she could overcome any hostility in this house to which she had come such a stranger, she strolled into the hall and up the staircase.

'Adrian! Lucie! Hi there! Anyone at home?' she called out gaily.

A soft, low-pitched voice, which she instantly recognized as that of Adrian's mother, answered.

'Who is it, please?'

Valerie saw a door ajar. A shaft of light spilled into the hall. Valerie pushed the door wider open and peered in.

'*Hello!*' she said in the same gay voice.

Now she found herself in Mrs. Ollivent's bedroom—a room which she knew almost as well as the one downstairs. Many a time she had come up here in the evenings with Adrian, during their engagement, to say good night to the old lady.

Blanche Ollivent sat up in bed, a single lamp shedding a bright light over the book she had been enjoying. She blinked confusedly through her glasses at the figure of the girl in the tartan jacket. For a moment she could not really see, nor had she the slightest idea who had spoken.

'Come in, my dear,' she said, 'Who is it? Are you a friend of Lucie's?'

Then she stopped abruptly. For now Valerie advanced out of the shadows and came into focus. Blanche Ollivent stared at that beautiful face, so well-remembered, with dawning amazement. The book fell from her fingers. Her tired heart gave an unpleasant and painful jerk.

'Good heavens, *you*, Valerie!'

Valerie laughed and drew nearer the bed.

'Yes, I expect it's quite a shock for you, seeing me again, Mrs. Ollivent.'

It was more than an ordinary shock to Mrs. Ollivent. The sight and sound of this girl after such a long interval and after all that had happened. She stared at the girl as though at a ghost.

'Where have you come from? Why are you here?'

'Didn't Adrian tell you that I was staying in Kyrenia?'

'No. Does he *know*?'

'But of course,' said Valerie with a tinkling laugh. 'We've met several times and we had an early-morning swim together only three weeks ago.'

Mrs. Ollivent clutched the bed on either side of her. She was trembling so badly that she could hardly sit upright.

'Adrian swam . . . with *you* . . .?'

'Yes, why not? We're old friends. At least we don't have to be enemies just because we broke our engagement. I'm married now. Haven't you heard? My name's Vanderlight. My husband

and I are in Cyprus on business. We're pushing off again next week, but I rather wanted to see a bit of Adrian before going.'

Mrs. Ollivent's bemused mind tried to understand what Valerie was telling her. Valerie married to an American . . . staying here . . . in Kyrenia . . . and Adrian knew, had been swimming with her? Adrian, whose heart Valerie had broken. Mrs. Ollivent could not begin to understand. But all her old dislike and mistrust of this girl returned in full force. She had never liked her, even though she had once accepted her for Adrian's sake. She had always feared there was nothing steadfast or truly lovable under Valerie's veneer of charm and beauty. And afterwards, when Valerie had left Adrian, which fact had been shrouded in mystery for his mother, she had hated her as far as it was possible for a woman as gentle as Blanche Ollivent to hate anybody.

Valerie, already a trifle bored, said:

'Isn't Adrian in?'

'No, he and his fiancée have just gone out.'

It was the first time Mrs. Ollivent had actually used that word openly, but she spoke it proudly now, full of her sincere affection for Lucie. Valerie put her tongue in her cheek.

'Oh, so Adrian is really engaged, is he?'

'As far as I know,' said Mrs. Ollivent coldly.

'Aren't you going to ask me to sit down and talk?'

Mrs. Ollivent, who felt chilled, and suddenly growing conscious of a frightening pain about her heart, strove to be calm.

'My dear girl, I really do not think that you and I can have anything to say to each other. You are married now to somebody else and I hope you will be very happy. But I cannot honestly say that I wish for any conversation with you. You once made my son bitterly unhappy and . . .'

'Oh, now listen, Mrs. Ollivent,' Valerie broke in, annoyed by this. 'I don't see why your sympathies shouldn't be with *me*. If we're going to harp back on the past, why do you suppose I broke my engagement with your son?'

'Really . . .' Mrs. Ollivent began to protest, her voice trembling. She was thinking: *Oh, dear, I don't want another bad attack. I must keep calm. I wish that Adrian would come back or that Nita would come upstairs. If I don't feel better in a moment I shall ring for her and ask her to show this girl out. How dare she disturb me like this? How dare she try to see Adrian and upset him and Lucie?*

160

Valerie continued to talk in a resentful voice.

'This is not the first time that it's been suggested that *I* was the horrid one who walked out on Adrian. It's beginning to annoy me. A girl doesn't break her engagement for nothing, you know.'

'I'm not interested,' began Mrs. Ollivent faintly.

'Yes, you are,' said Valerie in a rude voice. 'You and everyone else were interested enough to blame *me*. But it's high time you realized that I broke my engagement because Adrian let *me* down.'

Mrs. Ollivent gasped.

'How dare you say such a thing! Go away at once!'

'Don't say you don't know. Everybody in Kyrenia knows. . . .' Valerie was losing her temper now. And she had, in fact, no real knowledge of the old lady's critical state of health. She continued, 'My own mother advised me to break my engagement because Adrian behaved so atrociously . . . seducing that peasant girl. . . .'

She stopped, afraid that she had said too much. For Blanche Ollivent the words were like a dreadful blow. Her glasses fell off, and her eyes looked with sudden agony up at Valerie's angry face. When she spoke she heard her own voice as from a long distance.

'It isn't true . . . *it isn't true*. . . .'

'It is true,' said Valerie, full of the desire to justify herself. 'Everybody knows it. He was fooling around with Nicos Aliston's young sister. Nicos found them together in his studio one night and it was clear what they'd been up to. How can you blame me for breaking with him? I wouldn't have told you if you hadn't put all the blame on me. But what's it matter now, anyhow? I've married someone else and you say Adrian is going to marry Lucie Gresham. . . .'

Her words trailed away. She gave a gasp. Adrian's mother had fallen sideways on her pillows. Her lips were blue and her breath was coming in little gasps of agony.

Then Valerie knew that she had gone too far. She was genuinely horrified by the effect of her ill-chosen words. She turned and rushed out of the room, calling, '*Help! Help!*'

Nita came running out of the servants' quarters and up the stairs, Valerie, pale and shaking, pointed to Mrs. Ollivent's room.

'Go to your lady. I . . . I came up to see her and I found her

161

like that . . .' she gulped.

Nita plunged into her mistress's room. Then Valerie heard a cry from her which curdled her blood.

'She is dead . . .! *Mother of God* . . . my lady is dead!'

For a moment Valerie Vanderlight stood frozen. In that instant all her egoism and vanity, her senseless cruelty, fell away, leaving within her a welter of remorse which was to haunt her to the end of her days. For she knew that if Nita was right she had, in fact, been responsible for that death.

She was suddenly petrified with fear that Adrian would come back here, discover the truth and kill *her*. She wanted Bob . . . Bob who adored her and would never believe a word against her. Her teeth chattered. Her knees shook under her. Nita came running out of the room, her brown face convulsed, streaming with tears. Valerie whimpered:

'Tell . . . your master I called . . . but found your lady very ill . . . like that. . . .'

Nita hardly understood what Valerie was saying. In her peasant mind there was nothing but grief for the old mistress she had served and loved for many years. Mrs. Ollivent was dead . . . or dying . . . of that she had no doubt . . . but in case she was wrong she must get Loucas to telephone for the doctor. He understood the telephone. And the garden-boy must go at once to search for Mr. Adrian, who was out somewhere with Miss Lucie.

Nita stumbled down the stairs past Valerie, screaming for the old butler. Valerie, after one stricken look at Mrs. Ollivent's door, pulled herself together, followed Nita down the stairs and out into the night. She picked up her long skirt and began to run like one pursued by demons—away from Villa Venetia—down the road, back to the Dome Hotel.

TWENTY-SEVEN

IT WAS Valerie herself who gave Adrian the news of the tragedy that had taken place at Villa Venetia.

Adrian and Lucie were returning from their walk. In silence they strolled through the fragrant luminous night in which only the faintest breeze stirred the trees and sent in their direction a perfumed breath of jessamine from many gardens.

They were both sunk deep in thought. They had done all the talking that was possible and reached no happy conclusion. The main theme, of course, had been how best to take from Mrs. Ollivent all hope of the marriage that she had set her heart upon.

They had strolled down to the harbour and stood looking at the miracle of moonlight on the dark violet water, and up at the exquisite silhouette of the old ruined Castle etched against a star-spangled sky.

Kyrenia at night seemed to Lucie touched with magic. Whiteness of moonlight, blackness of shadow, grace and simplicity of design. Kyrenia was enchanted. On a night like this, walking beside Adrian, it should all have been so perfect. But it was marred now by the long-drawn-out anguish of hopeless love. Her one ambition was to keep from Adrian all knowledge of that love, so that she need never again be subjected to humiliation. So, during their many arguments and reviewings of the situation, she maintained a coldness, a withdrawal of herself which had the desired effect upon the man. He was confident that Lucie disliked him and the thought bred antagonism within himself.

If he had ever entertained any idea of turning this nebulous engagement into concrete fact he dismissed it abruptly after his talk with Lucie tonight. But—perverse like most human beings —the position intrigued him a little, and Lucie with it. What, he asked himself many times, had created such hostility between them, unless it was that she genuinely disliked him. But, if that was the case, why had she bothered to save him from assault that fatal evening? Of course it could be just that she had not wished the affair to upset his mother. He did not know. He was left with a sense of loneliness more intense than he had experienced when Valerie walked out on him.

'I suggest that when I go away next time you show my poor mother some change of front and I will write to her and do the same,' were his final words.

Lucie, her spirits at low ebb agreed.

'Very well. And after that I am afraid I shall have to go back to England.'

'To what?'

'Oh, I have friends ... and now my eyes are okay again I can always get a job at the Foreign Office. I have the qualifications.'

'Well, if you must go, you must. It seems that my poor mother will be the sufferer through all this,' and added with a touch of his old bitterness: 'Really, Lucie, if this is all you are prepared to do for her, why the devil did you ever make that preposterous statement to Nicos Aliston and start this trouble?'

She answered hotly:

'We needn't go into that again. I've already admitted that mistake. What do you want me to do about it now—turn myself into your loving future wife?'

'Hardly loving,' he said with a short laugh. 'No, my dear, that would be the final calamity ... two people who feel as we do about each other getting tied up for good and all. No! That's out of the question!'

There the brief dispute had ended, leaving him with that sense of loss, and Lucie with an agony of mind which she hardly knew how to bear. Every word he said had a razor's edge, slashing all her love and loyalty to pieces.

It was in this state of mind that they both met Valerie running down the hillside towards the Dome Hotel.

Adrian and Lucie stopped as they saw her. It would be too much, she thought, if things were to start up again between Adrian and *Valerie* tonight.

Then Valerie reached them. For a moment she stood breathless, panting and a little wild-eyed. She was not really sure what to say. She had not anticipated that she would run into these two. Adrian gave her a somewhat ironic smile. The beauty of her, in the moonlight left him unmoved.

'Hello—and good-bye,' he said with sarcasm.

But Lucie noted the look in Valerie's eyes, and the nervous clenching and unclenching of her long fingers. Something was wrong. She looked as though she had been badly frightened. Valerie decided on her course of action. She burst into tears, put out a hand and clung to Adrian's arm as though in need of support.

'Oh, Adrian, something *awful* has happened!'

'I knew it,' Lucie thought.

Adrian snapped:

'What? Where have you come from?'

'From Villa Venetia ... I wanted to see you and Lucie—to offer my good wishes, in person....' Valerie was stammering and her teeth chattered. Genuine tears of fright and self-pity were streaming down her face. 'Nita came running downstairs as soon as I got to the Villa. She ... said your mother had been taken very ill ... critically so.'

Adrian gripped Valerie's arm so fiercely that she cried out with pain.

'Has she had another heart attack? What did Nita tell you?'

Valerie blurted out:

'She thinks ... she said ... oh, I rushed upstairs to see her and help if I could.... Loucas telephoned to Dr. Jones.... But she ... your mother wasn't conscious.... I think ... she's dead!'

Lucie's heart gave a great jerk. Frozen, she gave a quick horrified look at Adrian. He had gone grey under his tan. She would never forget the look in his eyes. He let go of Valerie's arm, turned and began to run like a madman up the hill.

Valerie stood sobbing into her handkerchief, glancing over it at Lucie with a touch of slyness. She wondered if her story would be accepted. She could only hope that in all this chaos at the Villa the Cypriot maid would neither confirm nor deny it.

'Isn't it awful!' she began.

But Lucie had no time for Valerie. And certainly in that moment it never entered her head to doubt her story. All she could think of was the stricken look on Adrian's face. She, too, began to run home.

The next hour was chaotic. She found Adrian in his mother's room, by the bed, holding one of the delicate cold hands in his. Nita was sobbing. Old Loucas, in a quavering voice, maintained that Dr. Jones was on the way and should be here at any moment. But for the moment it seemed obvious that Blanche Ollivent was no longer alive. Or, if she was, she had sunk into a deathlike coma. Adrian was trying to assure himself that there was still life in that beloved body. He turned his head and looked over his shoulder at Lucie as she came in. The sweat

165

poured down his face. He said:

'Her drops ... give me the bottle ... fetch brandy ... Lucie ... massage her heart ... bring her back, Lucie. ... For God's sake do *something*!'

Sharing his anguish, she carried out his wishes. She took his place beside the still figure, but despair seized her as she looked at the ashen pallor of Mrs. Ollivent's face ... the pinched nostrils ... the blue lips. She put drops between those lips. She attempted massage, then the kiss of life. She heard Adrian questioning the weeping Nita. And now his voice rasped through the room, a note of suppressed rage and astonishment in it.

'You say *the young lady was already up in my mother's room* ... and came running down the stairs calling for *you*? Is that true? But how did she get in? Were you fool enough to take her up to see Madame. ... Good God!'

Nita broke in with a flood of words. No—no—she had not let 'Mees Valerie', as she called her, into the house. She must have come in by herself after *they* had gone. ... Nita had been eating her supper when she heard a scream from 'Mees'. ...

Lucie, soaked with perspiration after all her efforts, flung another glance over her shoulder at Adrian. He looked like a madman, his face convulsed with rage and grief.

'Oh, my God, *my God*!' he exclaimed to Lucie. 'Then Valerie must have come up here and said something ... something about *me* ... perhaps spilled the whole foul story. That's what killed her. Oh, Lucie, Lucie, is there no hope? If not, I shall go down to the Dome Hotel and ...'

'Hold on!' interrupted Lucie. 'Keep your head, Adrian, for God's sake! Wait for the doctor.'

But Adrian could not wait. He tore out of the house, but only reached the garden gate when the doctor's car drove up. And then the two men were in the Villa and Adrian was back in his mother's bedroom again.

Dr. Jones flung off his coat and rolled up his sleeves. He was a man of quick action. A good man in a crisis. He cleared the room ... turned Adrian and Nita out. He allowed only Miss Gresham to stay.

The next ten minutes were to Lucie a nightmare. All kinds of ugly possibilities crowded through her mind as she helped the doctor. She thought how ghastly it would be for Adrian if for the rest of his life he were to believe that his mother had died from the shock of learning the facts about *him*. The lies that the

166

rest of the world believed.

But Dr. Jones and Death were old enemies and had fought many battles from which the doctor had emerged victorious. And this was one. Blanche Ollivent's heart had not entirely ceased to beat. She had had one of her worst attacks. But he pulled her through. For a little while longer she was to be spared to the son who adored her ... drawn back from the Valley of Shadows. Arnold-Jones worked like a maniac that night, using every weapon that science and his own efforts could muster.

At the first sign of returning consciousness ... a vestige of normal colour ... a flutter of eyelids ... Lucie felt so thankful that she burst into tears. She ran out into the passage. Adrian was walking up and down. He gripped both her arms as she stumbled towards him.

'Has she gone? Isn't it any good?'

Lucie wept:

'Oh, Adrian, darling! It's going to be all right. She's still alive ... Dr. Jones says she is going to be all right....'

The 'darling' slipped out in that chaotic and unguarded moment. Adrian seemed not to notice it. A deep sense of relief flooded him. He picked Lucie's small sobbing figure right up in his arms and hugged her as though she were a child.

'Oh, thank God, *thank God*!'

Exhausted she leaned against him for one exquisite moment of happiness, her wet cheek pressed to his.

Arnold-Jones called:

'Come, you two—Mrs. Ollivent wants you....'

Adrian set Lucie on her feet. She followed him back into the bedroom. The doctor was rolling down his sleeves, one eye still on his patient.

'She wants to say something to you. Go easy, Adrian. She'll be all right now but ... she'll have to have extreme care and absolute quiet. Miss Gresham had better take complete charge up here and if she can manage to watch her tonight, let her.'

'Of course I can,' said Lucie.

Adrian knelt down by his mother's bed. Blanche Ollivent's eyes looked drowsily up into the blue ones of her son. She smiled faintly, then a look of painful anxiety replaced that smile.

'Adrian ... Adrian ... *that girl*....'

'Don't worry about her, darling ... just go to sleep....'

'I can't, till you've told me . . .'

'Told you what, dear?'

'Valerie . . . *Valerie* came here. . . .'

'I know.'

'She said . . . something terrible about you . . . and Nicos Aliston's sister. . . .'

Then Lucie darted forward. She knelt beside Adrian. She did not wait for him to answer. With an upward thrust of her jaw, she said:

'Don't believe one word that girl said, dearest Mrs. Ollivent. She isn't capable of the truth. She only repeated some horrid gossip. People always gossip in small places like this. There isn't a word of truth in anything she said. You know—*I know*—Adrian is the most *marvellous* man in the world. Aphra was his model. Nothing more, a stupid, vain girl anyhow.'

Mrs. Ollivent's eyes turned to Lucie and rested on her with affection.

'You have faith . . . then so have I. I will forget what Valerie said. She was wicked—cruel—never did like her.'

Adrian was speechless in that moment. But his heart went out to Lucie in a rush of warmest gratitude. Mrs. Ollivent whispered:

'You two . . . care so much for each other. You *are* going to be married . . . aren't you? I want it so greatly.'

Then Adrian with a tremendous effort laid aside personal pride and egoism. He felt that he had so nearly lost this beloved being tonight that he could and would do anything in the world to give her happiness and peace of mind. There was an expression of pleading in his eyes as he looked again at Lucie. But he put an arm around her shoulders and drew her gently against him.

'If Lucie will have me, Mother, there is nothing I want more than to make her my wife,' he said in a clear firm voice.

Lucie gave an involuntary gasp. But he drew her nearer—whispered against her ear as though kissing her.

'Don't argue, don't deny it. Don't do anything now, *please.*'

TWENTY-EIGHT

LUCIE felt that she had no wish to argue. In her dazed mind she was clearly conscious of only two things. One, that Adrian had made a definite announcement in a loud clear voice, that there was nothing he wished more than to make her his wife, and the other that the beloved Mrs. Ollivent was not going to die.

Later, when she had time for calmer thinking, it was clear to her that Adrian had only done this thing because he was in a state of shock. But for the moment she was content to stay in the shelter of his arm, feel his strong firm fingers on her shoulder and his breath against her cheek. She heard Mrs. Ollivent whisper:

'Adrian darling, you have made me so happy.'

Then Adrian further flabbergasted Lucie by saying:

'As soon as you are well enough to stand a ceremony, darling, we will have the wedding.'

Lucie's whole body was shaken by the wild beating of her heart. Her cheeks crimsoned. She turned a startled gaze upon him. But there was no mockery in those strange light blue eyes. He looked down at her squarely. He added: 'Will you marry me, Lucie?'

She could not say 'no'. She knew that Blanche Ollivent would be hanging on her answer. If this was another farce ... another game of 'let's pretend', then it was a cruel jest on Adrian's part. But she was still beyond reasoning. She heard her own voice give the answer—almost inaudibly.

'Yes, yes, of course.'

A little sigh from Mrs. Ollivent. The old lady's eyelids closed. For one agonizing moment Lucie thought that she had ceased to breathe, but Arnold-Jones was there with a finger on the delicate wrist. And he gave both Adrian and Lucie a quick nod and smile.

'She's all right ... she'll sleep now. Don't worry.'

Adrian stood up and drew Lucie on to her feet. She could not see. The tears were blinding her. She heard the two men discuss the old lady's condition. With Adrian's arm still around her, she stood listening, one hand pressed against her mouth. She did not even bother to wipe away her tears.

Dr. Jones would send a nurse up to Villa Venetia tomorrow

169

morning. He was going to ensure this time that his precious patient had absolute quiet and professional nursing. He could hold no particular brief for the distant future, he said. But providing that Mrs. Ollivent maintained her present strength—she had wonderful recuperative powers—she would recover. There was no cause for further alarm.

She heard Adrian say—with a return of the old grim note:

'Just as well, otherwise I'd have gone down to the Dome and wrung that girl's neck.'

Later Lucie found herself being led out of the bedroom and downstairs to the salon, where she dropped weakly into a chair and hid her face in her hands.

She heard the doctor's car drive away then Adrian's footsteps. Voices . . . Nita and Loucas expressing profound thankfulness that their idolized mistress had been spared . . . Nita going upstairs to sit in the sick-room and watch the sleeping patient until 'Mees' should take her place.

Now Villa Venetia was very quiet. Its former gracious tranquillity had returned. Lucie, face still hidden, tears drying, sat huddled up in her chair. She felt that they had all just passed through some terrible storm.

In the quiet of the night there was no sound but the chirruping of crickets and the gentle ticking of a beautiful ormolu clock on the mantelpiece.

When Lucie lifted her head she saw Adrian standing in front of her. There was no peace in his eyes, only unrest, and he looked deathly tired. But when he looked down at her tearstained, rather woebegone, young face, something near tenderness softened his gaze. He said:

'Thank you for helping me save my mother's life.'

'I . . . I did nothing,' she stammered.

'On the contrary, once we got here you were, as usual, most efficient. . . .'

She stood up, feeling enormously embarrassed.

'Thank you.'

'I thank *you* from the very depths of my heart.'

'I did nothing. And what little it was, you must know by now was . . . well . . . 'because I love your mother very much.'

'I could love you just for that, Lucie,' said Adrian involuntarily.

She turned her head away. Nothing that he said suggested that she, as an individual meant anything to him. Just that he

170

could love her ... because she loved his mother. He *would* marry her to please his mother. Oh, yes ... his devotion to the old lady was as fanatical as that. But the sweetness for Lucie was bitter. Suddenly she said:

'Oh, we *can't* marry ... it's out of the question. You said yourself that all this was just for the moment ... to save *her*. Tonight we had to renew our so-called engagement which is unfortunate. But it can be denied later. There can be no real meaning in what you told her.'

'Why not, Lucie?' he asked with an abruptness which took her breath away.

'Well ... you don't ... you don't really want it.' She stumbled over the words.

'At the moment, all I really want to do is to get hold of Mrs. Bob Vanderlight and commit murder,' Adrian said with a curt laugh, 'but at the same time you and I have got to get things straightened out. It is most important that when my mother wakes up again there should be no further disappointment for her.'

'But one can't just get married ... to please one's mother!' stammered Lucie.

'It has been done. A century ago most marriages were arranged for the convenience of parents, my dear Lucie.'

Now she gave some sort of smothered laugh.

'But this doesn't happen to be a hundred years ago.'

'Don't let's argue. We may as well be practical. My mother means everything to me and her dearest wish is that I should marry you. You love her too ... naturally not as much as I do ... but enough to wish to make her happy. You are alone in the world, and have no ties, and, you have told me many times, no particular man you are fond of. Why not, then, let us reach a purely business arrangement and get ourselves tied up?'

She was silent a moment. She thought that it was typical of Adrian Ollivent to make such an ice-cold proposal of marriage. It almost reduced her to hysterical laughter.

Adrian went on:

'I know you don't care a row of pins about me, and I don't blame you. I'm an impossible fellow. My poor mother, alone, has a misguided belief that I have charm'—he gave a bitter laugh—'but I'm not asking you to see the charm or pretend to love me. Only marry me, and at once, if you will.'

Lucie drew a long breath. How tired she felt! Too tired to

171

reason this thing out. But she tried to answer Adrian with his own cold logic.

'I quite understand. But I don't think it would work. "Arranged marriages" can't be a success.'

'Marriage as an institution never stands much chance of success. If anything, marriage with only friendship for a basis and incentive is the one sort which has chance.'

'That,' said Lucie, 'is ridiculously cynical.'

He shrugged his shoulders.

'As you wish. But look here, Lucie, you love my home and my mother. Why leave Cyprus and search for some mythical job? Why not marry me and make Villa Venetia your permanent home? You know my position. I have a fair income ... at least, what is left after paying the taxes ... but I can make you comfortable and I will do my best to make you a good husband. That is, as far as my disagreeable nature will allow,' he added, his lips twisted.

She looked up at him incredulously. So he really meant it! He really wanted to marry her and was talking about making a 'good husband'. She could hardly believe it. But the remorseless, chill quality behind it all seemed to shrivel her up. She did not know what to do. She wanted to accept ... she wanted to refuse ... and above all she wanted to turn and rush out of this room before she could betray her own heart's love for him.

She felt both his hands on her shoulders. Gently he drew her against him.

'Do you so loathe the idea of marrying me?'

'Oh, God,' she thought, 'don't let him start being kind. That would be too much. . . .'

He persisted:

'Well? Am I *quite* repulsive to you?'

She gave a weak laugh.

'D-don't be silly, Adrian!'

'Very well. Will you take on the new job of looking after my mother as a daughter-in-law, and me as a husband?'

'You ... you can't want it.'

'Oh yes I do. Strange though it may seem to you ... and although I am so often impossible ... I have an enormous respect for you. In fact, I like you tremendously.'

That was a concession, she thought, but her heart was crying out: '*You don't love me, though ... not one little bit.*'

He went on:

172

'Friendship and respect are two quite sound factors for a successful marriage. We used to get on well before the Nicos incident. Could you learn to be friends with me again?'

'I ... I don't feel all that unfriendly towards you!' Lucie stammered.

'Well, as far as the other side of marriage goes ... we can give it time. For a time we can keep the affair platonic ... if that suits you. But naturally, if I marry, I shall want children. My mother would like that.'

But this was too much for Lucie. Scarlet, furious, she shook herself free from his hands.

'Suppose I don't want that kind of marriage? Suppose I'm not willing to be made into a sort of burnt-offering!' she choked.

He frowned and shrugged his shoulders.

'I shall quite understand. But we might come to an arrangement. And anyhow, the sacrifice won't be all on your side, you know. What is more—you might get something out of it—you won't need to work any more.'

'You are absolutely heartless!' she exclaimed.

'Am I?' He looked down at her flushed, resentful young face and shook his head, 'Oh, well, I can see you refuse to meet me halfway.'

Then she surrendered.

'But I will! *I will*. Only be fair ... I just don't know where I am ... it's all so cold-blooded ... I don't know what to do or say. But I will marry you—if you think that is for the best, and that it will work out for everybody's happiness ... I will, Adrian, honestly; and it's—good of you—to ask me.'

An expression of relief came into his eyes.

'Do you mean that, Lucie?'

'Yes,' she muttered.

'Very well. Thank you.'

'Thank you, too,' she said in a strangled voice.

'It will at least make my mother completely happy. If you have no objection, I will arrange for us to be married as soon as possible ... here in this house. We will get the British Consul and the padre to come here. I think the sooner it is done, the more quickly my mother will recover.'

Lucie nodded her head.

'Very well.'

Now he took her hand and with all his old charm raised it to his lips.

'I really am grateful. You're angelic and very tolerant.'

She managed to keep her control.

'*You* are, too,' she said. 'You needn't think I don't realize I shall be—very honoured.'

'I'll try not to make you too unhappy,' he said, 'as for the honour ... well, I doubt if our friends and enemies in Cyprus will think you are doing well for yourself.'

That was the Adrian she knew best. She said:

'I couldn't care less what they think. Carol and Dex are my friends, but the others ...'

'Yes. By the way, what about Valerie?' Lucie saw his hands clench. 'I shall call that girl to account!'

'One doesn't know yet what she really said....'

'Oh yes one does. Mother told us. She spilled the whole story about me and my supposed attack on Aphra.'

'She really ought to be shot,' said Lucie in a low voice.

'If my mother had died, I should have been sorely tempted to do the shooting.'

'Well, don't do anything more about it now,' said Lucie in a low voice, 'it isn't worth it. It will only stir up a lot of mud. Fortunately for her, and for all of us, your mother is going to be all right. Don't see Valerie again, Adrian. I don't want you to.'

The words were out before she could restrain them. And at the unexpected possessiveness Adrian's brows shot up, and he gave an amused laugh.

'Oh! So my fiancée is about to exert her authority? Well, well ... I won't attribute it to jealousy, my dear, but I dare say you are right. I *had* better keep away from Valerie. I don't yet feel quite responsible for what I might do to her.'

'Go to bed, Adrian,' Lucie said, 'you look horribly tired.'

'So do you.'

'No ... I'm all right. I'm going to sit with your mother.'

'You can't stay awake all night.'

'I shall take a pillow and rug and lie on the *chaise-longue* near her bed. I may doze, but I shall hear her if she wakes and wants anything.'

'You're a good kind girl,' he said, with sincerity.

She bit her lip but made no reply. He added:

'I'll come and take your place after I've had a few hours' sleep.'

174

'There'll be no need. I can manage. I'm quite okay.'

He stretched and yawned.

'God! What a night it has been.'

She thought: *Yes, what a night it has been. And he has asked me to marry him and I have said 'yes'. I am actually going to be Adrian's wife. I shall live here in Villa Venetia. It sounds so wonderful. And it isn't wonderful at all, because he doesn't love me....*

He held out a hand to her.

'Come and say good night to me.'

She thought that he meant to kiss her. The idea held a mixture of fascination and terror for her. But to give herself away ... respond to his arms ... his lips ... no ... not now. Turning, she walked away from him, avoiding that outstretched hand.

'Good night, Adrian ... and don't worry any more ... I'll do all that you wish and everything will be all right ... I'm sure it will....' She was stuttering the words as she walked. She ran out of the salon and up the stairs. She knew that she must get away from him—or be lost.

The man stood motionless for a while. His gaze had followed the small figure out of sight. His eyes held a mixture of tenderness, cynicism and regret. Then he turned and, leaning his arms on the mantelpiece, put his forehead against them, conscious of the old blinding pain his his head, and an overpowering need for sleep.

TWENTY-NINE

EVENTS during the next two weeks were overwhelming for Lucie—so overwhelming indeed that there were moments when she felt as though she must sink under the burden.

But at least the primary object was achieved. For Mrs. Ollivent, with that resilience and courage which made her such a remarkable woman, rallied once more, and after a week of careful nursing was pronounced by Arnold-Jones to be past the danger mark. He had installed a very capable hospital nurse of middle age, who happened to be on holiday in Cyprus and was only too willing to go up to Villa Venetia and take a light case. It meant that she could live there in comfort, have all her expenses paid and prolong her holiday for a further month.

Lucie found herself no longer assuming a rôle which was purely hypothetical. She had become in fact Adrian Ollivent's acknowledged fiancée. Adrian himself put the announcement of the engagement in the local paper as well as in *The Times* and *Telegraph*. Gradually the letters of congratulation arrived— both from the Ollivents' friends, and Lucie's, which included a charming note from Lucie's former chief at the Embassy in Cairo. He expected to be in Cyprus on a job next month, he said, and would look them both up.

Every time Lucie received personal congratulations from people she knew in Kyrenia, she felt an embarrassment which she could not overcome. It still did not seem possible that it could be true. Yet she now wore Adrian's ring on her left hand. The day on which Adrian had given it to her was the happiest of them all.

Adrian was a changed man. He was no longer morose or disagreeable. There was a new satisfied look in his eyes as he went about the place. She could not quite understand that satisfaction. She took it for granted that the position was distasteful to him, but that he accepted it and was going through with the marriage for his mother's sake. But he amazed Lucie by his increasing good spirits. He treated her with the utmost friendliness. In no way was he a lover. Only in a brotherly way he would put his arm around her or drop a kiss on her cheek or her hair. He even seemed to enjoy planning for their future, and suggested a honeymoon in Europe. He was due, he said, for a business trip home. They would fly to Rome and then to Paris and later to London, where Lucie could visit her one surviving aunt and her English friends.

He asked her in a matter-of-fact way what kind of ring she would like and when she stamered that she 'would leave it to him' he refused to take that for an answer. She must have what she would like, he said. So, eventually, she admitted that she had a fondness for aquamarines which held all the shining pure blue of the Kyrenian sea. He teased her about this ... maintaining that she had modest taste. Then Lucie, who could seldom resist sparring with 'the great Adrian', said:

'Goodness! What did you expect me to ask for ... an enormous, fabulous diamond?'

He had given her a friendly smile and answered quietly:

'No ... in fact, I would never expect *you* to be a gold-digger. Anyhow, I like aquamarines too, and you shall have one. The nicest I can find.'

That was one of the most overwhelming things ... his desire to give her things. She had never known a man more generous; or more considerate of her personal wishes once he had taken the decision to go through with this strange marriage.

He flew to Cairo specially to buy the ring and at once flew back with it. He gave it to her just before dinner that evening. In a casual way he slid the ring on to her finger and said:

'Good luck, with my love and best wishes, dear ... hope it fits.'

Speechlessly, Lucie looked from him down at her engagement ring. It was the most beautiful aquamarine she had ever seen—large and square—exquisitely blue, translucent, glittering like ice. It was set in platinum with diamonds on either side. It fitted her finger perfectly because Adrian, ever practical, had measured that finger with a thread of silk before he went to Cairo.

Her cheeks grew hot and pink as she gazed at the lovely jewel. He had given it to her 'with his love'. *His love!* If only he meant that ... if only he could really love her as well as be her friend, she thought.

'Well,' he asked, 'pleased?'

She swallowed hard.

'I think it's the most glorious ring I've *ever* seen. Thank you so ... *so* much.'

He smiled, and was pleased with her appreciation. His affection for this girl, his respect for her character, was increasing daily. She asked for nothing. He had never known anybody take less advantage of a position, or be less of an egoist, than Lucie. There were moments when he found her almost too self-effacing. So with his growing kindliness and sympathy towards her, he felt an extraordinary desire to *give* to her. He was finding it new and delightful to have a woman to spoil ... someone young and appreciative. All the natural inclinations in Adrian, which were to love and to give, were stirring again. ... He had realized recently that his disaster with Valerie, and the bitterness of the

Aphra episode, had by no means killed his fundamental instincts.

That night, when he gave Lucie her ring, and saw her tremendous pleasure, he almost knew what it was to be happy again, and a long-standing need in his life was fulfilled. For this alone he felt a rush of gratitude towards her. And suddenly he pulled her in his arms and kissed her parted lips.

'Darling,' he said, 'I really think I'm going to like being married to you.'

The touch of his lips on her mouth made her senses reel. What he had just said was, itself, an intoxication. But she was so afraid that he was only trying to be 'nice' and make things pleasant and easy for them both. So she would not allow herself to respond too seriously. She returned his kiss lightly, covering her confusion with a laugh.

'I don't think it will be too bad being married to *you*, Adrian,' she said, then moved away from him.

The critical moment passed. The passion so suddenly rising in Adrian died down. He turned away, biting his lip. When he spoke again his tone was as light as hers.

'Mama in good form today?'

'Marvellous,' said Lucie, 'and Dr. Jones has spoken to Sister Walker and arranged for her to stay for another month, which she seems delighted to do.'

Adrian nodded.

'Excellent. She can take control until we get back from Europe.'

The colour stole back into Lucie's cheeks. She avoided his gaze. He could not dream, as he looked at that calm young face, of the fire that was raging behind the mask. The hot flame of longing to throw herself into his arms and pull his head down to hers again. That flame threatened to become a consuming fire. She was so much in love with him now that she felt sometimes that she would die of this love. Europe with *him* ... *as his wife* ... a dazzling prospect. But she said nothing ... she did not dare voice her thoughts. When he had gone upstairs she sat down and for a long time looked at her ring. She admonished herself.

Get a grip of your emotions, Lucie Gresham, or you'll have your heart broken in two. He doesn't feel as you do. He doesn't begin to feel it. All this with him is just skimming over the surface. You're a fool to let it go so deep with you.

But, fool or not, she knew that she could not change.

Life had grown so suddenly full of meaning that she did not know how to grasp it. She had never had so much in her life. Now she seemed to have everything, at least in the material sense. If Adrian was generous, his mother was equally so. She was never tired of giving Lucie proof of her delight in this forthcoming marriage which had now been fixed for the end of the month. Each day she seemed to find some little present for her future daughter-in-law. Lucie tried to stop the flow of gifts but still they came. An exquisite piece of jewellery which had been locked away and which Blanche Ollivent had not worn since she was a widow. Wonderful white lace which Adrian's father had bought her in Madrid. A lovely fan of carved ivory and old lace. Lengths of silk and embroidery ... and ... despite Lucie's protests ... a cheque, the size of which took her breath away.

'I have money and I do not know what to do with it. You must accept it, darling. I want you to look upon me as your mother. Buy what you need for your trousseau,' the old lady said.

So Lucie acquiesced. There was not time for her to buy much. She managed to find one or two attractive dresses, a coat and some embroidered lingerie made by the nuns in Cyprus. The rest, as Adrian suggested, she could buy in Rome or Paris.

The wedding was not to be held in the house, which had been Adrian's first decision. In spite of the fact that Mrs. Ollivent was not strong enough to leave her room, the old lady herself wished her son to be married in the English chapel which she had attended regularly until she became too crippled by arthritis.

'I believe in marriages which are blessed by the Church,' she said.

Lucie agreed, and for Adrian, as usual, his mother's wish was law. Mrs. Ollivent's other wish was that Lucie should be a 'white bride'.

At first Lucie shrank from the idea. This strange wedding, which was so obviously a marriage of convenience, did not in her opinion, call for full ceremonial and the 'blushing bride'. She would have preferred to wear a dress and hat ... and no fuss.

But here Adrian agreed with his mother. He wanted Lucie as a 'bride', he said. She found the idea startling and unexpected.

179

But he persisted that it appealed to him.

'You'll find in time that I share quite a few of my mother's old-fashioned sentiments,' he announced.

Lucie gave way ... too embarrassed to argue. But she thought:

'It all seems so *artificial*! I don't understand Adrian ... I don't suppose I ever shall.'

Mrs. Ollivent was delighted, and was able to realize one of her fond ambitions. Lucie was to wear the same wedding dress that she, Blanche, had worn when she married Adrian's father. It was perfectly preserved, a beautiful creation of rich creamy satin, the train exquisitely embroidered in silver true-lovers' knots—by the Italians. For she had been married in Rome. With it her Limerick veil, which was old and valuable and had belonged to Adrian's Irish grandmother.

The dress fitted Lucie with very little alteration. Blanche had had the same small slight figure. When Lucie first tried it on, she looked at herself in the mirror and stared unbelievingly at a really glamorous Lucie, looking incredibly slender and graceful in that clinging ivory dress. Pink cheeks ... shining eyes ... pale-gold hair gleaming through the rich lace veil. Mrs. Ollivent and Miss Walker, the nurse, with Nita hovering excitedly in the background, unanimously declared that it was all 'perfect', and that Lucie would make a most beautiful bride.

When Lucie burst into tears and ran out of the room, Mrs. Ollivent thought that she understood. It was just that she was a little emotionally upset at the moment: it was quite normal. Mrs. Ollivent did not doubt that the girl was quite happy. And Adrian was too. It was a long time since his mother had seen him show such enthusiasm for life.

Alone in her room, Lucie took off the bridal dress, threw herself down on her bed and wept until she was sick and blind. She almost felt she could not go through with this thing. She loved Adrian too much, and to marry him knowing that he was not in love with *her* seemed to augur a lifetime of frustration.

But she had burnt her boats. She could not back out of it now.

Carol was going to be her maid-of-honour. The American girl, since Lucie's engagement had become a '*fait accompli*', was just as pleased as the rest of them. Both she and Dex put themselves out to be agreeable to Adrian and establish some kind of friendship. They had not seen Valerie since that dreadful night when she had so nearly caused Mrs. Ollivent's death. Forty-eight hours later, it appeared she had left Kyrenia. According to Carol, Valerie suddenly announced that she felt ill and wished to fly back to America. So her blindly adoring husband had taken her. Which fact afforded Lucie no small relief. With Valerie's departure she felt that a sinister presence had been removed from Cyprus.

Only one dark shadow hovered. Aphra....

It was still a matter of bitterness to Adrian that the Cypriots remained hostile to him. His forthcoming marriage aroused much local interest and put a new complexion on things, because Lucie had made herself very popular during the summer months that she spent in Kyrenia. But Adrian knew ... and Lucie knew too, that they still believed that he had ruined Aphra.

The young Greek girl herself was seen no more in Kyrenia. She had remained in the convent in Athens with her aunt. Neither had Nicos returned. The Inn stayed shut. But one of his Greek friends whom Lucie met informed her that Nicos' exile in Athens was purely voluntary and not displeasing to him. For he had met an 'old flame' there ... an attractive young typist in the British Mission who was half Greek, half English, like himself. She had once been in Kyrenia on holiday and they had seen a lot of each other then. Now it appeared that their paths had crossed again and they were seen continually together in Athens. This news pleased Lucie. She had always liked Nicos and had never wanted him to be unhappy because of her. It delighted her to think that he had become interested in some other girl. And she had still some hope that Nicos would find lasting happiness when the friend with whom he was in touch passed on the news that Nicos was starting a chic little restaurant in the Greek capital instead of returning to Cyprus. So it looked to Lucie as though Nicos had found the answer to his problems, both in business and sentiment.

But the real moment of exquisite relief and delight for Lucie came with startling suddenness one hot summer's morning two days before her marriage to Adrian was due to take place.

She was in Adrian's studio at the time—it was midday—unpacking a parcel of canvases and some fresh paints which had arrived by air freight from Cairo yesterday. Adrian had promised to start his painting again. And his first portrait, he said, should be of his wife as soon as they got back from their honeymoon. Lucie had no particular wish to be painted, but she did want Adrian to resume interest in his old hobby.

So she had made him buy this fresh equipment when last in Cairo.

Adrian went down to the church to make the final arrangements with the padre. Lucie had been busy during the first part of the morning with the dressmaker who was altering her bridal frock. She felt positively excited as she stacked the new canvases in a corner, and thought about the day after tomorrow. She still could not believe that the great hour was approaching; that so soon she would be changing her name.... Lucie Gresham would be no more ... she would be Lucie Ollivent. Absolutely incredible! she told herself. And with Adrian continuing to treat her like a brother rather than a lover, and herself just a mass of repression, her wedding was bound to be a strain.

Yet she could recall many little incidents during this last week or so when Adrian had revealed himself in all kinds of new lights. It was a long time since he had uttered a harsh or sarcastic word to her. He treated her with amazing gentleness. He was always ready to laugh—to share a joke. He never failed to express satisfaction in their new partnership ... to admire some dress she put on, or praise a job she had done. Last night he had asked her to play for him, and when she stopped had touched her hair gently with his fingers and looked at her with what any woman might have fancied to be real tenderness.

'I could never ask to spend a more attractive hour than with you playing to me,' he said.

She thrilled to the praise and his touch.

She might even imagine he was growing truly fond of her, and that was a lot. But not enough ... oh, not enough, she thought, for a woman in love.

Old Loucas knocked on the studio door. He came in with a letter in a silver salver. Lucie took it and looked with interest at the Greek stamp and postmark. News from Athens—from Nicos Aliston.

She presumed that he was writing to tell her all the things that she had so far only heard about him second-hand.

She seated herself on the edge of the table and began to read the letter. It was closely written in the precise English writing of which Nicos was so proud. The studio was cool and dim, for the green shutters were closed to keep out the strong morning sunlight. Lucie was flushed from the exertion of unpacking.

One strand of fair hair had become loosened from its pins and fell across her cheek. In the cotton dirndl skirt and low-necked blouse which she was wearing today she looked much younger than usual.

Returning from the town, Adrian came upon her like that. So concentrated was she upon her letter that she did not notice it when he pushed open the studio door. For a few seconds he watched her and thought that she looked charming.

Every day since he had taken the vital decision to make Lucie Gresham his wife he had become more accustomed to and pleased with the idea. There had even been moments when he could imagine himself as her lover. Combined with that strong sensible character of hers, there was so much sweetness. But he was still of the opinion that she was indifferent to him. It seemed to him now that he must start in earnest to break through that indifference and somehow make their marriage a success.

What was she reading, he wondered, to keep her so engrossed? And then she gave a smothered cry and lifted her head. She saw him and sprang to her feet. Her eyes looked startled, but there was a kind of exultation in her face which interested him.

'What is it, Lucie?' he asked, and walked across the studio towards her.

She ran to meet him and gave him both her hands, looking as though she had suddenly gone a little crazy with joy. Certainly there was nothing repressed about Lucie in that unguarded moment. Her golden eyes shone up at him.

'Oh, Adrian, *Adrian*, how wonderful!' she exclaimed.

'What is wonderful? Has somebody left you a fortune?' He smiled and knew himself as delighted as a boy because she gave him such an unreservedly warm welcome. Whatever the joy was, she seemed to want to share it with him.

He was a little concerned now to see tears in her eyes ... brimming over ... pearling her cheeks. She gave a little sob.

'In a way—yes—it *is* a fortune ... better than one. It's just what I've prayed and hoped for all the way along. A miracle ... and it has come just before our wedding. I'm so terribly thrilled because it will make *you* so happy.'

He took the letter that she gave him but did not read it for a second. He had taken the hands she outstretched and his concentration was all upon her ... the flushed exalted face and the tears on her lashes. Once before he had seen those tears—when she lay sleeping on the sand at his side in Larnaca—and he had had an irresistible inclination to gather her in his arms and comfort her. But this was no silent appeal for comfort. Rather was it a wish for him to share in her unexplained delight. Something that would make *him* happy? What could it possibly be?

'Darling'—he used the word impulsively—'what *is* this all about?'

'Read it, Adrian. It's a letter from Nicos. I suppose it is cruel of me to feel so happy because life is all over now for poor little Aphra. She was so young and beautiful ... poor Aphra! But she did so much harm ... to *you*. I can't help being glad that she retracted it before she died.'

Now Adrian's smile faded. Startled, he began to read the letter. Little Aphra Aliston *dead*! That was a shock. As he read what Nicos had written to Lucie, Adrian felt that there could only be slight room in his heart for grieving. Sorry he was for the poor ignorant lovely girl who had tried to smash up his life. The grief anyone would feel for youth that dies before its time. But his individual feelings were of overwhelming relief.

Nicos said that for the last week or two there had been many victims in Aunt Caliope's convent of an epidemic of diphtheria. Aphra also had contracted it and it carried her off within a few days. Knowing that she was dying, she had sent for her Confessor and for her half-brother. Afraid to die with so grave a sin on her soul, she admitted that all the things she had ever said against Mr. Ollivent had been untrue. She asked that he should forgive her and that she should be pardoned by 'Mees' and anybody else who had suffered through her wrongdoing.

I know now, Nicos wrote, *that Mr. Ollivent was never guilty of the seduction of my sister. She did him a terrible wrong and I am guilty. All of us who have maligned him in Kyrenia must hang our heads with shame. I was completely taken in by Aphra's lies. She must have been crazy. But now the poor unhappy girl is dead and we buried her in the convent churchyard this morning, so I can only beg Mr. Ollivent to accept my profound apologies. I intend to come to Cyprus in the near future and offer them again in person. Meanwhile, I have written to my best friends and asked that the news should be circulated in Kyrenia. That is only just.*

It is a terrible blow to my pride and I do not feel I can ever hold up my head in Cyprus again, but I count myself a man of honour and could not live with peace of mind unless I did the right thing—which means everything in my power to refute the scandalous stories which have been spread on the Island about Mr. Ollivent. Everybody now will know the truth.

I have heard that you are soon to be married to him, Lucie, and send with my apologies my good wishes for the happiness of you both. I, too, hope to be married in the near future, but will tell you about that at a later date. . . .

Adrian lifted his head. Lucie's fair one had been close to it. With him, she was excitedly re-reading that carefully-written letter. Their gaze met. Adrian's face was a study in feeling. He drew a deep breath, feeling suddenly as though a great burden had been lifted from his shoulders, a burden that had crippled and almost broken him.

'Lucie!' he said, 'this really *is* wonderful!'

'I can hardly believe it. It seems terrible that it should have taken death to make that poor wretched child tell the truth.'

'So now you know,' said Adrian.

'But I *always* knew. I never doubted you.'

Adrian turned and looked at her.

'No—you never did. That is one thing I shall remember. You believed in me right from the start. You and my mother.'

'And now everybody else will believe in you. The news will flash round the Island. Oh, Adrian, it's *wonderful*! It's all been so unfair on you . . . so horribly unfair. But now they'll know. And no one can ever spit at your feet again like that horrible man at the Fair!'

Her voice rang out in the quiet studio. Then there was a silence. Adrian's blue gaze was fixed upon her. Slowly the red blood was creeping up under his tan. Once again he was conscious of her exultation. And it was for *him*! All this joy. . . .

With a sudden gesture he put an arm about her and drew her against him.

'Why are you so glad? Why does it matter to you so much?' he asked in a low voice. 'Is it only because you are worried about my reputation—because, as you have to bear my name, you want it to be an honourable one?'

Now her eyes were full of hot reproach.

'That's a beastly thing to say! You know I don't care about

myself. I'm glad for *you.*'

'Why? Why? I don't matter all that much to you, do I?'

She choked.

'Yes, you do, you do! Oh, you *fool*, Adrian! Can't you see that you do? Are you so stupid that you don't know that I simply *adore* you?'

It had tumbled out wildly—with no more restraint. And now Adrian caught her fast and knew that he held no unwilling victim, but a warm, pulsating woman who loved him ... who more than that ... who *adored.* The scales fell from his eyes and his own inhibitions were dissolved in the fire of her love. He pressed one cheek against the fair smooth head, his eyes shut, his heart leaping. He said:

'Oh, Lucie, Lucie my darling ... my *darling*!'

She surrendered to his embrace ecstatically.

There was no longer a single inclination within her to hide her feelings. Her joy in his established innocence had rendered her incapable of anything but a shining honesty, a pride in her own powers of loving.

'I adore you,' she repeated ... 'I always have done. ... And I have never been able to bear the idea that you don't love me.'

Now he, too, spoke without reservations and as though aware of the truth in himself for the first time.

'But I do,' he said, 'I love you with all my heart. We both seem to have been hiding our real feelings away from each other. I thought you disliked me after that night when I kissed you, and that you were only marrying me because of my mother.'

'I thought the same about you.'

'And now we know,' he said, and threaded his fingers through the soft fair hair, tumbling it about her shoulders. 'Lucie, Lucie ... you don't know how much I've wanted this to happen.'

She hung back a moment in his arms, still unbelieving and afraid.

'You can't love me, Adrian. I don't believe it.'

'Then I'll have to spend the rest of my life proving it to you, but I assure you it is so. I think I can safely say that I fell in love with you on the day of the Fair. I started to sketch you while you slept. I carry that little drawing of you in my pocket-book. Shall I show it to you?'

She put both her arms around his neck and hugged him like a child.

'Oh, no, no!'

'Why not?'

'Because I don't want you to let me go for a single moment. I want you to go on holding me like this,' she said in a smothered voice.

He laughed—full of tenderness. For a moment he strained her against him. Conscious that he was loved by this girl as it had never been in Valerie's shallow selfish nature to love. But the ghosts of Valerie and of Aphra, which had so long lingered almost maliciously in this studio, had been banished for ever. There was nobody but Lucie ... nobody in the future for Adrian except his mother and the girl he was going to marry the day after tomorrow.

'I love you, darling,' he whispered. 'I love you very, very much and you must never think otherwise.'

His long kiss—and yet more kisses—reassured her that she need not doubt, and that it was all true. He loved her.

She thought happily, in a kind of spiritual ecstasy:

'I want to climb St. Hilarion again when I'm his wife. Secure in the knowledge that I am his and that he is mine, we will stand together on the highest peak and look down upon the world. And I shall feel that the whole of that world is mine!'

Extract from Carol Dexter's diary of her visit to Cyprus.

If there's one thing I shall remember all my life it is the wedding of my friend Lucie to Adrian Ollivent in the little English church this morning—a glorious, glittering Cyprus day.

It is not so much that I was pleased to see my English friend look radiant and as truly beautiful as she did in her bridal dress. I know she was happy because she told me so last night when I went up to Villa Venetia to see her. She didn't say much because Lucie is a reserved type, but I could tell that a new note of confidence had crept into her personal life, and that she and the great Adrian had found some real bond of sympathy. But the remarkable thing which will live in my memory was the way in which the whole Kyrenian population took part in that marriage ceremony.

The Cypriots, every doggone man, woman and child, seemed to turn out in their Sunday best to do honour to the bride and bridegroom. If I ever thought the great Adrian unpopular I was wrong. When he appeared—he came down to the church with the friend who had flown from Cairo to be his best man—he found an amazing crowd ... an absolute mass of people ... thronging round the church. And as he walked to the door they threw roses at him and called out some kind of particular greeting in their own language. I was told it was the Greek for 'Good luck' and 'For he's a jolly good fellow.' They told me afterwards that Adrian's face was a study, and that he waved and thanked them, quite overcome.

There wasn't an empty seat in the church. Dozens who couldn't get in waited outside. The church itself was so full of flowers it looked like a garden, and Nita, Mrs. Ollivent's maid, said that the Cypriots themselves had come in earlier with hundreds of little bouquets from their own gardens as an offering.

The wedding ceremony was a simple one and quickly over. My friend Lucie looked quite angelic. Her sun-browned face was beautiful to see—so intense and yet so tranquil. She looked as though she was getting everything the world could give her. She always did love the great Adrian, and I must say he's changed a lot and that I got a bit of a heart-throb myself when I saw him standing there beside her. With those broad shoulders and fine head, he really is quite a good-looker.

When they came out of the church, with the organ playing, I followed, and I was startled by the cheers they got from the crowd. It was as though the whole of Kyrenia fired big guns. They just roared, and they put out their hands to pat Adrian's arm or touch Lucie's veil. All so smiling, behaving as though they had just seen something very special.

Well, I think I agree. It was very special, and I had a lump in my throat when I saw the great Adrian pick his wife up in his arms and carry her to the car.

They drove up to the Villa very slowly. A lot of Cypriots followed, running, pelting the couple with flowers. Dex and I, from our car could see Lucie waving at them like Royalty, and trying not to cry.

We had champagne and wedding cake, a jolly party, in Mrs. Ollivent's bedroom. And she looked as happy as anybody and stood up to all the excitement.

I helped Lucie dress. They were to take the afternoon flight to Cairo and then on to Rome. I mentioned to Lucie that I was a little surprised by the enormous personal triumph she and

Adrian seemed to have achieved on their wedding day. She gave a funny little secret smile and said: 'It's obvious they really love Adrian, these people. Until now they've not understood him. Now they do.'

I agreed. And I told her, too, that I had never seen a man look more in love with his bride, whereupon she gave me a beautiful smile and said: 'Yes, I think he is in love with me. In fact, I know he is. I'm the luckiest and happiest girl in the world.'

And there it all ends. And as I told Dex after the pair had gone, I reckon little Lucie IS the luckiest and happiest girl in the world—except, of course, myself!